W9-BDQ-091

A City for Lincoln

Also by John R. Tunis

IRON DUKE
THE DUKE DECIDES
CHAMPION'S CHOICE
THE KID FROM TOMKINSVILLE
WORLD SERIES
ALL-AMERICAN
KEYSTONE KIDS
ROOKIE OF THE YEAR
YEA! WILDCATS!

ODYSSEY CLASSIC

A City for Lincoln

JOHN R. TUNIS

An Odyssey Classic
Harcourt Brace Jovanovich, Publishers
San Diego New York London

HBJ

Library of Congress Cataloging-in-Publication Data

Tunis, John Roberts, 1889–1975
A city for Lincoln/John R. Tunis.
p. cm.
"An Odyssey classic."
Summary: Don Henderson, basketball coach for the Springfield Wildcats and head of the Police Department's Juvenile Aid Division, comes up against town politics that threaten his work with the youth and convince him to run for mayor.
ISBN 0-15-218580-1 (pbk.)
[1. Juvenile delinquency—Fiction. 2. Corruption (in politics)— Fiction.] I. Title.
PZ7.T8236Ci 1989

[Fic]—dc19 89-2035
Printed in the United States of America

A B C D E

Introduction

When I was a boy reading through the Tunis shelf at my public library one summer, I kept putting this one off (along with the one with the World War II picture on the cover, *Silence Over Dunkerque*). I put it off because it didn't look like one of Tunis's sports novels, and at the time I wanted sports novels only. "A City for Lincoln." It sounded like a biography of Young Abe as a woodchoppin' paragon on the plains, or something in that mock-historical line. I got enough boyhood-of-the-presidents stuff in school; on my own time I wanted fun, and from Tunis, I thought that meant sports.

One day, in despair because I had read everything of Tunis's except this one and the World War II novel (which I never *did* read), I flipped it open and began to read the first chapter. Well, all right! It *was* a sports book—in fact, it was the sequel to my beloved *Yea! Wildcats!*, picking up the saga of the Springfield, Indiana, high school boys' basketball team at a thrilling point: the Wildcats in the state finals tournament, with the game the next day! Tom Shaw, Jackson Piper, and the rest were assembled under coach Don Henderson; Peedad Wilson was dispensing good-humored sagacity from behind his newspaper desk; the townfolk (chastened by the events in *Yea! Wildcats!* but still excited) were all a-twitter. I couldn't get to the checkout desk fast enough.

I couldn't get to the end of the book fast enough either, but not for the usual reasons. *A City for Lincoln* is the strangest and most surprising of all Tunis's novels. It begins abruptly with the *end* of a sports story (the classic Big Game, without any buildup), then turns into a cops-and-robbers tale with kids as the cops, and ends up as a compelling civics lesson. After the first few chapters, we are done with basketball, deprived of firsthand action, because Tunis forces us to share the point of view of Coach Don Henderson, stricken with nerve-induced gastritis and trapped on the trainer's table, away from the court, doomed to interpret crowd noise as news of how the Kats are doing. Very odd indeed.

Even odder is the fact that one doesn't miss the

basketball. The social dramas that pick up where the hoops leaves off are very gripping, not just for their melodrama but for their crucial importance to the lives of characters we have come to care about. Tunis cunningly provides a continuum between the sports and the sociology by making these characters carry the story from the one sphere to the other—not only Don and Peedad but Tom Shaw (and his father, J. Frank, the Big Boss Man) and other kids we have seen do well in uniform. As we watch them participate in decisions that deeply affect the quality of life in their city, we realize we have perhaps been a little condescending in our regard for them: We saw them as jocks and expected them to play games for us—just as we expected Tunis to be a jock writer and write up the games. We had no expectations about the rest of their lives; in fact, we weren't terribly interested in them as whole people.

One wrongheaded attitude Tunis loves to expose is that by loving kids when they have numbers on their backs, we are being strong, caring adults with a productive interest in "youth." Tunis delights in showing us our error. Being a sports fan is not the same thing as *working* with kids. Sometimes, it even means working against them. And playing organized sports is not the same as growing up either. Don Henderson, concerned as always to avoid any kind of paternalism, finds a new way to put large responsibilities directly into the hands of Springfield's young people in *A City for Lincoln*. The results are fascinating.

The story takes its last strange turn when Don Henderson finds himself leading a charge to get the adults in town to assume similar responsibility for themselves—in this case, by converting a privately owned utility into a municipal operation. Ironically enough, this issue also comes down to a contest—a game, if you will—in which winning or losing is the final question, and Don runs for mayor of Springfield. Tunis, bringing home the irony, closes the book by narrating the election with a sportswriter's eye for key strengths and weaknesses, strategic gambits, and momentum. And this time, Don isn't shut off from the action; he's in the middle of it all.

So are the kids. The contrast with that early basketball game is important. Then, Tunis pulled the controlling adult off the case and let the kids play their game unto themselves. But now, in an election—which is surely an adult affair—he doesn't exclude the young people as he did Don. This, he is saying, is the real thing, this matters, and everyone should be involved.

Nothing meant more to Tunis than what he saw as the spirit of America: its creativity, generosity, and fearlessness in the service of self-determination. He had no use for rich conservatives who amassed their fortunes and grew afraid of change; he had no use for serious traditionalists who sought to bridle the spontaneous adventurousness of the American experiment. In several books he lampoons right-wingers who label every innovation "bolshevism" and advise the "lower classes" simply to pick themselves up with good cheer and rise to prosperity. These lampoons, written in the 1940s, have come to life in a way that would not surprise Tunis. Instead, they would confirm his conviction that we should let kids take responsibility for themselves first, and then for the future of the United States.

A City for Lincoln rings with John Tunis's celebration of our natural American goodness and spirit, represented best of all by the fearless young. He seems to be showing us for the first time that we can entrust to them higher tasks than simply to execute a coach's defensive strategy in a basketball game. We can give them the right to create our future. It really is *their* future, as Don Henderson points out to the town fathers of Springfield—and who are we to construct it ahead of them? With this novel, as with all of his books, Tunis does his part: he places the story in the hands of his young characters and then places the book in the hands of young readers. The parallels are intentional. Tunis knew that a book, in the hands of a kid, was a call to responsibility. He trusted his readers to *make* something out of his stories, to turn them into thought and action.

—Bruce Brooks

A City for Lincoln

1

As Don passed through the gym, he noticed a dozen little shavers of eight or nine out on the floor in their stocking feet. Their arms were hardly long enough, their hands scarcely big enough to get round the basketball and hold it. Yet hold it they did, with sureness and poise. Concentrated upon their game, they paid him not the least attention. Shrill, excited cries echoed over the empty gymnasium.

Forgetting his aching head, Don stood watching, listening to their shouts and appeals. That's basketball, he thought, that's basketball in Indiana. Basketball, the game of the people, of all the people, the game every Hoosier understands, young, old, rich, poor. The game of hoops nailed to barn doors and trees and garages, the game of the small towns of the U.S.A.

The Springfield Wildcats and Don Henderson had come through—first in the sectional games of the State High School Basketball Tournament, then in the Regionals and a week ago in the Semifinals at Muncie. Now it was the day before the Finals; the grand climax of the year for every citizen of Indiana. And the Springfield Wildcats were in the Finals. They would play in Indianapolis tomorrow. Hour by hour, all over Springfield, the fever increased. Old ladies shopping in Maher's grocery and the A & P discussed fast breaks and inside blocks. Businessmen went without lunch, deserted their offices in a search for tickets. Around the lobby of the Springfield House a group stood, hoping every minute someone would turn up with an extra seat. Basketball was the only topic of conversation; in stores and shops, along Buckeye Street, in Joe's Lunch, and before the Indiana Theatre. In Mike's and the pool parlors along Superior Street with their signs inside, "No Minors Allowed," where the high school boys foregathered as dusk descended; outside the *Journal* Building where sixty bikes decorated the curb while their owners argued over Tom Shaw and Jackson Piper and waited for the Special Basketball Edition to come down; everywhere was a single thought—the game. And only one question was asked—got a ticket?

And there was one person on whom the pressure grew every minute of the long day. The coach of the Wildcats was the most important person in Springfield, well aware that if fortune was kind, within a matter of hours he would be the most important citizen of all Indiana. This fame carried a penalty. In the Middle Land the basketball coach is the friend of everyone and everyone's his friend. When his team comes through to the Finals, one out of 775, he has more friends than ever. They all know him. He'd better know them, too.

Dizzy with fatigue, Don went down the stairs of the gym and, nearing the coach's room, heard the warm deep voice of Russ Brainerd, his assistant.

"Pants, medium weight, size 32, twelve pairs."

A young voice answered like an echo. "Pants, medium weight, size 32, twelve pairs."

That would be Perry. Perry Taylor, the tough kid the cops had had so much trouble with. For the first time that feverish day, Don smiled. That experiment was working out.

The coach's room was small, lined with shelves of equipment. A pale thin boy stood counting the stuff on the shelves, while Russ, leaning against the bench at the end of the room under the window, checked the items on a pad.

Don slumped into the folding wooden chair. It creaked loudly. There was but one chair in the room. The more chairs, the more people in the tiny space; the more people, the more confusion. Hence one chair.

He hauled the batch of tickets from an inside pocket. Wrapped round it was a sheet of paper with a list of names. He sorted the tickets out. Now then, here's two for Doc Showalter, here's two for the Kennedys . . . one for Chris . . . one, nope, two for . . . hold on a minute . . .

He found himself shuffling the tickets aimlessly. Russ's voice interrupted him.

"Shoes, pro model, two pairs of eights, three size twelves."

"Shoes, pro model, two pairs of eights, three size twelves. Check," echoed Perry Taylor.

Shoot! I'm so tired I don't know what I'm doing. This head of mine hurts the worst way. Now let's see, let's get this straight, two for the Doc, one . . . nope, two for Chris . . . that leaves . . .

•

In the main building above, the new principal of the high school slapped down the telephone on his desk and started briskly toward the door. Along the outside room was a counter, and behind it three girls were working at desks. One called as he went past.

"Mr. Storey! Cambridge City."

He wheeled, walked over to a switchboard on a small table in one corner, took up a receiver and flipped a switch. "Yes . . . yes . . . who? Oh, hullo, Bill, hullo there, didn't recognize you, boy. Yes. Yes, sir, yes, we are, this town is really wild tonight." There was a note of pride in his tone. For Springfield was a Hoosier town. And if Anderson went haywire over the Indians, if Evansville threw the town into the river when they won and Logansport became mad over the Berries, Springfield was not behind them in affection and enthusiasm for the Wildcats. "Bill, I sure wish I could. Every single one gone, Bill, every one. Why, I could get rid of two thousand right here now. O.K., Bill, sorry." He replaced the receiver, but before he could move another girl called from behind the counter.

"South Bend. *And* Lafayette. Who'll you take first?"

He stood motionless for a second. "South Bend." Again he flipped a switch. "Hullo? Why, yes, yes, of course; of course I recall you, Mr. Stevenson. I remember you very well indeed. I sure do. Why, I'd like to oblige you, sir, just can't do it. Cannot . . . no . . . how's that? Yes, sir, we aren't even taking care of our own folks here in Springfield. Yes, that's right. How's that? Don? I don't hardly think he has; you can call him, though. He's over in the gym now; his number is 4673. 4673, that's right. You're welcome."

As he replaced the telephone, the girl immediately called him. "Lafayette. And Fort Wayne. *And* Rushville."

The principal turned toward the outer door. "You can't locate me. I'm out of the office. Be back in an hour." He stepped quickly into the corridor, closing the door behind him.

•

Doc Showalter, Springfield's leading osteopath, opened the door of his office in the Merchants Bank Building, and surveyed the crowded waiting room. He was a big man, with brown, friendly eyes behind his glasses. His coat was off, and his fingers were deep in the pockets of his vest.

He caught an eager eye.

"J. Frank," he said, nodding his head.

The man on the couch flipped a newspaper together, rose, and went through to the inner office. The Doc paused, the doorknob in his hand. He waved a finger.

"See you just a minute, Mrs. Green."

Inside, J. Frank Shaw took off his coat and vest, and stretched out upon the hard table. Doc Showalter went to work with practiced fingers. He talked as he worked.

"Well, how's the boy? How's Tom today, J. Frank?"

"All right at breakfast. He's taking the whole thing in his stride."

"Good boy, mighty good boy, Tom. Don couldn't have done anything this year without him. Just about won that Fort Wayne game last week. I think they'll win tomorrow, I really do."

The man on the table grunted. An old player himself, he was an expert and everyone else in Springfield, including his son and the coach, had to listen when he discussed basketball. "Doc," he said, "you must realize one exceptional player isn't enough in Indiana. To win here you must have two exceptional players. That's why we didn't come through last season—one reason, that is."

"Why, yes, h'm . . . mebbe . . . h'm . . . I suppose." The Doc continued to talk as he went on working. "Yes, only this year he has Jackson Piper. I swear, that kid looked sweet to me out there this last month. He's taking those passes from Tom. . . ."

The other grunted under the Doc's ministrations. He said nothing for a minute. Then he remarked quietly, "Colored boy, isn't he?"

The Doc straightened up. Then he leaned over and resumed work. "Sure. What's that got to do with it? On the left side, J. Frank, left side . . . please."

"Not for my team!"

"No? Why not?"

"Not for my team. 'Course if Henderson wants to use him, that's his affair. He never would take advice from those who are older, who've forgotten more basketball'n he'll ever know. Nope, you take a colored boy, now; they're fine when things are easy. When a team's on top of the heap. Push 'em round a little, and they just aren't there."

"Mebbe. Over here, J. Frank, over here, and on your back, please." The Doc patted the table by the window. "But I still like Henderson's methods. Seems to me he's done pretty good since he came to town, considering the material he's had."

The patient rose and moved across to the adjoining table. "Material! Material!" His tone was blistering. "Material my Aunt Emma! Lemme tell you one thing, Doc. And you . . . can paste this . . . in your hat, too. Speaking . . . as an . . . as an old player . . . y'understand. . . ."

His last words were lost in a kind of gurgle. For the Doc had him speechless. His big palms were round J. Frank's throat, and he was moving his head from side to side. If the patient was unable to talk, however, the Doc was not.

"Tell you what, J. Frank, I'm kinda worried about Don."

"So! Whatsa . . . whatsa matter?"

"He's all in, that boy. I b'lieve if the season

was to last a week longer, he'd crack. Why, he's been on the verge of a nervous breakdown, pressure he's been under these last weeks, since winning the Conference. Everyone's after him. Now sit up, J. Frank, sit here on the side . . . back to me."

•

When Don finally came out of the basement and up the side steps of the gymnasium, it was black outside. The parking space was empty of cars, the front steps were deserted. He stood for a minute in the darkness, thinking.

I'd like to go to Walgreen's and get something for this old head of mine, but that soda clerk and old man Tuttle and the whole world and his wife'll be on my neck if I do. Guess I'll just go home the back way and keep out of sight, keep away from folks. I don't want to see a soul tonight.

He crossed over, went along a block and turned into Michigan. The cold March wind cut him as he rounded the corner, and he put up the collar of his coat. The wind and the sharp night air should have made him feel better. They didn't. The more he walked the worse he felt. Up ahead a man was unlocking a car by the curb. Don came up, went past. Then he felt a sudden pain in his stomach, a pain that doubled him over. He stood leaning against a tree, panting, when someone grabbed his arm.

"Don! You're not well, you're not yourself tonight."

"Oh! Hello, Peedad, hello. . . ."

Peedad Wilson, editor of the *Evening Press*, said nothing. He had one of Don's arms in a tight grip, a grip that was comforting. They stood speechless for a few minutes. Then the pain began to lessen; slowly it disappeared. Don straightened up.

"I'm better. I'm O.K. Thanks, Peedad."

"You aren't, you're a sick man." He turned him round and walked a few steps to the car. He opened the door.

"I'm going to take you home and put you to bed. You should be away from the telephone and those people at your boarding house tonight; you come with me." He pushed him in the car. Don sank into the seat with relief. The pain was almost gone; but his head still hurt and he felt weak. Despite the chilly air there was perspiration all across his forehead.

The old fellow went round and climbed in

behind the wheel. "Why, you're trembling, Don, you're trembling all over. Mustn't let this basketball get you down."

"Be finished tomorrow night, Peedad."

The old man looked at him and said nothing. Then he started the car and moved out into the street. It was quiet and deserted. In a couple of blocks they crossed the little bridge over the Wildcat River, and saw South Washington up ahead, the long avenue that nearly bisected the town. At the edge of the city limits, it turned into Route 69, the straight highway south to Indianapolis.

Immediately they were plunged into basketball again. The town was alive, feverish with excitement. They stopped, waiting for a traffic break. There was no traffic break. The line of cars going south to Indianapolis poured past one after the other; a whirr, a flash of lights, another whirr, and another flash of lights. There was emotion even in the procession of automobiles. For it was a caravan, a kind of modern pilgrimage to Mecca, a mechanical pilgrimage roaring on into the blackness of the flat farmland, toward the city, and the lights of the Field House, and the Finals of the State Tournament. The next day had begun even before it had arrived. The day when the Wildcats would meet their greatest test. Because here they're all tough. Here no team is a set-up, no one is a pushover. Here they try hard; they play hard; they play to win. That's basketball in Indiana.

2

It was peaceful, stretched out on the couch in Peedad's living room after dinner, and restful, too. No telephones. No demands, no one asking for tickets. Just the old man sucking on his pipe in the easy chair, and the sounds of dishes clattering in the kitchen sink out back. Don looked at his watch. Almost nine o'clock. By this time tomorrow we'll know how we stand.

"Feel better, don't you, Don?"

"Yes, I do. That stuff you gave me fixed me

up. I'm mighty glad you happened along just then."

"Wish you'd change your mind and stay all night."

"I'd like to, Peedad, but the evening before the Finals it wouldn't be wise. If anything happens, I have to be where they can get hold of me."

"I wish you would, just the same. Don, tell me. You won the Conference this year, you got a better team'n you had last year. How you account for it?"

"Why, Peedad, the improvement is due to one thing this year—Tom Shaw."

"You mean he's better? How could he be? Wasn't he an All-State center last year?"

"Yes, he was. But he's improved all right. He doesn't foul so much, he carries himself better, and he's foxier, oh, much foxier. Point is, having won the Trester Award and all that last year, he could have made lots of trouble this fall. Some boys would; the Award has ruined some boys. He could have been fat-headed and troublesome, yes, and quarrelsome, too. Tom isn't that way, he just isn't that sort of a boy."

"Takes after the old man, hey!" Peedad lifted

his shaggy eyebrows and glanced ironically across at Don.

"I dunno, Peedad. I dunno 'bout that. I'd hardly say J. Frank's exactly quarrelsome."

"What! After that scrap you had with him last winter! He's not quarrelsome, not a bit, so long as he has his own way. I remember last year you telling me what a wonderful citizen he was, and how much he did for the town and everything, and my saying . . . Remember what I told you?"

Don remembered.

"I said J. Frank Shaw's a fine man until someone disagrees with him. If you cross him, watch out! Play ball with him, same as everyone else in town, and things are dandy. Cross him, and you'll wish you hadn't; you'll soon discover who runs Springfield, Indiana. You found out pretty quick, as I recall."

"Yes, I'd admit that. Tom isn't the same kettle of fish, though. Tom's different." He thought of the tall boy with the crew haircut, saw him sitting on the bench, listening attentively while he explained how to work out some problem, how to outsmart some better team, how to pull the Kats through a tight game. Hang it all, he thought, as he had often before, what makes the J. Frank

Shaws? Once the old man was like Tom, once he was quick and keen and active, a master of the fast break; once he could pour that ball in like nobody's business. Once he was young and warm and generous to other kids, helping them sink baskets and make the winning shots. Once J. Frank was like Tom. Once.

"Nope. I'd have to admit you're right. Tom isn't the same as J. Frank. Point about Tom is, the publicity that kid has had would have ruined most players. Not Tom Shaw. He's the same as ever."

"Yes, I can see that."

"I knew from the start of the season, I told Russ back in the fall before we began practice, that he'd either cause me all the trouble in the world or be my greatest helper. Peedad, I don't mind telling you he's carried far more than his share in our games so far. Lots of times he feeds the other players like Jackson who actually make the baskets; they look good at his expense. Remember my first season, Peedad, when folks all said I put him on the team because he was J. Frank's boy, because he lived on the west side?"

"Now he's the high scorer for the Conference."

"Correct. But he doesn't let it affect him the least little bit; he doesn't let it influence his play for the team. Most games he's carried more than his share, but usually you can't notice it from the stands."

"I haven't had a chance to see any games this year," Peedad said. "Don, tell me something that interests me a lot. You seem to have right good luck with boys. Don't you ever run into trouble? Take last summer, for instance, when you had charge of the Recreation Program in the park. Did you have any trouble with the bad ones?"

"Peedad, I don't really believe there are any bad kids, leastways not many. One or two, one or two perhaps, just a few. There're not many bad kids, Peedad, but there's a plenty of bad parents."

The old man nodded. "I hope you're right. I only hope so. But still and all, there's a couple of gangs in this town that make me wonder sometimes. Now take those boys who broke into the high school last winter."

"Happens I know all about that. Perry Taylor was one of my boys who got mixed up in it. The police said they busted in to steal clothes; that's not true, they didn't. They broke in to play basketball."

"How do you know?"

"Well, they caught this Taylor boy. Now Perry's a kid I had quite some trouble with in recreation work in the park all summer. I finally straightened him out, and I know him; he tells me the truth. And he told me the whole story. Look, Peedad, remember when you were a boy. Well, suppose you were a kid, and you listened to that game over the radio last February, and then suppose you got steamed up and wanted to play yourself. Where'd you go to play basketball in Springfield on a Saturday night?"

The old man hesitated. He knew the town. Yes, where? Where in Springfield, Indiana, can a boy play basketball on Saturday night? What do we offer kids here in town? What do we give them to keep them busy? Sure, the clip joints are all running Saturday nights, and the Steak House, and the gambling spots, Mike's and the pool parlors along Superior Street. But where can a boy play basketball? We wanted a winning team, we concentrated upon the varsity and let the kids of Springfield take care of themselves, that's what we did. We left them here by themselves, with no place to go.

Where could a boy play basketball in Springfield on Saturday night? "Why, the Y, I suppose," he said.

"There was a dance on there that evening. Peedad, those kids wanted to play and there was no place for them to go 'cept the gym. It belongs to them, it belongs to the Wildcats, so they broke in and used it, that's all."

"Yes, I know, I realize all that, Don, but there's some tough kids hereabouts. That gang from Depot Street across the tracks, for instance, they go round letting the air out of tires in parked cars and . . ."

"That's no crime, that's just kids."

"Yes, but wait a minute. Then they gang up on our lads who deliver papers. The *Journal* has had all sorts of trouble, so have we. They'll set on a boy and beat him up and even steal his bike. They've done it several times. Why, we had to send two of them away from town; we sent two boys off to reform school. Now what do you do when you come across real bad ones like that? How do you handle 'em?"

"Peedad, lemme tell you something. Seems like to me when kids are really bad, it's 'cause they crave attention and don't know any other way to get it. My belief is that if you do find a boy who's bad, nine times out of ten you'll turn up a dad who's no shining example."

The little man sucked on his pipe and looked at Don attentively for a minute. He was thinking. "H'm, yes, h'm . . . sure. But specifically, how do you handle those cases, one of these bad boys? Looks to me like you'd have had trouble this summer. Just how do you handle 'em?"

"Well, I dunno. Each one I handle different, I guess. First-off, I try to find out what a boy's real interests are. Take this young Perry Taylor, for instance. Everyone assured me he was a tough cookie, teachers couldn't do anything with him, always sullen and surly-like, always in mischief, hooking rides on freight cars, breaking windows, pinching oranges from the fruit store. Well, anyway, Perry was just plain mean. So I tried to find out what interests him. Big league baseball? Nope. Swimming? Fishing? No, didn't ring a bell. Did he collect stamps or something? Never tried. One night late last fall I took Perry home in my car. 'Perry,' I says, 'what on earth interests you?' He didn't seem to know. So I asked him, 'Well, what do you like to do best in all the world?' Peedad, he didn't answer for quite some time, maybe fifty, sixty seconds. Then he comes out all of a sudden. 'Know what! I like to go out and hunt for walnuts.'

" 'Oh, you do, do you!' I looked at his hands right away. Sure enough, his fingers were all walnut stains. 'Perry,' I says, 'how are the walnuts this year?'

" 'Oh,' he says, 'they're fine!'

" 'O.K., get me a peck.'

" 'A peck?'

" 'Yessir, you go gather me a peck of walnuts. All cracked and ready to eat. Deliver them up to the house.'

" 'How much? How much'll you pay me?'

" 'Perry, I leave that to you.'

" 'You leave the price to me!' You see, Peedad, no one had ever accepted him that way before. 'Uhuh,' I says, 'you set the price. You set it; I'm not a mite afraid you'll cheat me.'

"Well, sir, well, Peedad, next night that darn kid showed up with a peck of walnuts, the finest walnuts you ever saw, all cracked and ready to eat. I wasn't home, so my landlady asked him how much I owed him, and he said sixty cents. That's the regular price. So later I told him, 'Perry, that's just fine. Get me another peck.' And he did. Pretty soon he got to hanging round the locker room of an afternoon; he got to helping us with the clothes and straightening things out; he was a good little worker, so now I'm breaking him in to act as manager after Red Crosby graduates. Storey says I'm taking chances, says the boy has a bad reputation, says he steals. Says he's no account. I ain't afraid, I trust him, and I b'lieve the boy'll turn out O.K. He's a good, hard worker, and smart. Well, I've talked quite considerable, Peedad; it's done me good, too. I feel relaxed. I forgot all about that game for a couple of hours. Thanks lots, thanks." He rose and stretched. "Guess I'd better be getting along."

He paused. The old man sat there without speaking. He was thinking. After a while he nodded his head slowly. He said nothing. Then he got up. "I see," he remarked, nodding again. "I see."

He saw a good deal further than the coach of the Springfield Wildcats realized at the moment.

3

Everyone pretended to be busy. The boys hung up their jackets and coats and spread out their clean clothes on the benches. Doc Showalter, who acted as team physician and knew almost as much about basketball as the coaches, was cutting up pieces of surgeon's plaster which he was sticking by one end to the edge of the rubbing table. Red was laying out the solution for the Doc, passing chewing gum around, moving back and forth with quick, active steps. Everyone seemed to be busy except Don.

He yanked off his coat and hung it on a hook, and walked across to the door. The dressing quarters looked exactly the same as they had the previous year; clean, modern, odorless, impersonal compared to the small, smelly lockers of the gym back in Springfield. Well, this was it. Once again they'd come through when they had to, once again they had climbed into the State, into the last game of all.

The boys dressed rapidly. From their movements, as first one and then another rose from the benches and began chucking balls back and forth, he realized how tight were their nerves. Only Tom Shaw seemed cool and contained. He threw the ball as he always did, with a kind of flip, a hard ball, fast.

"Watch it! Watch those fingers there, Tom. Not too hard, boys; not too hard, Jackson. Here, slip up on the table and let the Doc fix up that ankle of yours . . . there. How's it feel today? Does it hurt? It doesn't! Good. Not too hard there, Chester. Watch those fingers, boys, you aren't warmed up yet."

Now everyone was dressed and ready to go. The clock over the door said ten minutes to eight. Don understood their feeling, their craving for action, their desire to get started and get it over with, to have the relief of motion and movement and body contact. He understood their anxiety as the moment they had been working for together since fall came closer; the test they had been aiming at through the whole season, through the Conference games, the Sectionals at home, the Regionals at Marion, the Semifinals at Muncie. It was here, almost, and they were so tense and tight they could hardly bear the suspense.

And Don was the most nervous one of all! More nervous even than the new players, the boys like Earl and Chester who had never before been in the State, or Jackson Piper on whom so much depended this evening. He noticed Earl toss the ball mechanically, catch it again, shove it round his back, and throw it with his left hand, the gum in his mouth moving jerkily all the while.

Jackson rose from the table, stood up on his weak ankle, tested it, hopped up and down carefully, made a couple of quick starts, then stopped and nodded his head. The Negro boy was a beautiful sight with his sinewy arms and legs. Now everyone was ready, even the slowest of the subs had finished putting on the familiar red suit, the red jersey with the number on it, the red satin pants. Several were hauling on their jackets with the word WILDCATS in blue across the front.

"O.K.! O.K. there, Tom, put on that jacket. You too, Chet, don't take cold now. Everyone set?"

The team and the subs ranged themselves on the long benches by the wall. Their heads went down over their knees; their jaws were the only part of their bodies in motion.

"Last year—" Don looked up and down the long line—"last season . . . last year, we came in here thinking when we beat Anderson in the afternoon we had the State. We didn't pay much attention to Bosse and they clipped us by a point. This year we won't make that mistake!"

There was an involuntary movement of the hands along the bench. Clap-clap, clap-clap, they went. A few murmurs rose. "Let's get this one . . . this is the one we want."

"Yep, let's get this one. Only one thing, don't play faster'n you can think. We're gonna shift on blocks, but don't shift until you see there is a block. On the offensive bankboard, go in there with your eyes open. Does no good if your eyes are closed. And keep your hands up, everyone.

Carry your hands where they'll be ready alla time."

His voice rose and fell, now high, now low, commanding their attention. "Tom! You'll be the judge; get out there and move. Remember, you gotta balance your offense and defense, gotta be balanced. . . ." A sharp pain suddenly struck under his heart. He hesitated a minute. It passed and he went on.

"Most likely they'll start faking at the gun. Don't let it bother you, don't let it get you." He turned to Otis Kling, the track coach who had scouted Bosse for them. "How's 'at now, Otis? Did that Number Seven do all the shooting last week? Mostly he did? Good! That's your man, Chester; he's fast, he's tough, and he can shoot. Yes, sir! Now they're gonna be on Tom, naturally; they're gonna jam him to death same's everyone else has all season. They think if they stop Tom they can beat us; they're planning to stop Tom. That's your chance, Jackson; you go. When Tom comes across, you fake to him, and go!" The jaws moved in unison along the bench.

"Earl! Occasionally last week you tipped off who you were gonna throw to. Watch that, boy. And see that basket, see it. Don't just chuck that ball anywhere. Shoot it up there, lift it up there like it's supposed to go.

"Jackson, you're on Kates. Now this man Kates, I had him, oh, some years ago at Center Township. He's a drivin' fool, a drivin' fool; he loves to play basketball, he goes in there, he's got balance and body coordination. Smart, too; the only man in the Conference who fooled Tom last season." His voice was higher, now lower. "He's good, sure he is. *If* you don't hold your position. Remember, Jackson, remember that. He'll get an inch on you every time, so work him, work him to death. You be in position, you make him turn the corner. He's sneaky, oh, he's awful sneaky, and fast; we found that out last March, didn't we, Tom? You bet we did. Whatever you do, keep your eyes on that ball. This year, the same as last, he's been doing a lot of dribbling, so watch him every second. Jack, play like you played against this man Wilson in Muncie last week, and you can handle him."

There was that pain again. It was a kind of stab under his heart, a pain that made it difficult to breathe. He had to wait a minute or two, and turn half away so they wouldn't notice it. On the bench one boy's knee twitched, someone's head jerked back involuntarily, and two hands clapped. He realized the tension they were under, the emotional strain that gripped them all, even Red, even the Doc and Russ standing behind him.

"Le's see now . . . what else? Oh, yes, one thing; Kates likes to catch the ball, throw up his empty hand . . . like this . . . see . . . and then throw the other way with his right hand. Just a trick, that's all; it fooled us some that first half last year, so watch him, Jackson, watch him alla time. I depend on you. Remember, we outscored this same club 16 to 7 last year in the second half.

"Tom-boy . . ." He stepped across and ruffled the big fellow's hair. This is the last time, he thought. The last time he'll play for the Wildcats, or for me. The last time he'll be jumping up there under the bankboards, the last time he'll be pulling the team together, hauling them along to overtake the other side as he did on this floor last March, and at Muncie a week ago. This is the last time. Today and that's all. He'll be through high school. He won't be on the team next year.

The boy's expression didn't change; his jaws continued their everlasting motion. Yet his face was taut and strained like Don's.

Gee, this is the last time, Tom was thinking. I never hardly realized it before. The last time I'll be seeing Don over there on the side look toward me, confident-like, even when we're behind, when we're doing badly even. The last time I'll be slugging it out for the Kats, for Don who stayed with me and taught me all I know about basketball, like he stayed with Jackson this year when folks said colored boys quit in the pinches. Gosh, this is the end. It's here now, and it hurts. The last time . . .

"Tom-boy, you're the boss. You take charge, you're captain. You watch 'em, you call time, you set the tempo, you run the show. And whatever you do, follow up, boy, follow up, follow up under that basket. I'm counting on you under that basket, Tom."

He's been with me through everything, through my whole stay in Springfield, Don thought. Through the thin times that first year when they laughed at us, and the good times when we came up, when we were winning and when we were losing; he really made this team. He made Jackson Piper, too; he brought us into the State once again; why, he's even made my reputation as a basketball coach! That's what he's done, that's about all. And this is the last time; it's here now.

He glanced at them, saw Chester's red mop of hair, and Earl's nervous tension as he sat locking and unlocking his fists, and Buck McClure turning a ball round and round in his palms, and Jackson's skin glistening in the electric light. But what he really saw was Tom Shaw, reliable Tom, the tall boy with the giant arms and legs. Tom's head came up slowly, those blue eyes turned toward his and blinked a little.

He feels it. He understands, he feels it too. This is the last time.

"Fellas, get out in front, get out in front and stay there! Whatever happens get out in front. And move that ball; whatever you do, move that ball. Just one more thing. I want you to have some fun tonight. . . ." He paused a second as that strange, stabbing pain gripped him beneath his heart. It was deeper and fiercer. He held his side until it lessened.

"Boys, we've had quite a struggle this year, but we've come a long, long ways since that first game we lost to Rossville last November. Basketball has to be fun. It has to be fun. Last year I felt we had a better ballclub than Bosse, even though they edged us out. I honestly felt we were the better team. They've got a veteran club this season, but I think we have a better one, I really do. And I'd like for you to go out on that floor and prove it. You can. . . . I believe you will. . . . I feel you'll beat this bunch today. . . ."

The pain was worse now, much worse. He turned away from them, as the rasping of benches and the sound of a dozen voices echoed together across the room.

"Le's go, gang . . . le's go, Kats . . . we'll take this one . . . le's go, Wildcats . . . yea! Wildcats! The old fight . . . le's go, gang . . . the old fight . . ."

4

Tom was the last to rise. He knew something was wrong, noticed the agony on Don's face as he turned away. Towering over everyone, the tall center stepped across to his coach, now leaning against the rubbing table. The boy's hand was out.

Don grasped the great wide fist, surprised to find it moist. Why, he's as nervous as I am! His hand's all wet.

Tom, in turn, felt Don's hand. He was astonished to find it was damp. He looked at him, observed the drawn face. Don's not well, Tom thought. Don's in pain!

"Hey, you guys! Hey, Doc! Chester! Hey there, Red . . ." The hand in Tom's grasp suddenly went limp, and Don slumped from the edge of the rubbing table to the floor.

They picked him up, Tom and the powerful Doc Showalter and Red and Russ Brainerd, and laid him on the table. The Doc leaned over, feeling his pulse, listening to his heart, watching the spasms of pain stab across his face. While all the team and the subs crowded around, open-eyed.

The Doc raised his head. "Russ! You'll take the team out there. Leave him here to me."

The boys moved away. And the Wildcats left the room for the last round of all, with their coach stretched out in pain on the rubbing table in the locker room, his assistant in charge of the team.

The hallway beneath the stands was packed with fans eating hot dogs and drinking cokes. As the team edged through the mob, snatches of basketball conversation came to them from the waiting throng.

"I'll say those Hatchets were lucky . . . I'll say . . . And he makes a fast break about as well as anyone in the Conference. . . . That Richmond bunch pulled the darndest three man defense on us. . . . I understand there's a big package riding on Bosse this evening . . . sure, the hot money. . . . Hey, Flatfoot, what's cookin'? . . . There go the Kats! Hi, there, Tom! . . . That's Shaw, the big one. . . . Is that Frank Shaw's boy? . . . Yep, you know J. Frank, don't you? Great guy, Frank is. . . . There's Piper, their colored forward. . . . He's the lad that Tom sets up alla time. . . . There they go. . . . There go the Kats. . . . Yea! Wildcats!"

They worked their way through the crowd and along the passageway to the floor, minus their coach, without the man who had fought and worked with them, who had helped them pull through to the last round of all. The Bosse team was already out under one basket practicing free throws. Across the arena, four girls in white stood in a line, each with an arm on the arm of the one in front. They were leading a cheer.

"Yea, Bulldogs! B-U-L-L-D-O-G-S! Fight—team—fight!"

The Wildcats gathered round Tom Shaw at the edge of the floor. Above them were the thirteen thousand howling maniacs in the stands, the two rival yelling sections shouting at each other across the arena. The boys put their arms around each other's shoulders and leaned over, heads down. This was the last time. They were going out for the last time of all, and their coach was back in the lockers, twisting in pain on the rubbing table. The sight of his agonized face was before every one of them as Tom spoke.

"Fellas . . . we don't know what-all's hit Don. All we know is, he's out. So we just gotta go in there and knock these guys off without him. What's more . . . we're gonna do it, too. C'mon! Le's go, you Wildcats!"

Back inside the dressing room, the Doc was feeling Don's stomach gently, pressing it here and there, bringing bursts of pain to his tightened lips. He continued, watching the expression of agony sweeping across the face of the coach on the hard table below. "Does it hurt there . . . there . . . no, no . . . lie still, Don . . . well, I know . . . but you can't . . . you cannot go out, that's all . . . well, Russ'll handle 'em. You're sick, you're a sick man."

Looking up, Don saw serious faces bending over him; Otis Kling staring down wide-eyed, and Red Crosby with a frightened expression, and the big brown eyes of the Doc with his firm, concentrated look. Even through his pain he felt their concern. For by now the pains were intense, all up and down his stomach as far as his chest. It must be his heart. That was it, his heart. All athletes had heart trouble at one time or another, he reflected. Then he noticed Red, Red who should have been out on the bench.

Me, too, I should be there. Russ can't handle 'em against Bosse; he hasn't the savvy, he hasn't got the experience. I've got to get out with the boys somehow. I must get out there with the team, I must. . . .

He tried hard to sit up and struggle to his feet. Without a word, the Doc gave him a gentle push and back he slumped. No strength; no strength at all.

Then they started to remove his clothes; his coat, vest, shirt, trousers. Someone threw a couple of blankets over him. Otis appeared with a hot towel which he wrung out, tossing it from hand to hand, and finally placed it on Don's bare stomach.

Don heard the Doc saying something to Red Crosby. Vague words came from far away. "Here, Red . . . you take this prescription . . . take my car . . . here's the keys . . . and the car ticket . . . nearest drugstore . . . tell 'em who it's for . . . filled immediately, y'understand?"

The Doc turned back to the table. Don could see his eyes peering anxiously down. "Just as hot as he'll stand it, Otis, as hot as he can stand it."

"Now then, Don, you lay still. You've got an acute case of gastritis. Nerves, that's all, just plain nerves. You've been overdoing things for the last four months, going day and night; now it's caught up with you. You're paying for it. Keep quiet now and do what I tell you, and most likely you'll be all set in a few hours. What's that? They'll lose without you? Well, if they lose, they lose. You've told 'em everything, Don; you can't steer the ball into the hoop for 'em; you can't do 'em any good out there right now."

A roar swept suddenly into the dressing room. It only died down for brief seconds throughout the next forty minutes. The game had begun, and the Springfield Wildcats had taken the floor for the Finals without their coach.

5

The quick, sudden silences were harder to bear than the crowd-roar which almost continually filled the dressing room.

Like this one. A kind of lancinating silence, a silence that stabbed you, that hurt, a silence that was more painful even than the pains all through your stomach, pains that reached up to your chest. That silence, now. That would be Jerry Kates taking the ball out. Kates, getting ready to come down the floor.

There he is, standing there calmly, one hand on his hip, bouncing the ball with the other, surveying the court, collected, relaxed, sure of himself. Watch him, Jackson-boy, watch that man! He's coming down now, slowly, past the ten-second line. Hear that roar! He's coming toward them, almost insolently, dribbling the ball first with his left hand, then with the right, seeking an opening, a chance to break through, eyes on his opponents, not the ball, moving a little to one side or the other . . . then . . .

There he goes! There it comes, that spurt, that burst of speed which puts him around the block and under the basket, turning to throw.

Suddenly Red's excited voice came out of the haze above him. "We're ahead, twenty-one to eighteen. Tom sank a long one, and Jackson hit two charities. . . . I think we've got 'em now." And he disappeared.

"How much time? Hey, Doc, how much time?"

"Didn't say, Don. Not much left, I'd guess. Four-five minutes, mebbe." He tossed the hot towel from one big paw to the other, expertly. "You feel a mite better, don't you? You do, son? Good. Jest lay still there, lay still."

Yes, but I should be out there. I ought to be

there, on the bench beside the subs, watching every move, diagnosing their offense, 'cause Russ just hasn't got it. The experience; he lacks experience, that's what he needs. I ought to be out there with them, shouting at them as they come up the floor, reminding them what to do. Set up, set up that offense, boys . . . set it up!

An enormous roar came into the room. "Gee! What was that, Doc, that noise? They must have evened up."

"Nope . . . no . . . that's most likely another foul or something. You lay still there, Don."

Five minutes to go. Five to go and three points. Anyone's game. I gotta be in there, I really must get there some way. Russ is in front of the bench now, kneeling before one of the subs he's sending in. He's talking to him. Get that ball, Dale, get it and break away whenever you can. Never mind those set plays, never mind . . .

Or maybe he's telling Jack to press Kates. Likely they aren't pressing him the way I told 'em. They forget, those kids, they forget when the going gets tough. Stay in closer there, Jackson, stay in closer; you're giving him too much room. . . .

I oughta be there, this is really awful. This

is worse than any game I ever played, than any game I ever coached, much worse.

The cheers came in, distinct now over the steady crowd-roar. "Yea! Wildcats! Yea! Wildcats! Fight—team—fight." Don could see the stands, shoulders heaving up and down in unison, mouths open together, bodies moving forward in a common effort, in perfect rhythm. "Kats . . . Kats . . . Kats . . . Yea! Wildcats!"

And now the substitutes on the bench were half-rising as Tom comes slowly down the floor. "Pour it on, Tom, pour it on! Keep going, Wildcats, c'mon, Kats . . . get tough . . . get tough out there, Kats. . . ."

Once again Red, breathless and crimson of face, came dashing into the room with another report. "Twenty-seven—twenty-one. The boys are hot again now . . . those guys are shot-happy!"

Ah, so it was our side, it was the Wildcats who were making the noise! Twenty-seven to twenty-one. Six points. "Hey, Red, hey there, Red, how much to go? How much time left, Red?"

But Red moved fast. He was gone, vanished from the room, probably back on the bench by this time. And probably Russ was standing suddenly, jumping up and shrieking at the umpires as coaches always did about this period at the end, pointing out some lad on the other team.

"Hey! How 'bout that? How 'bout that for travelin'? He traveled . . . that li'l boy in red there."

And as usual, the umpire, knowing coaches, would pay no attention.

Then that roar. That wild, almost savage shriek, a shriek which could only mean one thing. Bosse has scored. And again . . . and again, louder now, and louder still. Bosse was crawling up. Those veterans of the court, with poise and balance, were not yet licked. They were crowding the Wildcats, showing that experience will tell as the game edges into the last final minutes.

If only I were out there beside them, with them, instead of trapped here, helpless on this table.

Silence once more. Then that roar, mounting, mounting. Must be Kates. That's Kates all right. Stay in close, Jackson, for goodness sake stay in close. Yep, that's Kates all right, I can tell. He's dribbling down the floor. He's weary, too, and there's a lock of damp hair plastered over his wet forehead as he bounces the ball with his right hand, looking all the time the other way, stopping, pivoting, turning, passing the ball behind his back to a teammate, taking a few steps and then receiving it in return, slapping it on the floor several times, while big Jackson dances before him, arms outstretched, mouth open . . .

There it goes! He darts under, he's in there, he's one-handing that ball up and into the net. . . .

Again the mad, frenzied outburst. It could only mean one thing. He saw the Doc's brown eyes above him waver. The Doc had heard it, also.

"Well, there's only one play in basketball that counts. Putting the ball through the hoop." The big, friendly guy had to say something. He said the first thing that came to mind. No use kidding at that moment; they both knew their basketball too well.

"Wish we could get the score. They're picking up on us all right."

The Doc, wringing out a towel on the floor, said nothing. Like Don, he realized the exact progress of the game outside by the noise barometer they were reading inside the locker room.

Impossible as it seemed, the noise increased. Now they're pouring from the stands, the cops and the firemen and the ushers are kneeling and making a barrier round the court with outstretched arms, and the crowd is pushing out of their seats, down there to the surface of the floor, right up to the floor itself.

It was Red's panting voice. "Two points ahead 'n' two minutes to go!"

Two points and only two minutes to go! Anyone's game. Bosse had crawled up. The noise was louder and shriller now, it broke in continuous waves of sound as the clock ticked off those seconds. The Doc glanced at his wrist watch, but said nothing. A minute and a half . . . a minute fifteen . . . less than a minute . . .

There! Someone is shooting now. Perhaps Tom's up under the basket, tapping it in; perhaps the ball is rolling round on the rim, round and round and round, endlessly and forever. . . .

It's in! Somebody has scored. Is it the Wildcats? Is it Bosse? Now . . . listen . . . listen to that! That could mean anything at all. They looked nervously at each other. Either side might have scored.

Then came the greatest roar of all. It's a tie, or else Bosse is ahead.

Even the Doc forgot his patient, forgot the hot towel in his hands, and stood, his head half-turned toward the door. They waited alone in the big, silent room, while on the floor the Wildcats fought savagely for victory, for their coach stretched out in pain on a rubbing table back in the lockers.

Don forgot his agony, forgot everything as he listened to the storm. Yet he was unable to tell what had happened. It lasted longer than any noise had lasted all evening. Whatever had taken place was something important.

Then the quiet of the room was smashed, broken, torn apart. Stomp-stomp, stomp-stomp came the feet through the door. A dozen voices, panting, exhausted, hoarse but happy, came to him. And he was surrounded; by Tom with the sweat glistening all over his red face, by Jackson with his flashing grin, by Chester and Red and Earl and Buck McClure and the others.

"We did it for you, Don! We licked 'em for you, Don. We clawed 'em up; we beat 'em all right. Yea! Wildcats! Yea! Wildcats! We licked 'em for you, Don, we got 'em for you!"

6

Pandemonium. The boys and the subs pushed around him, and he managed to sit up, wringing their damp paws, slapping their moist backs, shouting at them in triumph. This is it, boys, this is what we worked for, planned for, hoped for. We've won the State; we're the champs!

The room filled up, people slapped at them, called to them, yelled names deliriously. At the door old Jake, the guard, was trying to keep from being submerged by a tidal wave of visitors. When he stopped one, a dozen swept past. Inside, the noise and confusion were terrific. Now the cameramen, half a dozen, ten or more, were ranging them up for photographs. Buck and Earl had the tattered remnants of the nets hung round their necks. They knelt before the little group of photographers, their wet, tousled heads up, joy on their faces, still panting from the exhaustion of those last minutes.

"Just one more, please, just one more, please, just one more." The bulbs flashed and burst in the smelly room. The cameramen yanked plates from their machines, stuffed them into side pockets, and shoved in fresh negatives. Once again the bulbs exploded, sending little clouds of smoke into the thickening air. Then the group of tired, exultant players dissolved, swallowed by the mob of friends, fathers, sportswriters, teachers, and relatives who by this time had completely taken possession of the place.

A figure came through the crowd toward Don, now leaning on one elbow on the rubbing table. It was Dave Conwell, the rival coach.

"Don! I'm awful sorry to hear you're sick."

"It's nothing, Dave, just a slight attack of gastritis. I'm coming around, I'm O.K. now. Say, it's darn nice of you to come over, mighty nice."

"It was a swell game, Don; too bad you couldn't

have seen it. A swell game and a swell bunch of kids you got. We're all agreed we couldn't have lost to a nicer gang."

"Thanks, Dave, thanks lots, thanks."

"Yes, sir, and I mean it, too. Now you take care of yourself. Where's that colored boy? I'd like to shake his hand. He sure ruined us this evening, him and that big center of yours. Couple of grand kids."

Then a familiar face began to edge through the door and into the crowd around the table. He wore an elaborate ulster carelessly unbuttoned, with a blue silk muffler round his throat, and his hat was at a rakish angle. He neared Don, surrounded by people.

"Don, this is too bad, your being laid up like this. I'm sorry to hear you were knocked out."

"Oh, thanks, J. Frank, thanks. I'm coming along. Just a quick attack of gastritis, that's all. I'm O.K. now."

"Gee, I wish you'd been out there, it was great. Well, congratulations, boy! I always knew you had it in you, knew it when we first picked you up that night at Center Township three years ago."

The circle about Don looked at J. Frank with

respect. Someone whispered his name to someone else. "J. Frank Shaw!"

Don grinned and accepted the outstretched hand. Why not? It was J. Frank at his most agreeable. Darn it all, Peedad Wilson picked me, held out for me against this fella. But what's the use of crabbing at a time like this? You can't help liking the big guy, thought Don, feeling warm and comfortable in his smile and the genuineness of his handshake. Now that's really good of J. Frank. After all, he's a sportsman, say what you like.

"Thanks, J. Frank, only I didn't do it, y'know. The boys did it, Tom especially. You really oughta be proud of him."

J. Frank threw back his shoulders complacently. Everyone round was listening and he realized it. The knot of people turned to him as he shook his head modestly. "Tom's a good boy. We don't always see eye to eye on things, but he's a good kid. Mighty near played himself out this evening, too."

Then someone else pressed in. Art Beckner, the coach of the Bearcats, came up, and Sandy MacMann of Fort Wayne wrung his hand, and then he saw Mr. Stansbury, the Superintendent of Schools. Now I've arrived, Don thought. I've taken the Kats into the Finals of the State two years in succession and now we've won. Even J. Frank Shaw wants to make up and be friends, and here's old Stansbury. Shoot, it's O.K. with me. I'd like to be friends with everyone.

"Hullo there, Doc . . . thanks lots, Art. Sure, I'm O.K. now . . . thanks, Jimmy . . . great bunch, yeah, you bet . . . wasn't he something off those bankboards . . . he always is . . . thanks, Mr. Stansbury. Why, I'm all right now, thank you . . . just a sudden attack of gastritis . . . yessir, yessir, thanks, Harry, thanks a whole lot, they tell me you really ran that game tonight, Harry, you really did . . . thanks, Hank, thanks, Joe. Yep, I'm coming along. Why, hullo there, Sid . . . you bet, I feel much better, yeah, no foolin'. *Hey*, you men there, don't stay in those wet clothes, get those wet clothes off right away. Hear me? Hullo there, Bill, hullo. Glad to see you. Yes, we did; yes, we had some luck, I guess. . . . Thanks . . . thanks very much. Glad to meet you, pleased to see you, sir. Yes, sir, great bunch of kids, thanks lots. . . . Yep, I'm coming along, I'm better. . . ."

Funny thing, he *was* better, too. The pain had

almost gone, and he wasn't as exhausted as he had been. When you win, you aren't tired. Victory conquers fatigue, even the fatigue of that long and exhausting day. The players, joy on every face, wandered round in a dream. It was the dream that a few like Tom Shaw had dreamed almost every night for three years, and especially during those past six months, those weary, anxious months. When you lived only for the next weekend and thought of nothing beyond Saturday night; when the least slipup, the smallest mistake, the veriest piece of luck, the ball falling outside the basket instead of inside as it rolled around the rim, could have made that dream impossible. Now it had come true.

And no one really believed it.

"Sure thought they had us this evening, didn't you? . . . Naw, I never did. . . . Me neither. . . . Looked like you'd shoot; I thought you'd shoot that time, Chet. . . . Aw, he hooked me, why, you saw him hook me. . . . I tell you I saw him, sure I saw him. Yeah, these officials are always tough on me; they hate me for some reason, I dunno why. . . . That shovel pass right then. . . . Boy, were we hot out there this evening. . . . Jackson, you sure poured it on them

7

Me an' Jackson, me an' Jackson Piper," said Perry to the kid pushing the little cart loaded with planks. "You and Jackson Piper!" said the boy, jeering at him.

"Yessir," said Perry stoutly. "Jackson Piper's a friend of mine. Say, he won that game, didn't he? Didn't Buck Hannon say so?"

Back in Springfield that afternoon the kids left behind there, which meant the great majority, had turned to. Carts, bikes, wheelbarrows, and the backs of ancient Fords were loaded. Trees, branches, broken boxes, wooden planks, any inflammable material that wasn't nailed down was begged or borrowed and hauled to the middle of Forest Park. Soon a mound, a large mound, appeared; it grew even bigger as dusk fell.

"Suppose they don't win! Suppose they lose this evening!"

"They aren't gonna lose. They'll beat Bosse, you just wait and see!"

All Springfield was confident, all Springfield was sure of it. Young, old, boys, girls, men and women—everyone felt victory in the air. That they had felt the same way the previous March and been disappointed, made no difference. Perry Taylor was especially certain. For the best of reasons he did not go home to dinner, but stayed downtown, eating two hamburger sandwiches at the Greek's. A chilly mist from the Wildcat River descended over the town, and he was glad to be able to listen to the evening game in comfort. This was by no means difficult that evening in the center of Springfield.

The Greek had a small radio turned on most of the time; naturally at the moment the game came first. There was a radio on the cigar counter near the entrance at Mike's, and most of the other pool parlors along Superior where the gamblers congregated had radios, too. Walgreens had a small portable in the rear of the store, and another out by the soda fountain. A dozen, twenty, thirty, then a hundred kids gathered by game time. The Goody Shoppe on Indiana Avenue was jammed, every booth full of high school boys and girls listening. The audience at the Steak House was older but just as intense; so was the fashionable crowd in the packed Grill Room of the Springfield House.

Perry found he was too nervous to stay in one spot long, so he journeyed around, getting a snatch of the battle here and a snatch there, a few minutes in Hook's drugstore, a little in the taxi office on West Walnut. All over town Buck Hannon's excited tones penetrated the air.

"There goes Jackson Piper . . . a fast break . . . a fast break down the floor . . . he flips to Tom . . . takes a shovel pass back again . . . he's in the clear . . . he's under . . ."

Gee! If Jackson scores now, we can't lose!

Then in five minutes Perry was over at Mike's or the Elite Pool and Billiard Parlor, where Buck was also king for the moment. In a thousand, ten thousand, twenty thousand homes all over town that evening, the same voice came in from radios, tense, excited, conveying the drama of that battle in the Field House fifty miles away. Springfield lived for Buck that night and Buck that night lived for the game.

Or almost all Springfield. Strangely enough, among the few people who were not interested in the Finals at Indianapolis were some of the younger citizens of the town. Their indifference did not keep them at home; on the contrary, it sent them outdoors. They were a mixed group of boys, a few about the age of Perry Taylor, boys like Mike Cray and Roy Miller and one or two others from the high school. Most of them, however, were older. They all lived in the same neighborhood in the northeast section of the city over by the railroad tracks. Perry knew them—so, too, did the police force—as the Depot Street gang.

If you follow the Nickel Plate out north, you'll eventually come to the new Warner Gear plant. To avoid a walk of almost a mile, workmen living in that section cut through the fields, and then across the tracks just above Depot Street where it runs beside the railroad. Thus a kind of path which had by custom and usage become an unofficial thoroughfare had been made. In and around this path through the fields was the official headquarters of the Depot Street gang.

Like the workmen in Warner Gear, they knew the railroad and its habits. They knew when the fast freight went through, when to look out for the Fort Wayne express, and when to expect the Flyer. They even knew some things the workmen did not know. They knew when the signal boxes were inspected, and when Harry, the railroad detective, could be anticipated in the vicinity. A chilly Saturday night in March was not one of those times.

It was dark that evening when the Depot Street gang met together after supper, and the tracks out by Warner Gear were deep in shadow. So they didn't hesitate. First, by the aid of a flashlight, they took the locks off the signal boxes. Then they pulled the levers and cut a couple of freight cars standing outside the plant to be unloaded. This took little effort and was agreeable work, since it could cause trouble. Once finished, they crossed the tracks and scampered toward the center of town, picking up a few recruits and associates on the way.

The fun would be downtown and at Forest Park the remainder of the evening. That was the high spot of the night's excitement and entertainment. They walked in that general direction, hooting and cat-calling from time to time, shouting at each other, yelling at two girls who scurried past on the opposite side of the street, amusing themselves by shying rocks at telegraph poles. Nearing a street corner, someone had the idea of tossing a good-sized rock at a street lamp. It missed. Another boy found half a brick in the gutter, and threw that with care. It missed, too. Then another took a hand in the sport, and another. Suddenly there was a crash and a shattering of glass. Darkness covered the corner and the vicinity. The boys scuttled rapidly out of the region.

Three blocks further along they tried their luck once more, only to be warned off by an indignant citizen going past. Their remarks to him for interrupting the fun, as they slouched down the street, had an ugly ring. Two blocks nearer the center of town they paused, collecting a supply of stones, and let them go simultaneously at the corner street lamp. It took a couple of concentrated volleys to bring it crashing, and the ensuing darkness with it.

Another corner, another street lamp as target; a few more volleys, and once again this region was without illumination. Their combined efforts and the continued practice were having their effect; they were blacking out corner after corner on the first round. Occasionally they were scared off by annoyed cries from porches or upper windows, or by some passerby, but the streets were mostly deserted. Every policeman in town was on duty in the business district for the celebration, as they knew. Now they were approaching the center of the city, and the game became more dangerous.

Soon lights showed up ahead. The gang strolled along Superior, pausing at the storefronts to look in the windows. Mike's was open, and several boys popped in to hear that the Wildcats had won the State. They reappeared, yelling. This seemed cause for a celebration of some sort, something particularly special. They stood together, deciding what should be done. Several obvious suggestions were in order. They could let the air out of the tires of all parked cars on the side streets. This was tempting yet hardly daring enough. It would be exciting to smash in a plate-glass store window a few blocks up Superior Street. This was tempting but too risky.

Too many cops downtown. One boy mentioned the bonfire, and thought that starting it and having it burn out before the arrival of the team would be fun. But that would be difficult to accomplish with half of Springfield already gathering in the park.

Those citizens who were not already there, now that the game was over and the team had won, were now on their way toward the park. The streets were full. Men were pouring from the bars and taverns. The whole district was alive and excited. "Well, the boys did it; they won the State at last. They've won! We've won the State. Yea! Wildcats! Yea! Wildcats!"

A stream of cars passed steadily up and down the main streets in the business blocks. Some were decorated with colored paper streamers, some bore big signs, YEA KATS. WE KNEW YOU'D WIN. All had their horns going full blast. The town was in fete. And the police force, grouped around those half dozen squares of downtown Springfield, was alert and ready for trouble. When a town wins the State for the first time in its history, you're prepared. If not, you'd better be!

So the gang stood there, jostled by the growing throng in the growing excitement, not quite knowing what to do next. Occasionally a boy from school or some older man went by and turned to look at them as he moved along. The Depot Street gang! The Depot Street gang on the loose tonight.

Over on the next block, Perry Taylor was waiting, uncertain, also. He knew the team would undoubtedly be met somewhere outside town, probably at the junction of South Washington with Route 69. Beyond any question, the mayor would go out to meet them, and the school band in cars, so Perry figured that by standing prominently on Superior near Mike's he might see them as they left, and he might be able to hook a ride out to greet the team. Then he would return with them to the celebration in the park. He hoped to be one of the first to welcome them, and particularly his friend, Jackson Piper.

While he stood on the curb, watching and waiting, his eyes darting up and down the traffic-jammed street, things were happening in the block behind. A cop saw the Depot Street gang and told them to move along. They wandered aimlessly down Buckeye, past a row of stores, pausing to look in the windows. Just ahead a man turned into a passageway known as Dugan's

Alley. It connected the two main streets, a narrow lane barely large enough for small trucks to squeeze through to deliver merchandise to the back door of the Bon Ton Store that fronted on Superior.

One of the boys saw him turn in, and walking quickly ahead to the entrance of the alley, stood there watching. The man stumbled along a little way, stopped, then lurched on. Now the boy was joined by two or three others, their eyes on the staggering figure moving down the passageway, which had brick walls on both sides. It was narrow, it was dark, it was deserted. The whole gang followed, attentive to that reeling figure ahead. He had most plainly been celebrating the Wildcats' triumph, and here might be some easy money if he had any change in his pockets.

"Here! Gimme that flashlight!" The flashlight was long and heavy, with a knob at one end. The boy grasped it firmly by the smaller part, and walked up behind the man now leaning against the blank wall of the store. He took one rapid look at the crowded street behind him; then raising the flashlight he struck the man on the head. The man dropped. Just at that moment the glare of an automobile lamp flooded the dark alleyway, lighting up the figure slumping to the ground and the boys grouped around him.

They ran.

Perry Taylor, standing on the curb of Superior just a few doors from the alley, his attention fixed upon the passing cars, was suddenly startled by the sound of a police siren. It rose over the blaring of horns and the noise in the street around him. All at once a figure dashed past. It was Mike Cray. He was pursued by another figure that jostled Perry as he ran—Roy Miller.

"It's Casey . . . it's the cops . . . the prowl car . . ."

The siren came nearer. People were turning to look; somewhere up the street a cop started running toward them. Perry was frightened. Cops! Panic seized him. Unthinkingly he ran, too, down the street behind the flying wedge of the Depot Street gang. At the nearest corner they broke up, running this way and that, some straight up Superior, some around and down Michigan, into doorways, drugstores, lunchrooms, anywhere. They vanished from the earth. All except Perry. He ran straight into the arms of Andy Anderson, the chief of police.

8

Don had finally succeeded in breaking away from the celebrating crowd in the dressing room in Indianapolis. He left the squad in charge of Russ Brainerd, and came on ahead to Springfield with Dick Lewis, the sports editor of the *Journal*. At the junction of South Washington and the highway they slowed down for the traffic light, and the officer on duty recognized the white press card on Dick's windshield. He blew his whistle, held up his hand, and came over.

"That you, Dick?"

"Sure is. How you bearin' up, Joe?"

"Well, looks like we've got our work cut out to prevent 'em from tearing the town apart. When's the team coming up?"

"They stopped off at Westfield to eat. They'd oughta be along in about an hour, I'd say."

"I was looking for Don. He's with 'em, ain't he?"

"He is not. He's here, right side of me."

"Hullo, Joe, what's up?"

The big policeman edged up to the window. He leaned inside. His voice was lower. "Don, Andy wants you to get in touch with him at police headquarters, right away. Seems he has one of your boys there."

"One of *my* boys?"

"That's right."

"Who is it, d'you happen to know?"

"Kid by the name of Perry Taylor. They caught him slugging a drunk in Dugan's Alley."

Slugging a drunk? No, not Perry; not Perry Taylor. There's some mistake, there's been a bad mistake here. He tried to speak, but a wall of fatigue surrounded him. The words refused to come.

"The chief says will you please drop in first off before you go to the park. Kid won't talk, won't say a word, boys can't get him to open up. He says he'll only talk to you, says you're the only one he'll talk with. Will you stop off at City Hall as you go past?"

•

Two officers sitting on a bench in the entrance to police headquarters in the basement of the City Hall rose as Don entered. Their coats were off, and their blue shirts indistinct in the one light over the desk behind the grille facing their bench. Andy Anderson, the chief, was at the desk.

"Here he is now! Congratulations, Don, fine work, boy. The team sure went to town for you . . . the Kats were really hitting tonight, weren't they? Congratulations, Don, you did a job all right." Big Andy came round from the grilled part of the room, his hand out. "Great stuff, Don; put it there, boy."

"Yeah, thanks, thanks, boys. Where's Perry?"

"Him? Oh, he's upstairs. You had it mighty tough for a while this evening, didn't you, Don? We figgered you was in trouble there when they hauled up on you toward the end. Say, that colored boy just about saved you with those free throws. Only what happened on that foul in the second quarter? How 'bout that foul they called?" Another officer, hearing the voices, came from an inner room. "Hullo, Don, congratulations!"

"Thanks, Harry, thanks lots. Chief, what about my boy?"

"But, Don, that foul there . . ."

Don ran his hand over his forehead and shoved his hat back on his aching brow. "Look, boys, look, I've had a long, hard day, a mighty tough day what with one thing and another; fact is, I'm kinda confused. Let's us tend to this kid; let's get this kid straightened out before we talk any more basketball. What say?"

"That's O.K., Don. We'll go right up and see him, so's you can get away. The crowd's gathering at the park already; they've collected a bonfire as big as all outdoors. What a bonfire they're gonna have; had to call the fire department out. What a pile those kids gathered! Come this way, Don." The chief led him down a passageway, through a kind of anteroom where there was a table strewn with comic magazines.

He was talking all the while. "Seems like this Taylor kid and half a dozen others tried to roll a drunk in Dugan's Alley there in back of the

Bon Ton. Man was drunk, and these kids set on him. They picked up a flashlight the boys used; guess this Taylor . . . here . . ."

They went through another room where several detectives were sitting, and came into a hall where the chief removed the bars from a heavy steel door. "He's in here, where we usually keep 'em while they sober up." They entered a large square room, entirely unfurnished except for a stone bench in the wall on three sides. Several unconscious drunks were stretched out along the stone bench, and alone, apart, in the far corner, a miserable boy was huddled. When he saw Don, his face gleamed and he jumped up and came over.

"Why, Perry, Perry-boy, what on earth . . . I didn't expect to find you here."

"Don, you won. You won all right tonight, didn't you?"

"Sure did, we cleaned up Bosse this time, Perry."

"Tell me 'bout it, tell me all about it, Don."

"Not here. Chief, can I take him inside?"

"Why, certainly, come along." The two men with the boy between them went back into the detectives' room, where there were a rolltop desk, a large table, and files on all three sides. There were also several men tipped back in their chairs, waiting.

"This is no good, Andy. I can't do anything in here."

"Right this way, into the question room." He opened another door and led them into an adjoining chamber which in reality was a small replica of the horrible place they had left; a small, square room with a concrete bench built into the wall and nothing else.

Don felt hot. No wonder kids don't stay straight, when you shove them into jail with crooks and drunks. No wonder.

"I'll just leave you alone, Don."

"O.K., Chief; O.K., Andy." The heavy door shut. He took hold of the boy's arm with a hand none too steady. "I'll tell you the whole thing, Perry, the whole game from the start. Only first off, you must tell *me* something. What happened? Exactly how did it happen?"

The boy opened his mouth, started to talk, shut it again. "You've got to tell me the whole thing, tell me the truth, Perry. I think I can help you, I really believe I can. But you must tell me everything."

The youngster looked at him. "Gee . . . I dunno . . . nothing . . . I dunno."

"But, Perry, come now, what happened? You were caught down in Dugan's Alley. . . ."

"I was not."

"Well, you were caught near there, you were in the alley."

"I wasn't, neither."

"Perry, you telling me the truth?"

There was a long moment of silence; then Perry looked at him resentfully. "Think I'd lie to you?"

Don glanced down at the little figure on the bench, noticed the thin, checked shirt that he had worn all fall in school, at the faded, stringy necktie, now under one ear. The boy looked him back squarely in the eyes.

"Nope, I don't hardly believe you would. Suppose you tell me what happened from the beginning."

"I'm standing there . . ."

"You were standing where?"

"On Superior near the alley, waiting for Jackson, for Jackson and the team. Then the kids come running out of the alley, and . . . I dunno . . . I got scared. . . . I ran, too."

"But you must have done something to be scared of."

His tone was positive. "No, I never did!"

"You didn't do a thing? You weren't in the alley at all?"

"No."

"You didn't even know a drunk was rolled in the alley, I suppose?"

"I do now." His voice was firm, his glance steady. It was a situation that could puzzle a strong, healthy person, and that night Don was neither.

"Do you know who did it? D'you think you know who it was?"

He nodded.

"Oh, you know! Will you tell me?"

The boy looked down. There was a long silence, and finally Don said, "Maybe they're friends of yours. Are they?"

The boy nodded again.

"Oh, I see. And you claim you had nothing to do with it even though your friends were mixed up in it?"

He looked up quickly. "That's right, Don."

The thing was complicated. Don hesitated. You believe him—and yet. He took another tack.

"Perry, are you often out late on Saturday nights?"

To his surprise, Perry said bluntly, "Sometimes I am."

"Oh, you are? What for? What for do you go out late on Saturdays?"

The silence lasted and lasted. Don could see he was getting nowhere. The cap twisted in the boy's hands. He shrugged his shoulders. No wonder the cops could get nothing from him. Don looked down at the slender figure with the rumpled head of hair, the blue denim pants, the frayed sweater. At his stubborn mouth and chin, almost breaking down but not quite. "I'm trying to help you, Perry. Tell me now, what do you usually do on Saturday nights?"

Suddenly without warning, Perry slumped on the bench, sobbing. "I . . . I . . . I . . . stay out late unless I can go to Jackson's."

"Now, don't cry. There's nothing to worry about. Where do you go?"

"To Jackson Pi . . . Piper's house, when I can."

The handkerchief was grimy and sodden. It had not been washed for a long time, if ever.

"What for do you go to Jackson's? Tell me, Perry, tell me now."

"Count o', count o' . . . my dad." The tears flooded again, he sobbed and sobbed and his sobs shook Don's arm which was around the boy's shoulders now.

"I don't hardly understand. What's your dad—what's that got to do with it? Perry, tell me, I want to know. I'm trying to help; I want to be your friend. Don't take on now. Just tell me, boy. You know me, you know I'm your friend. Sure you do. Then tell me, what's this about your dad?"

"Saturday nights . . . he comes in late . . . and beats me."

Then Don understood. He understood things he had seen in the gym and paid little attention to. Now he remembered them. And he thought, How little I know about these kids. I think I'm close to 'em, I like to believe I feel and know more about 'em than the teachers in school, yet how little I really know! He began to understand the whole picture now, to piece things together. "So . . . you wanted to go to Jackson's for the night, eh?"

No reply. The head nodded through the sobs. "Is Jackson your friend? Is Jackson your best friend?"

"Yeah. Long time since . . . since we went

to Roosevelt together. We've been friends a long time. Don . . . Jack . . . he did O.K. this evening for us, didn't he?"

"I'll say. Just about won that title for us, him and Tom Shaw. So you go to Jackson's, do you? Mrs. Piper, does she take good care of you, Perry?"

"She's a nice lady." The sobs had diminished to an occasional gasp.

"O.K. Now dry your eyes, Perry. Here, you just use this; you take my handkerchief, it's bigger'n yours. There, that's right. Now, boy, you wait here; you wait right here while I slip down and have a word or two with the chief."

The boy reached for his arm. He held it firmly. "You'll come back, Don, promise you will. You won't leave me here alone, will ya? Promise, Don?"

"Of course not, Perry, of course not. Think I'd leave you now, boy? Don't you fret; I'm right with you alla time, every minute. You just sit down and take things easy. There, that's better. Now don't worry, I'll be back, I promise."

He stepped to the door and opened it. An officer was seated in a chair tilted against the wall just outside. Don went down the corridor to the main entrance in the basement. Andy was still at the desk under the green light behind the grille. The two officers were putting on their coats to go to the celebration at the park. "Come along, Don, we'll take you over in the car. They can't begin without you. They'll be waiting for the coach to show up over there."

"The team won't be in town for a little while yet, boys. They have to eat. I'll be over a little later. Andy!"

"Come in, come in. Would he talk?" The chief leaned over and pressed a button which unlocked the gate of the grille. The door clicked, and Don pushed in, sinking to a chair. He tried hard to pull himself together as he sat beside the chief at the desk. Suddenly he had nothing left, nothing to fight with, he was through, drained, finished.

It was going to be a battle to convince this man, too.

"Andy, I've talked to the boy. I've known this kid quite some time; he's no stranger to me. Of course I realize he hasn't any too good a reputation round town. On the other hand, I've never found him a bad kid. Tough, yes, but not bad. Seems tonight he was just standing on Superior waiting for the parade, and got picked up."

"Ah! That's his story."

"Look, Andy, it may not be true. Then again it might. Remember when you were a boy, remember how scared you were of policemen? As I get it, he sees this gang running, he's frightened and starts to run too."

"So he says!"

"Well, has he ever been brought up on charges of this kind before?"

"Why, no, I can't say he has."

"Have other kids in town?"

"You know we've had quite some trouble with certain elements in town lately; you know that. The Depot Street gang and those kids on the north end."

"But not Perry."

"No, but he's a bad lot, Don. He knows all those boys; he's been hauled in with 'em for hooking rides on freight cars, one thing and another."

"Did he ever steal?"

"I suppose so. I couldn't prove it."

"Know anything about his home life?"

"Not much."

"I do. His mother's dead. His father works in the steel mills. Drinks, too, on Saturday nights."

"Hold on. That wouldn't be old Manny Taylor, would it?"

"Yeah, that's the man. He drinks on Saturdays, Andy; then he comes home and beats the kid up."

"So the boy claims, hey?"

"And I happen to know. I've seen him often enough hobbling round the gym of a Monday, even seen bruises once or twice and wondered what they were. Never thought to ask. Don't speak well for me, does it, Andy? You get to thinking of the few boys on the team, and . . . well . . . somehow the others don't seem so important. Till something of this sort happens."

"Manny Taylor . . . Manny Taylor . . . why, sure."

"You know what this lad does? Spends Saturday nights at the Pipers' place."

"Jackson Piper's?"

"Uhuh. Seems they're pals. Been pals ever since they were in junior high, over to Roosevelt. The Pipers are the only folks in town who'll take him in. No-good kid, tough boy, see?"

The chief of police whistled. The pattern was clearer now. He began to respect this Henderson. Why, he's done a job on the boy, he's gotten the dope.

"Think he knows who did it?"

"I'm sure he does."

"The Depot Street gang?"

"He won't tell. But I may be able to find out if you'll give me a chance."

"Well . . . what do you suggest? What do you want to do with him?"

"Filed charges yet?"

"Not yet. We wanted to get him to talk before we took down a statement. We waited for you. With that dad of his, I kinda think reform school is the best place for the boy."

"Chief, let's us think this over a day or two. Let's talk it over carefully with the judge. Let's not rush into the thing; what say we wait awhile?"

"How about the boy in the meantime?"

"The boy's coming home with me."

"With you! He is *not*! This is a serious thing; suppose his yarn isn't true, suppose he's kidding you, suppose he . . ."

"Andy, listen, these boys don't lie to me."

"But look, Don, you gotta go to the celebration in the park. How can you look out for him?"

"Why not? He can come along, too."

Andy Anderson suddenly became the tough chief of police. He leaned back and hit the desk with his fist. Two pens in an inkwell jumped as he did so. "He will like hell. I'll tell you what he'll do. As soon as you leave him for a moment, he'll hitchhike out of town so fast you won't see his dust. And I'll tell you which way he'll go—he'll go north. We'll pick him up in Logansport tomorrow—that is, if we're lucky."

"Not if he promises me he won't!"

"Promise! Kid like that . . . promises not worth the powder to blow 'em to hell."

"No, you're wrong there, Andy. He won't lie to me. He'll stick, you wait and see. Look, as you say, we can send this kid to a reform school. O.K., then what? End of two-three years he'll be back in town, a graduate crook, and you'll have a smart, resourceful criminal on your hands. Let's not jump into this, Andy. Let's us see if we can't put this kid on his feet. He hasn't done anything really wrong, he's not hopeless, not by any means."

"It's irregular. I don't like the idea. We oughta file charges in any event. If the *Journal* gets hold of this . . ."

"I'll fix it up with Deke Noble. He's on the desk tonight. I'll fix it up with Deke before I go to bed. Deke understands, he's a good guy, he has kids of his own."

"It's irregular! If I didn't know you, Don . . .

Well, you be responsible; you're responsible. If he skips town and I'm dead sure he will, it'll be up to you to fetch him back. Or else!"

"I'm responsible. I'll see he shows in court Monday morning."

"You going to the celebration and everything, it's most irregular. I intended to file charges . . ."

"Leave it to me. Trust me on this, Andy. Let me handle the boy. I believe I can take care of him and get the information you want." He rose. "Just lemme have a word or two. You wait outside the door."

They went out, the chief mumbling as he did that it was all most irregular. They passed the officer outside the room, and Don entered, shutting the big door behind.

"Perry, c'mon over here. We're gonna leave this place, you and me. But before we go, we must remember this thing isn't settled by any means; we'll both have to face up to it on Monday in court, and you must tell the story as you told it to me, to the judge. This evening you're coming home with me. Now wait a minute, hold on a sec! First off, you've got to promise something. If I get you out and take you to my place tonight, you've got to make me a promise. Promise you'll stick."

"I promise, Don."

"Tonight we're going to the celebration in Forest Park. For the team, y'know."

The boy straightened up, he became animated for the first time. "Yeah! I helped gather wood for the bonfire. Gosh! Say, will Jackson be there? Jackson just about won that game for you tonight, didn't he, hey, Don? That's what Buck said over the radio; he said Jackson played a wonderful game."

"Right, Perry, he just about won it for us. Now we two are going off to the park, and I'll be up there on the platform with Tom and Jack and the boys, and you'll be down with the crowd. These officers here seem to think you won't stick; they think you'll run out on me, that you'll beat it from town. I don't. I told 'em so. Perry, you don't foul, do you?"

There was scorn in his tone. "Naw . . . I don't, you know I don't."

"I know it, sure I know it. You'll stick with me until Monday?"

"Yeah."

"Promise?"

"I promise."

His dirty paw was moist like Tom's and Jackson's in the Field House. For just a second Don glanced down at the grimy face with the fear gone now, with confidence and trust coming into it. He turned and threw open the door.

"O.K., Chief, this boy's gonna take in the celebration at the park with me tonight."

9

Judge James leaned back in his swivel chair. His room in the modern County Court building was luxurious. The *Journal*, proud of the building, the newest and largest in Springfield, always spoke of "the Judge's commodious quarters."

"This isn't only what happened last Saturday night, Don, it doesn't concern only that Depot Street gang; it's the whole problem we face of the youngsters of Springfield. We intend to set up what we shall call the Juvenile Aid Division. It will be part of the police department. As director, you'll have full authority and complete jurisdiction of all cases that come before the department involving minors. You handle 'em the best way you know how. When you have something serious, you investigate and hand the offender over to the City Court, and he'll be tried just as he is now. When a case isn't serious, when it concerns a first offender, it's yours. We'll give you power to put kids on probation, to make 'em report to you, to fine 'em or do whatever you believe necessary to straighten 'em out. Well, Dale . . . that's about the size of things, isn't it?"

The mayor, sitting across the room from Judge James, glanced at Don to see how he was taking the offer. Then he nodded to the judge. "I'd say so, that's about the long and short of it, Judge."

They both gazed at him. There was rather an anxious look in the judge's gaze. Don shook his head, more in confusion than anything. He sat without replying. Then he shook his head again. Leave basketball, leave basketball and take on a headache like this new Juvenile Aid Division! This wasn't funny.

"Why, Judge, I dunno, I hardly know what to say. . . ."

Fearful he might refuse, the judge jumped in quickly. " 'Course we all realize, Don, that this is something entirely new in town; it's an idea that's never been tried before, it may need some working out; we appreciate it's an experiment, but we all feel you're the one person in town who's closest to the kids, to the boys and girls of Springfield. We know it won't be easy. Most of our youngsters here are all right, but there's an element in town that's been causing us a whole lot of trouble in the past year or so, and frankly, we just aren't sure how to handle 'em except to set the thing up this way."

"I don't believe I can do it."

"If you can't, no one in Springfield can," said the judge with conviction.

"That's correct, Don, if you can't, no one in town can," echoed the mayor.

"But see here, I never tried anything of this kind before; it's all new to me; it's a job I'd have to learn."

"You had to learn how to coach basketball, didn't you? Why, yes, it is a new idea; these times call for new ideas, and young fellas like you to carry 'em out. We usta have a lot of younger men in politics; even had a Young Democrat and a Young Republican Club here before the war. They disappeared somehow; they don't function anymore. We need younger men to carry on; we want you to take over. Don, this work with kids is mighty darn important. And besides, sixty-five percent of the work of the police force is with children; take some of that burden off their hands, and you'll be doing a big job. Help the police stay on their regular duties. Now everyone says Don Henderson is the person to head this up, to get it off to a good start, they tell me you know the kids better than . . ."

"Who's everyone, Judge?"

"Why, everyone in town . . . Peedad Wilson . . . and . . ."

Don smiled. They always go to Peedad Wilson when they're in a jam, don't they!

Folks in Springfield chuckled and grinned whenever you mentioned his name; yet when something went wrong, they turned to him to find a way out. Not to J. Frank Shaw who really ran Springfield; who owned the Merchants National Bank, and several stores, and had a controlling interest in Station WSWP, not to mention a hand in real estate and insurance and just about everything else in town. It was true that the business men at Rotary on Tuesdays laughed when they spoke about the *Press*, Peedad's paper. But there was always a kind of affectionate note in their voices when they talked of him. It was also true they called Frank Shaw, "J. Frank," with respect. With more respect, perhaps, but in different tones.

"I always thought Peedad was a friend of mine."

"Oh, he is, he is, he likes you; he's for you, Don. He thinks you've really got what it takes to put this thing across." The mayor, never very quick on the uptake, tried to reassure Don.

"I'll bet if Peedad is for the idea, J. Frank isn't," said Don, glancing out the window at the Montgomery Ward sign on the store across the square. "You know, there's a lot of things you have to think about in this town."

A car started noisily outside. The two men twisted a little in their chairs. They exchanged a glance which Don didn't miss. Dale Pennington's friendship for J. Frank Shaw was no secret in Springfield.

"Harrumph, harrumph," said the judge,

twisting uneasily in his seat and turning his pipe around in his fingers.

Yes, thought Don, that's how things are. J. Frank's a practical man, and Peedad Wilson's an impractical old geezer, the editor of the *Press*, the afternoon paper; never made any money, never will; just about exists on the Democratic advertising in the country. An editor, that's what he is, not a successful businessman.

Yet a thousand people in Springfield loved old Peedad for every one that loved J. Frank Shaw who ran the town. Life's funny, thought Don, still looking out at the green Montgomery Ward sign across the square.

"Harrumph, harrumph," went the judge, knocking the ashes out of his pipe. "Point is, J. Frank's far too busy with civic affairs and all to understand some of the things happening in town."

The judge's logic was hard to follow. Too busy with civic affairs. Well, isn't this a civic affair? And how come, if he's so busy with civic affairs, he doesn't see what's happening right under his eyes? Doesn't make sense to me.

"Besides," added the mayor, "he happens to have a good boy. Trouble with J. Frank is, he judges all kids by Tom. Now Tom's an unusual boy."

He has other troubles, too, thought Don, remembering how J. Frank had interfered with his coaching the year before, and tried hard to get him thrown out of town. He rose. "Well, all I can say is, I'm mighty pleased you wanted me, but this is kinda out of my line. I've got to think it over. There's lots of angles to be considered. I'll let you know first thing Monday morning."

"Fine, Don, fine!"

"That's great, Don. You let us know first thing Monday. Remember, we need you, the town needs your help the worst way."

He closed the door and went into the hall, ringing for the elevator. Mattie, the Negro girl on the elevator, said something but he hardly heard her words. Now then, shall I go right across the square to Peedad's office or shall I wait till this evening and see him at home? They'll be watching from the judge's window to see where I go. Shucks, what do I care? They know Peedad's my friend; they know I don't want the job, and I don't either, I darn well don't.

The battered wooden stairs across the square contrasted with the limestone entrance to the

Court House. Don went up one flight. Peedad's office seemed unusually dingy compared to the quiet, clean and modern chambers of the judge. The old man sat at his rolltop desk as usual, a green eyeshade on his forehead. He whipped it off, a warm smile covering his face, and leaning over removed some proofs, newspapers, letters, bills, envelopes, folders, calendars, and other things from the only chair in the small room.

"Come in, Don, come in. I can't say I'm surprised to see you."

"Peedad Wilson, I always figured you as my best friend in town, and here you go wishing this headache on me."

The old man chuckled and put his feet on the desk in the middle of the mountain of papers he had moved from the chair. "Guess they didn't look very far."

"Guess they didn't have much choice; guess no one wanted the job."

The old man put his hands behind his head. He was serious now. "Don, this here's the most important thing in Springfield at present."

"Why, Peedad? Why is it?"

"I don't hardly need to tell you why. 'Cause

it's working with kids; 'cause on what happens to them depends what kind of a town we have fifteen years from now. Whether this nation stays a democracy, as we hope, some of us, depends on the towns like this all over the country, and what happens here in this town depends on the kids. They'll be Springfield, Indiana, in fifteen years, remember. And in twenty years they'll be running the show—I hope."

"Not if J. Frank can help it, and he's good for another twenty years, easy."

"He may be, he may be. It doesn't matter. He's on the way out, Don, and all the rest like him. Their day is over, only they don't know it yet. Now look, Don, you've got to tackle this thing. You're the only person to head up a Juvenile Aid Division, the only person in town the kids all know and respect. They believe in you, they think you're fair, they feel you understand their point of view; they know you'll shoot straight, and they realize you won't stand for any funny business, either. Especially the ones who saw you fire your whole varsity team two years ago."

"But, Peedad, there's so many complications."

"What?"

"Well, first off I'd want to know how Andy Anderson takes the idea."

"I can tell you. We've been into all that with him. He's for it. Why not? It takes a headache off his hands; why shouldn't he be for it; why shouldn't he support you?"

"Will I get one hundred percent backing from him and the other boys on the force? Otherwise it's no use."

"Absolutely. That's understood, but we'll thrash all that out with him in detail."

"How 'bout J. Frank? You can't tell me he likes the idea."

"No, he does not. But he has no public office."

"Peedad Wilson! Stop playing foxy. What did J. Frank say to this idea when he first heard it?"

"Oh, the usual thing. Sometimes I think we haven't any juvenile problem in this town; we only have an adult problem. He said it was pampering kids, said it was pouring money down the gutter, said real estate in Springfield couldn't stand a two mill raise in the tax rate, said . . . about what you'd expect. Soon's he found out your salary was going to be the same, soon's he discovered it wasn't going to cost the town money and might actually save 'em some dough in the long run, he agreed. He'll go along."

"Maybe. If he does I'll be surprised. How about authority? I'd need authority to enforce discipline, to put across whatever I've decided."

"You'll have it, Don. You'll have the boys on the force behind you, and the mayor, and Judge James. The Council has agreed to pass any ordinance you might want, like, f'rinstance, a curfew law."

"We don't need that in Springfield, Peedad."

"H'm. Ever seen the streets downtown after a basketball game at night? Kids roaming round until all hours."

"I know. I'm aware of that. But the curfew isn't the way to stop it. Pass a curfew law, and kids think it's smart to break it; they think that's fun. I remember how I felt once. Anyway, if a boy violates the curfew law, it's his parents who are responsible. Besides, the law is not enforceable. What are you going to do; arrest 'em? No, sir, that's not the way out."

"Very good, what is the way?"

"Best way is to grab the kids on the streets after ten and take them to the City Court. Bring their parents in, too, and warn 'em plenty. Publish this in the newspapers, announce it in all the schools at Assembly, tell 'em we'll pick kids up on the streets at night. Then pick up a few and let the rest know you mean business."

Peedad rose. "I rather guess we needn't go any further. It's a mean sort of mess you've had shoved in your lap; but I believe you're too good a citizen to refuse. You've got to take this job. Or am I sizing up Don Henderson wrong?"

10

The conversation started pleasantly enough, but before long both men were annoyed. They sat in Mr. Storey's office, not beside the desk near the entrance where even with the door closed everyone in the anteroom outside could hear what was going on, but at the table in an alcove to one side where they were alone and secluded. Notwithstanding his annoyance, Don tried to be patient, pleading, attempting to get his point across.

"But look, Mr. Storey . . . I know all that . . . yes . . . but, see here, Mr. Storey, if we don't . . ."

The principal, kindly, timid, fearful, tried hard to explain, to get his point over to the impetuous young man at his elbow.

"Nope, Don, that'd never do, never. I tried that at Marion coupla years ago; didn't work out there and it wouldn't here. I'm older'n you; I know these boys and girls."

I know 'em better'n you can ever hope to, Don thought, because I see 'em when their character shows up, when they're faced with a crisis, when they're really what they are. I mustn't say that to him, it would only make him mad. Somehow I must *convince* him.

"Well, but if it's their show, it's up to them; they've got to run this thing. If they aren't in on it from the start, if we appoint people *we* want to sit on the bench, they won't have any confidence in the thing. Why should they? Seems to me they ought to elect their own representatives, same's we do. Oughtn't they?"

"No, Don, I'm sorry I can't agree. That would never work out; it would be most irregular."

There it was again. Irregular. Everyone in town talked that way about kids. If you attempted to keep a boy out of reform school, it was irregular; but if you put him away for three years so he could learn thoroughly to be a crook, it was regular. If you ran the student newspaper in school, if you supervised the distribution of basketball tickets so only one boy or girl out of ten got to see their teams play, it was regular. But if you treated them as citizens capable of making their own decisions and choosing their own leaders, it was irregular.

Gee, I wish to goodness I was mayor of this town for a couple of weeks. I'd do some things that really would be irregular.

Mr. Storey perceived his bewilderment. His kindly face peered anxiously at Don; he was a worried and an apprehensive man. He placed his hand on Don's knee in friendly fashion, trying to persuade him.

"I'd like to help, Don, I want to go the limit with you on this. I'd like to go along if I possibly can."

Great Scott, I'm not asking for the moon. I'm merely saying kids are human beings and have a right to be treated that way. "Look, Mr. Storey, tell me something. We talk about building character and all that, why don't we trust kids to manage their own show. I teach my teams how to play; then I send 'em out and expect 'em to use their intelligence and initiative. If they come up against a tough problem, if they meet a new defense, well, they've got to solve it for themselves out on the floor. Or get trimmed, that's all. They do, too, that's how they won this year; when the boys ganged up on Tom, Jackson cut loose; when they tried to stop Jackson and Tom, too, Earl was dropping 'em in."

"Yes, but Don, don't you see . . ."

"D'you think, Mr. Storey, that we older folks in town do so well managing our affairs that we should try to tell the kids just how to run theirs? Look at the mess we make of things uptown. They couldn't do any worse, could they?"

"Yes, but Don, after all, I'm responsible. I'm the principal. I'm responsible, you know."

What he really means is that he's a newcomer here in town, that he doesn't take any chances, that if there's any trouble the school board won't like it. "Mr. Storey, won't you let me try this, just let me try this? It's their show. Why not see whether or not kids can run their own affairs?"

He's weakening. I believe he's weakening!

Suddenly by something in the man's face, by

the way his fingers twisted in his lap, Don saw he was being persuaded against his will. By George, I believe I can convince him. I believe I can if I stay with it!

•

The auditorium was filled to cracking. Ordinarily it seated only seven hundred, but inasmuch as there were over twelve hundred in the school, the kids sat everywhere, on the sides of the balcony, in the aisles. They stood against the wall on the floor; they perched on their haunches under the platform where the orchestra usually held forth. Don, walking to and fro on the stage, watched them pour in; more and more and more, and still more in an eternal procession. Occasionally he got a glimpse through the doors in the rear of Mr. Storey fluttering around, nervous, upset, worried, in the hall.

To tell the truth at that moment Don was worried also.

If this gang ever cuts loose . . . No, sir, I believe in 'em! I believe in 'em as responsible people. If I do, I oughta let 'em run their own show in their own way.

At last they were all inside. Not an older person, not one teacher in the room, either. The noise, the confusion, the bobbing up and down, the twisting and squirming and squeaking of chairs, the sound of twelve hundred shrill voices talking simultaneously was overpowering.

Then from the wings of the stage the dispossessed orchestra began "The Star-Spangled Banner." Several hundred chairs thumped and bumped, twelve hundred pairs of feet scraped the floor; it sounded like the rumble of an avalanche.

"Oh . . . say . . . can . . . you see . . ."

Once again the scraping of feet, the thumping and bumping of chairs, and they were seated.

Red Crosby stepped up to the mike. There was scattered applause and some rather ominous wisecracks came from the floor, but as soon as he started to talk they listened.

"We've been called here as you know on a serious matter. It's something that concerns us all. Our friend Don Henderson, the basketball coach, will explain it to us."

Twelve hundred machine guns crackled, twelve hundred pairs of hands spanked together and continued to do so. Don stood looking at them, waiting a minute before he began.

Well, this is it! The first few minutes will

decide how things go, the first few minutes will be the toughest.

"Friends, men and women—I shan't call you boys and girls because you're citizens of a Republic. That's the reason you've been called in here today, because as citizens you have responsibilities, that's why we're meeting here now." He paused. No sound. No scraping of feet, no coughing, no restlessness, no movement through the auditorium. Why, he thought, treat 'em like people and they'll respond like people. Ask 'em, and they'll always come through for you. By George, I believe I could do anything I wanted with 'em at this minute.

"As you all realize, there's been quite some trouble in Springfield lately, a gang war which held up newspaper deliveries, some casual bike stealing, a little breaking and entering, some petty thievery in the stores, and then last Saturday night after the Finals, a bunch of boys tried to roll a drunk in Dugan's Alley. It didn't take much time to catch these boys, but that's not the point. The point is the City Council is worried; they don't hardly know what to do or how to handle cases of this sort. So they've kind of passed the buck to me!"

A ripple of laughter burst out. It died away quickly as the smile left his face. "Yes, I'm going to leave school for a while. The rumors you've been hearing are true, and Russ Brainerd will take over spring basketball this year. I'm leaving temporarily, but I don't anticipate it'll be for long, six to eight months, maybe, not more. I've been appointed to head up the new Juvenile Aid Division of the city. I've accepted on one condition. That's up to you people." He hesitated and looked them over, up and down, the ones he knew, the ones who were only familiar faces to him, the younger kids in the balcony, the older ones downstairs.

Then he leaned forward. "I'll accept . . . on one condition. If you'll help. Will you do it?"

"YES!"

Ever hear twelve hundred young voices say YES? When they say it, they mean it. The word echoed to the roof, bounced back, shocking Mr. Storey who stood anxiously in the hall behind the closed door with a bunch of teachers. Just that one word, spoken together, all of them, as if they had rehearsed the timing. Then silence over the auditorium filled to cracking.

"O.K.! I'll take the job. And you'll help. Now here's the setup, and let me say first why this is being put up to you in this way. Because it concerns you, and you, and every kid in Springfield, and because it does concern you, because you've got to take part in it, we've asked your help. In a democratic country the citizens are expected to assume responsibilities in time of trouble; you're all citizens, you have a responsibility. You're the Springfield of 1960; don't ever forget that. If we're going to have a decent town in the future, it's up to you here, now. You've got to take part and help make this a better city.

"Here's the setup. We intend, that is the Juvenile Aid Division with the approval of the Council and the mayor and the chief of police hope, first off, to establish a Junior Court. This court will function for you people. It'll be run by you people. It'll administer sentences such as you see fit. This court will consist of three judges, a girl and two boys. Your job here today is to elect those judges, and you'll also have to elect a prosecuting attorney. . . ."

"Chester! Chet Davis! Chester!" Shouts rang through the room, and laughter. Chester's propensity for arguing, his love of verbal in-fighting was known throughout the school.

Don smiled. "Anyone, anyone you people select is O.K. with me. A prosecuting attorney and a defense attorney, because this is a serious matter and we intend that everyone who comes before the court shall have a fair trial. I've asked your help; you've promised it. O.K., now get to work. Remember, this court will have authority to make its decisions stick, and its decisions will be respected and obeyed by every citizen of the town, young and old. The police force and the chief are behind us. So your job right now . . . this morning . . . is to choose the members of the new court. Any questions . . . if not, I'll turn the meeting over to Red, and leave."

There was no applause as he walked over to the wings at the side. From behind as he went out came Red's high-pitched tones.

"Now . . . now . . . they's a number of kids with slips of paper'll pass up and down so you can all vote. But first of all, we gotta nominate the candidates. We'll put their names on this blackboard. I now throw the meeting open for any suggestions you may have."

A storm greeted these words. Don heard the storm as he went through the wings and into the hall beside the auditorium. The storm rose, higher, higher still; the building seemed to shake. Gosh,

I hope everything's all right in there, I hope they'll get through it O.K. Nope, you have to trust 'em; you have to believe they'll come through; that's the only way.

He walked slowly up the hall beside the auditorium and turned the corner. In the entrance hall outside the auditorium a group was standing near one of the two main doors. Mr. Storey, with Dave Wallace, the dean of men, and Miss Perry, the dean of women, and several teachers made up the group. They were all listening. The noise from within the room was truly frightening.

"There!" The principal turned as he saw Don, almost with relief. "There! I told you, I told you it was irregular, Don. Listen to that!"

Inside the big hall a thousand cannibals were devouring human flesh, a regiment of infantry was storming a line of trenches in battle, a mob of howling dervishes were fleeing in the desert before the sirocco. And a bunch of young Americans were settling their problems in their own peculiar manner.

The noise presently died away, and Red's voice could be heard explaining something. Then tumult again. The chairs rocked, voices shrieked, pandemonium covered the hall within.

"I must get in. I must stop this. They'll tear the place apart; there ought to be some older persons in there." Mr. Storey reached for the handle of the door.

Don was quicker. He stepped in front of him. "Wait a minute, Mr. Storey, just wait a sec. Let's give 'em a chance on this. Why not show 'em we believe in 'em? How would it look if we rushed up front right now?"

Mr. Wallace instantly came to his assistance. "They're loud, they're boisterous; that's only their way, Mr. Storey. I think Don is right. We should let them work this out the best way they can. Don't you think so, Miss Perry?"

The stoutish woman adjusted the glasses on her nose. She spoke calmly, which was difficult at the moment as the noise rose feverishly from the hall, but she spoke with determination. "I certainly do. I've heard adults make just such a rumpus over at the City Hall in the last presidential campaign. No one interfered, either."

"Listen!" The noise died away somewhat, and Red's thin pipe came faintly through the swinging doors.

"Shut up, you kids."

To the astonishment of the little group outside,

the barbaric sounds vanished. Then his tone came plainly to them again.

". . . And after you've voted, and after you've folded your ballots and given 'em to the tellers, you'll pass out and go right away to your homerooms. Now, any more nominations . . . any more nominations?"

There was a shout, a yell, a question from the balcony, a dozen queries from the floor, and a hundred voices broke in. Mr. Storey hovered nervously round the door, waiting expectantly for the place to fall apart, hoping apparently to take Don off guard and dart through. But Don stood firmly preventing him.

By golly, I'll keep him out if I hafta throw him out. I surely will.

It was hard, nevertheless, to watch the agonized expression on the face of the principal as the tumult inside grew louder and louder. Then there was a sudden wild burst of hand-clapping. Some favorite had been nominated. Another burst, and another.

"Most irregular, Don, the whole thing is most irregular."

"That's right, Mr. Storey, that's right. And it's irregular for kids to steal bicycles and prevent other kids from delivering papers. That's what we're trying to prevent."

Sudden silence. The silence lasted this time. A faint rustling of papers; otherwise silence. The quiet inside the auditorium seemed to worry the principal almost as much as the noise.

Then a chair banged loudly. And another.

The swinging doors suddenly came forward, smacking Don in the back and nearly knocking him over. A boy appeared, his mouth open when he saw what had happened.

"Gee . . . I'm sorry, Don!"

"Go to your homeroom, go to your homeroom immediately, Sidney," said Mr. Storey, paying no attention to Don who was almost knocked down by the blow.

Bang-bang, bang-bang-bang-bang went the chairs. More boys came out; then two girls arm in arm, talking violently. "Go to your room, Jim, go to your homeroom, girls, go immediately please . . . go to your homerooms. Dave, will you and Miss Perry step over to the other side and take charge of the doors there; see they all go to their homerooms at once. Don and I'll stay here."

But there's nothing to take charge of, there's

nothing to take charge of. These kids are all right. They know where their homerooms are.

Bang-bang, bang-bang-bang. It was a barrage of slamming seats now, and a Niagara of youth sweeping out the doors and into the hall. They were excited, yet sober; their faces were tense and eager, yet serious at the same time.

I know, thought Don, as he watched them pour through the swinging doors. I understand, I remember the first time I ever voted. They were serious and exalted, too, because they were being treated as people with minds of their own, as citizens of a Republic.

Gradually the banging subsided; the last boys and girls came up the aisles. Mr. Storey locked first one pair of doors and then went toward the other, perceiving the emptying auditorium with a sigh. He was relieved! By great good luck, by the grace of God, by the fortune which favors the brave (in this case the principal of the Springfield high school), a riot or worse had been averted. And the building was still standing.

So his demeanor plainly said.

Now the last stragglers had left, and he stood holding open one side of the doors, while Red Crosby, in his blue sweater with the crimson S in front, came down the steps from the platform and up the aisle toward him. Red carried by the handle the tin cash box in which Mr. Storey usually kept the receipts from the basketball games; it was stuffed so full of ballots it wouldn't close.

Red's face was elated, but he also had a soberness in his elation. He came up the aisle toward Don and Mr. Storey beside the door. It was to Don he spoke as he came out of the auditorium into the main hall.

"Now comes the tough part—the counting of the ballots. Looks to me like to make it really democratic, Don, we'd oughta have a committee count these ballots."

11

Say, this is going to be rich, this is gonna be a lot of fun. Imagine! Tom and Earl and Mary Jo Leonard making like judges! Imagine that! Will they be wearing long black robes or beards or what?

The whole business was a lark to the twenty-two boys and girls charged with traffic violations and ordered to appear at the first session of the Springfield Junior Court that Saturday morning. They began showing up early, parking their bikes, standing on the steps of the courthouse in the spring sunshine, talking, laughing, kidding each other.

"They got you, did they, Jim?" "They grabbed you, hey, Stinker?" "Sure, me, I'm a criminal, I am. I'm Cactus Pete." "I'm a criminal, too. Hey there, Milt, you going to court?" "D'you get pinched, Jake? Say, maybe they'll send us all to jail for life." "Maybe so. If they do, my pa'll just have to bail me out before night, that's all, 'cause I tend furnaces." "I wouldn't mind a bit going to jail, Harry. Take it from me, I'd rather go to jail than go to school." "You betcha." "Me, too." "Say, that's right. I'd a darn sight rather go to jail than try to write those English themes for Miss Burton." "So'd I; lots. 'Cept Saturdays. I'd sort of hate to lose out on Saturdays, the pictures and the basketball games 'n' everything. Just about everything happens on Saturdays."

They piled up the three flights of stairs, talking noisily. The doors of the courtroom on the third floor were shut and locked. So they stood about the corridor, chattering, almost eager to begin. Tom Shaw and Earl and Mary Jo with beards! "Say, that's something! This is gonna be a circus!"

Exactly as the clock struck nine, the doors were unlocked by Jay Hanwell, the big football tackle, and the whole mob poured inside, laughing, talking, excited. Somehow the chattering lessened and their tones died away as they squeezed into the benches behind the rail that separated the court itself from the rest of the room. Notwithstanding their levity, the place impressed them. It was an enormous, high-ceilinged chamber, paneled in oak, with the judges' chairs set at the wall in front of an American flag. A modern light above gave the court a kind of theatrical appearance. The table for the clerk was below, with a swivel chair and a cushion covered in checked cloth on the chair. There were a table for the attorneys and a row of chairs for witnesses, all facing the judges' chairs. This was inside the rail. Outside were rows of seats for perhaps one hundred persons.

Something about it all made them suddenly solemn; the flag behind the judges' chairs; the sober look on Jay's face, his lack of attention to their greetings and subdued whistles as they tried to speak to him; Chester's back, while he busied himself with some papers at a table inside the enclosure; Red Crosby at another table, working

Say, look, what is this, anyway? This was all supposed to be a joke, this was gonna be fun. We were gonna kid Don, and make with jokes and all. Now Don isn't here; there's no older person here. No making with jokes, either, no wearing beards or anything.

Tom leaned over the bench and spoke in a low tone to Red, who nodded. "Oh, sure." He faced them again. "Please answer present to your name." Then he called the list of names. They all were present except one boy.

"Roy Miller . . . Roy . . . Roy Miller not here? Not present? The clerk of the court will have the Juvenile Aid Division call his home, and if he's not there send a prowl car out."

"He works Saturday." "He delivers groceries for Maher's on Saturdays," said two voices from the benches.

"That's right. The clerk will have an officer check at Maher's store immediately." The big football player slipped from the room as the boys and girls stirred and looked at each other. Say, we thought this was gonna be just a joke, this Junior Court!

"You want to plead guilty or not guilty?" Red waved the papers in his hands. "If you plead guilty and save the city the trouble of prosecution, you'll be let off with a fine or lighter sentence. If you care to plead not guilty, you have a right to counsel and we'll assign one to you. But if you are convicted, your sentence will be heavier. Everyone has a right to be tried by Justice Metzger in the City Court if he wishes; you don't have to plead guilty here unless you so wish."

Say, something's wrong. This isn't working out the way we expected, not at all. This was gonna be a lot of fun, this Junior Court, with Mary Jo and Tom wearing beards. We were going to have a good time. Now, what's this about sending that cop out for Roy Miller? Sounds like they mean business.

"Should you care to plead guilty, please step forward and the court will impose sentences."

The twenty-two offenders glanced at each other soberly. No one moved at first, then two, then three, four, half a dozen, until finally the whole group slouched forward inside the rail to stand before the three judges sitting above. The judges, who had their heads together, took no notice of the waiting defendants, a fact which did not put the latter at their ease.

Tom Shaw finally rose. "You citizens of Springfield have all pleaded guilty of violating traffic regulations in one way or another. This is a serious offense. Last year six kids that most of us know were killed because they disobeyed the safety laws of this town. When you act like that you endanger your own lives and those of others, too. You have no excuse, whatever. . . ." He stopped to glance at a paper in his hand.

"First off, those caught without bike licenses. Everyone has had plenty of notice about these licenses; they've been on sale for two weeks now. You've read that there has been less bicycle stealing since the Juvenile Aid Division put this system into effect last month, and there's no reason for your failure to get 'em. They only cost fifteen cents; kids north of the Wildcat River get 'em at the branch office on West Superior; those south, at the main office of the Bureau of Motor Vehicles in the City Hall. We have decided to give you people a suspended sentence and allow you another chance. If you're picked up Monday without a license, we'll take severe action next Saturday. Next week we'll crack down on you.

"Now, the fourteen defendants who violated

regular traffic rules. I see . . . that is, the judges here see no extenuating circumstances. We therefore sentence you all to write out and hand in a careful five hundred word essay on safety in traffic. In this essay you will explain why the rule you violated was necessary, and why it has to be upheld. This is to be handed in to Miss Burton at the high school"—a groan went up from the boys and girls before him—"before nine o'clock Monday. If it isn't there at nine, or if in her opinion it isn't satisfactory, you'll be asked to do it over. Should she consider it bad, you'll be summoned to court next Saturday and given a far more severe sentence."

Five hundred words! Why, that's over twice as long as our regular weekly themes. Five hundred words will take all day today and to-morrow to finish!

"I can't do it."

"I gotta work today."

"I was going to the Indiana-Purdue game."

"My dad wanted me to help at the store."

Bang-bang. Bang-bang. Jay's gavel hit the desk. They had failed to observe his return. Silence fell.

Tom glanced down at them. "We aren't interested in what you happen to be doing or would like to do today. You can write these essays or not, just as you please. This is a first offense for everyone here, and we want to let you off easy. But unless you turn in a clean, well-written paper of five hundred words by Monday at nine, and unless Miss Burton signifies to the court that it is satisfactory, you'll be back here a week from today. You won't find things so simple then. Mary Jo . . . anything you care to say? Got anything to add, Earl? Cases dismissed."

There was dignity in the court; there was dispatch also. The clock on the wall over the heads of the judges showed 9:26 A.M.

The kids turned, piled back to their coats and hats on the benches beyond the railing. Five hundred words! To Miss Burton of all people. She's an old meanie, she makes you spell words right, and . . . everything. Five hundred words! Gee!

Then the door opened, and Officer Curtis entered with an angry, red-faced boy at his side. Roy Miller, the town's bad boy, the kid who lived on Depot Street by the railroad tracks, who was mixed up in gang wars and auto stealing and almost all trouble in the city, had refused to obey the summons of the Junior Court. He looked round savagely. The law was nothing new to him, so he was not intimidated; he did not see any particular joke in being hauled up before his acquaintances, either.

"This way . . . step in here . . . inside the rail," said Red Crosby. "The City of Springfield, Indiana, against Roy Miller. The defendant stands here . . . over here."

Behind the rails the others were watching. For this was the first, the authentic, test. This prisoner was tough and knew it. His scorn of the law was obvious enough to everyone in the room as he stepped forward, surly, contemptuous.

"Hey, I gotta work, I gotta job."

Bang-bang. "Silence in the courtroom."

The blue-coated officer moved inside the rail and stood with folded arms beside Jay Hanwell. He was a big chap who looked bigger and more imposing than ever.

"Roy Miller, d'you plead guilty or not guilty to riding on the wrong side of the street on a bicycle, to going through a traffic light at the corner of Buckeye and Superior, to riding without a license, to failure to appear here in court this morning in response to a summons served on you by Officer Curtis at your home last Wednesday night?"

"Guilty? Sure, I suppose so. What's it to you, Red?" He stood looking at them defiantly, at the three judges with their heads together, at the boys and girls gazing from their seats with mixed awe and admiration. He was undisturbed by the legal atmosphere, the paneled room, the flag behind the three judges, even by the cop standing beside Jay, the only tangible evidence of the law. No good to ask this boy to write essays; he just wouldn't.

Tom Shaw rose. "Roy Miller, we find you guilty on all counts. The sentence is to have your bicycle impounded for a period of one month from today."

The others gasped. They're really tough; they really mean business, don't they? Will they get away with it?

Roy stood a moment in rage. Then he burst out. "Ya can't do it! I work at Maher's. I deliver groceries for him. I got a right to my bike. Or I'll lose my job. You can't take my job away; you can't do that to me."

Tom paid no attention to the outburst. He interrupted, turning to the officer at the side.

"Officer Curtis, you'll take the defendant back to Maher's store, impound his bike and run it to the police station. It'll be held there in the basement until . . . until . . ." Tom glanced at the calendar hanging beside the bench. "Until the second day of May, next."

"Yes, sir," said the officer. "Hey, you! C'mon!"

•

Late that afternoon, following a long day in the new offices of the Juvenile Aid Division in the courthouse, Don Henderson walked slowly home. He happened to pass the Bureau of Motor Vehicles. Inside was a mob scene; outside a line of boys and girls stretched far down the street. They greeted him as he went past.

"Hi, coach." "Hi there, Don!" "Hi, coach."

"Hullo, gang. What gives here?"

"Bike licenses. They're really getting tough with us. We're after our bike licenses before Monday."

News spreads fast in Springfield, Indiana.

"What can I do for you, son?" he asked.

The youngster didn't reply. Instead he extended a folded paper. J. Frank opened and glanced at it, the agreeable smile vanishing as he did so. The boy was watching him closely. So was the attractive receptionist behind the switchboard across the room. The man realized they were watching, and he knew perfectly well that many other people were watching at that moment also.

In fact the whole town was watching J. Frank right then—the men at Rotary, his friends in the Springfield Club, his business acquaintances, his family, and especially his son. They were there, at his side, waiting to see what he would do. That was why he did not quickly tear up the paper and toss the pieces aside, which was his first impulse. J. Frank was intelligent and seldom acted without thinking carefully. To be sure, the agreeable smile left his face, yet he was not unpleasant as he nodded to the boy.

"Very good. I'll be there. Saturday at ten!"

With no further conversation he went into his office, closed the door and, after hanging up his hat and coat, sat down at his desk and studied the paper. It was apparently legal, duly stamped by the clerk of the City Court. The summons, for that was what the paper was, invited him to appear in Junior Court at ten the following Saturday.

J. Frank lit a cigarette and glanced out the window. A few days before, while getting his car away from the curb in a hurry, he had grazed a boy's bicycle, and now the lad was making trouble. Many citizens would have called Andy Anderson on the telephone and arranged things; others would have gotten in touch with the boy's father and offered to pay ten dollars. Either method was difficult for J. Frank. Too many people in town knew him, and far too many knew about the summons by this time. The fact that he had helped set up the Junior Court, or at least given his verbal approval to the whole Juvenile Aid Division, rendered his position even more delicate. As did Tom's place on the court. To pay no attention to the summons was impossible. Fortunately he realized this.

And the more he reflected the better he felt about his decision. To ignore the summons would mean everyone in town could accuse him of not supporting constituted authority. It would mean that the first prominent adult hauled into the

Junior Court was repudiating it. As the man who ran Springfield, J. Frank couldn't afford that luxury. But he enjoyed a fight, and this one promised some fun. It promised a good opportunity to slap down Don Henderson, that fresh young Henderson who had grown too big for his boots since he won the State. In any event he would be there in court and try to run things, and J. Frank was confident he could stand Don on his head.

In basketball, yes, he knows basketball, but in a court of law he's beyond his depth. I can make a monkey out of him in that court. Why, I can make him so ridiculous he may have to leave town. Besides, I doubt if this court has any jurisdiction over me; I don't believe they have. I'll fight, I'll go to the mat on this thing.

•

It was the next Monday morning. Andy sat in Don's office at the rear of the County Court Building, looking out the window. His cap was shoved back from his forehead; he tilted in his chair.

"Don, it was something, boy! I really wouldn't have missed it for all the tea in China."

"I'd like to have seen it. He isn't any too fond

of me, and I was afraid he'd think I'd put the kids up to it, so I felt I'd just better stay away."

"Most of the town felt different. The room was packed; you couldn't have got more than . . . why, you couldn't have got two more people inside. You see we've had adults up there before a couple of times, sentenced 'em and made it stick, too. But J. Frank Shaw is something pretty special."

"Yes, he's something else again. I'd sure like to have been there."

"Pretty near the whole town was. Y'see, Don, to Frank all this Junior Court is a lotta nonsense, boys and girls just pretending, that's all. It simply doesn't appeal to him. It's an idea he doesn't understand, it's out of his line; so when this boy catches him cold . . ."

"Andy, how did it happen? I've heard so many stories. Just how did they nab him?"

"Why, first of all, it seems this boy, Rex Carson, came along and parked his bicycle at the curb behind Frank's big Cadillac. Now Frank, he's in a hurry to get down to a director's meeting in Indianapolis that morning, so he comes out of his office, jumps into his car, backs up and crashes into the boy's bike. He says he didn't know what happened; that's the bunk. Instead of getting out and seeing what's what, he thinks, Aw, it's only a boy's bike. So off he drives. But the boy happened to be coming out of the Five and Ten just that minute, and sees the whole thing. He knew J. Frank and his car; he gets the number; he files a complaint as he has a right to do in the Junior Court. So then the fat was in the fire; they have to issue a summons for the old boy, returnable Saturday morning."

"Say! That's something. Was the bicycle badly damaged?"

"Yes, it was crumpled up some, the front wheel. Y'know, I bet ten people called me at headquarters, asked me to fix the whole thing up, not to let it go to court. J. Frank didn't, though, I'll say that for him. He was willing to go through with it."

"Yes, he thought he could beat it, that's why. He believes the whole idea is silly; he dislikes this juvenile work, and he saw a chance to make the whole thing look funny."

"Might be. But you know there's not a boy in town would have passed sentence on him 'cept Tom. And not a kid would have stood up to him like Chester Davis, either. That boy really knows his stuff. He'll be a lawyer someday, and a darn good one, too. Well, J. Frank took it all as a joke at first; he comes into court very pleasant and smiling-like, nodding to the folks he knew in back on the benches, just a lot of good, clean fun. . . ."

"I know. I've seen other adults come in just the same way. They felt it was fun at first, too."

"That's right. Well, first thing, he refuses to recognize the jurisdiction of the court. Says they have no authority to try the case or pass sentence, either. Up jumps this Davis boy, and reads him the city ordinance under which the Junior Court was established, giving them authority to hear cases of the kind between two kids or between a kid and an adult. Then he quotes the 'Bicycle Act' of 1939, and sets out the fines and penalties in a case of this sort. So they have the big boy cold. Frank, he starts to splutter the way he does when he gets mad, and the clerk of the court tells him he's out of order, and before you can say a word, the three kids have sentenced him to pay to have the bike repaired and ten bucks damages!"

"Did he pay?"

"You bet he did; he had to. He glares at Tom,

then he glares at the officer standing there, and this defendant, this Rex Carson, and then he sees all his friends on the benches in the rear and hears 'em snickering, so he realized he was licked. He peels off the cabbage like it was poisoned money and hands it over. The pay-off came when Tom went on to sentence him twenty-five bucks for leaving the scene of an accident. . . ."

"Oh, boy! Twenty-five bucks! Of course he'd drop that in one night at the country club in a poker game with Wilf Benson and his buddies."

"Think nothing of it. Or chuck it away in the slot machines in the Springfield Club at noon. But to pay it over as a fine, say, that really hurt. I thought he was gonna tear the place apart. Then the officer just stepped over and touched him on the shoulder, so he sat down and wrote out a check, so mad he could hardly see."

"Say, isn't that something! That just about makes it official; that just about ties it all up; we've made it stick on J. Frank Shaw. Now it's really official. Wait till this gets round town; wait till they hear it at Rotary. Just wait! We won't have any more trouble about getting this court across with folks in Springfield now. They'll see we mean business at last. Know what, Andy, I believe it does more good for an adult to be hauled into the Junior Court than into City Court, because it causes them embarrassment. J. Frank thought he could lick it. Why, he'd have given five hundred bucks to have been out of that whole thing. He imagined he was gonna make a monkey out of those kids. Well, sir, he got fooled, that's all."

"Bet he did. Not the first one, either."

Just then the door opened and Don's secretary stuck her nose in.

"Yes?"

"Boy by the name of Norman Hanscomb says he wants to see you. Says you sent for him yesterday."

"Hanscomb . . . Hanscomb . . . oh . . . a colored boy? Bring him in. Nope, don't go, Andy, don't go; stick around."

A skinny, frightened Negro boy entered the room. He saw the chief of police and hesitated on the threshold, uncertain whether to come in or to cut and run.

"Come in, come in, Norman." He placed the boy on a chair, then sat down behind his desk facing the terrified youngster.

"Norman, what school do you go to?"

"Roosevelt."

"Oh, Roosevelt. What grade?"

"Seventh."

"I getcha. Miss Stacker and Miss Crane and Mr. Eaton. That right?"

"Yessir." His hands twisted in his lap.

"Whose homeroom?"

"Miss Crane's."

"Uhuh, Miss Crane, a nice lady." The boy glanced nervously from the policeman in uniform to the coach behind the desk. "Play basketball up there, I suppose?"

The black head nodded.

"Where?"

"Forward."

"Forward , that so! Looks like you'd be a tough customer on a fast break. They teach you the fast break up there, don't they? Well, I suppose you'll be coming down to me someday."

"Yessir." The hands twisted, but less anxiously.

"Hold on now! I think I remember you! Aren't you the lad who ran rings around Washington School in that game I refereed last fall. Wasn't it you?"

The boy nodded, his fright gone now. In fact there was almost a smile on his face. "Why sure, why sure," continued Don. "Chief, this kid is the Jackson Piper of the Wildcats two years from now. He's fast, and he can hit, too, believe me." He turned to the policeman. Then suddenly he swung back in his chair to the boy and leaned across the desk.

"Norman! Why'd you steal those gloves?"

The boy froze. He couldn't speak, he could hardly open his mouth. He was rigid with fright. "I . . . I . . . I . . ."

Don looked him in the eyes. "Why did you steal those gloves from the Five and Ten, Norman?"

The boy's head wavered from one to the other, from the big police chief in blue, watching, to the man behind the desk staring at him. "I . . . I . . . I . . ."

It was too much. He broke down and burst into tears.

Don rose and walked round to the side of the weeping boy, putting his arm round his shoulder. "All right, Norman, all right. We aren't gonna send you to jail. Just tell me the truth now, how many pairs of gloves did you steal in all?"

"Fu . . . fu . . . fu . . . five."

"You quite certain it wasn't six?"

"Uhuh. Six."

"O.K. That's all I wanted to know." He patted the boy on the shoulder and sat on the edge of the desk close to him. "You took six pairs of gloves valued at a quarter a pair from the Five and Ten. Now listen, Norman, I'd like for you to get this straight."

The tears peeled off the eyelids of the youngster, but he raised his head as Don continued.

"Norman, I want to explain to you what this Juvenile Aid Division is all about, and why you were brought in here. It's been organized to help kids who get into trouble and ordinarily would have to appear in the City Court as first offenders. When you come in here, there's no official record of your case. I investigate it, and decide what shall be done. Maybe I'll decide to settle the thing myself, maybe I'll pass it along to the Junior Court to have it tried, and the offender sentenced by his own crowd. Get it? Understand?"

He nodded. Apparently he understood.

"Now ordinarily I'd shoot this case into the Junior Court so quick you wouldn't know what struck you. I'd let them dispose of it, and they're tough, Norman. But I ain't a-gonna. For one thing, you're a first offender. And I want this to be the *only* offense, the last time. Understand, Norman? I've been making quite some inquiries around, and it appears you're not a bad boy. You help your mother, and . . ." He referred to a paper on his desk. "You took these gloves to sell so you could buy a license for your dog. Correct?"

"Yessir. Trixie, now, if she doesn't have a license, they pick 'em right up."

"I know. I know all that. Only it isn't any excuse for stealing. You can earn money, same as other boys do. You must learn that stealing is a crime, and there's no excuse for it, none whatever. I've talked this all over with Mr. Harrison, the manager of the Five and Ten, and he says he'll accept payment for these gloves and won't press charges. Provided, and here's the catch, you are willing to pay back the buck and a half."

"Ain't got no money." He started to cry again, wiping his eyes with the back of his hand.

"That's just the point. Can you wash cars? You can? O.K. then. Take this card to the Pure Oil Filling Station on Superior Street, and show it to the boss there. You ask for Mr. Phillips.

He says he'll give you a chance to wash cars on Saturdays, and he'll pay you fifteen cents a car. All the money you earn you must take over to Mr. Harrison to pay for the gloves. Understand?"

"It may take lots of weeks."

"You don't have to pay it all back at once. You pay as much as you earn as fast as you can. But you must pay something every week, and you must report here every Saturday after work and tell me how you are getting along. When you have it all paid up, Mr. Harrison will give you a receipt, and you bring that back here to me to file. Understand? You take this card to the filling station on Superior; you wash cars; you get paid; you bring the money straight over to Mr. Harrison. I've written the manager's name on this card. Here 'tis. Now, get going, and whatever happens don't let me catch you stealing again. Remember, Norman, I surely will if you do."

The boy mumbled assent, grabbed the card, and vanished.

Andy rose. He stretched, nodded his head. "When you get too old to coach basketball, Don, and would like a steady job in the department, come round to police headquarters and see us."

13

Quite a difference, thought Don, quite a difference.

His mind went back to that dismal and exhausting night of the Finals, the night when he was so beaten he had to stay in the dressing room while his team clawed and chewed its way to victory; to the dejected and beaten kid in the frayed coat who sat in the police station, thin, scrawny, undernourished. This boy had not merely filled out in the months since the end of the basketball season; his attitude had changed.

"You feel some better since you had your tonsils out, don't you, Perry?"

"I sure do, Don. I dunno, things are sort of different now. Gosh, I'm so darned busy down there at the gym, what with spring practice and getting ready for next season and all, I haven't time to think. Y'see, Don, Red, he has so much on his hands with the Junior Court, he's had to turn a lot of things over to me."

"I know. That's fine. How much do you weigh now, Perry? You weighed yourself lately?"

" 'Most a hundred!"

"Say! You've gained . . . you've gained a lot. Isn't that something! I'm awful glad. Drinking that milk every day?"

"Sure am."

"Fine. Now one more thing before you go, Perry; you might help me out on this. I wanted to ask about this boy Roy Miller."

The expression on Perry's face changed.

"Him?"

"Yeah. You useta see quite a bit of him one way and another, didn't you?"

The boy half turned toward the wall. "Uhuh."

"What about his home life, his family?"

"Lives on Depot Street, with his grandma."

"Think Roy is happy at home, Perry?"

"Nope. I don't hardly think so."

"Well, he's been running round pretty fast and loose lately. Would you say offhand he's the ringleader of those kids the other side of the tracks, that gang over on Railroad Avenue and along Depot Street?"

"Yeah. Him and Mike Cray. I don't get to see much of him; leastways not for some time, Don."

"Then you wouldn't care to guess . . . speaking off the record, you understand . . . you wouldn't be able to make a guess as to whether he stole that bike or not?"

"Why, sure he did."

"What makes you say that?"

"Heard the kids talking about it in the lockers yesterday. They know."

"That so! Well, thanks, Perry. I won't quote you on this. The police know he did it; that is, they're fairly sure he did, but he won't come clean, and the evidence is shaky. Oh, Perry, one thing more. I've arranged for one of the best officers on the force to conduct a physical education class each Saturday morning for the kids in town. I want you to go. It'll build you up, and it's important for you to go every week. Begins next Saturday in Jackson Park." He stood up, stretched across the desk, his hand out. "Keep in there pitching, boy. Remember, a good manager makes a good team, and a bad one can hurt it plenty. What with Tom gone, and only two veterans next year, I'm gonna need all the help I can get in the fall. And mind you drink your milk, Perry."

"Yep, I will, Don. And thanks."

The boy went out the door and Don immediately took the telephone up. "Miss Stevens, call Chief Anderson." There was a minute's pause, and the phone jingled. "Hullo . . . Andy . . . that you, Andy? How are you? O.K.? Well, I'm ready for that kid now; send him over."

"O.K., Don, I'll have Casey take him over. Say, he's a tough nut. If you can get anything out of him you'll be going some. I'd have to admit he has us licked here."

"I don't know's I'll have any luck, but lemme have a crack at him, Andy. Seeing as how I know him fairly well, I might have a try at it."

The file was on the desk before him, all the documents; the reports from the truant officer, the findings of the Junior Court, the report from the city's probation officer, the letters, the recommendations, the testimony from the pastor of his church, the whole sorry, sordid story. The story of a citizen of Springfield, Indiana.

He was deep in it, turning over the papers and letters as he had turned them over a dozen times before, when there was a knock at the door.

Now for it! "Yes?"

Casey, the big cop, stood outside with a defiant lad. "All right, Hank, let him come in."

The boy entered and, without being asked, knew what to do. He sat silently in the chair, while the man with folded arms regarded him across the desk. There was no one else in the room, and neither of them spoke for a long moment.

"Well . . . you let me down. You let me down, didn't you, Roy?"

The boy wore a frayed leather jacket, his pants were torn, his shoes scuffed and worn. Of this Don saw nothing; he had seen it all before. Besides, he was looking into the boy's eyes.

No answer. Not a word from the truculent figure opposite.

"Tell me, Roy, what happened?"

"I dunno." His shoulders rose slightly. Under

Don's gaze he wavered, his eyes began to seek the floor.

"Roy! See here! I kept you out of reform school last month, remember? The police, they wanted to send you straight off to reform school. But I fought them, I stood up for you, I brought you in here and talked and argued with you, and tried to explain things. Then I went to bat for you with Anderson and the force. Didn't I? Didn't I, Roy?"

The boy nodded.

"Yes, I fought for you, that's correct, and I figured you liked me well enough not to let me down." There was another long moment of silence in the room. "Roy, you know something? These things hurt."

He glanced up quickly. Yes, no fooling, there were traces of pain and sorrow visible in the eyes of the man with the folded arms across the desk. The boy's eyes fell back to the floor again.

"This really hurts me, Roy, it hurts. I'm gonna tell you something now, something you don't know. I've been . . . ordered . . . to put you in jail!"

Quiet. Quiet over the room. Neither moved; neither seemed to breathe. Outside, beyond the closed door, the girl in the adjoining office was clattering away at a noisy old typewriter. As if nothing was happening, as if your whole future wasn't at stake, wasn't in the balance, as if you weren't going up the steps of the big gray stone jail already. Going up . . . up . . . inside.

A door slammed somewhere down the hall. The typewriter continued its clattering. Neither the man nor the boy spoke.

Without warning his arms came down, he placed his hands apart, flat on the desk, palms down, and leaned over. "Roy! I know you stole that bike!"

No surrender. No breakdown. No tears, no weeping. This boy was not Perry Taylor, nor Norman Hanscomb, either. He was tougher fiber. With a curl on his upper lip he came back at his accuser across the desk.

"O.K.! I took the bike! I took the bike, so what you gonna do? What you gonna do, send me to jail? G'wan and send me! You want a guy to work, you want he should get a job and go straight, then what? You took my bike away, you and your stooges at the Junior Court, Tom Shaw and Mary Jo and that gang from the west side."

No crying, no tears, no breakdown. Now his face was aflame and his chin was up, and the expression in his eyes had changed. There was all the difference in the world in those eyes; they were rational again. There was release in them.

But no breakdown. Just the soreness and the rawness and the bitterness against society. "All I wanted was to work, to be let alone, to keep my job . . . you an' your stooges. Them kids from the west side. That big stiff . . . him and his pals. Thinks 'cause he's a basketball player . . . I wouldn't have took it if you hadn't swiped my bike first. It's mine. I earned the money for it myself; I bought it, my grandma never gave me one penny. I earned money for it. And you took it away from me! So I got me another. It's unfair, and I hate this town. Everyone's unfair, everyone's against me in Springfield. I hate it!"

Don waited, waited until the torrent had subsided and the boy was cooler. He waited until there was a space of silence between them.

"Yes, I realize all that, Roy. But that doesn't excuse you. Does it? You had a hearing in a court of law."

"You! You and . . . yer stooges!"

Don refused to bite. "Look now, Roy, see here a minute. Suppose you got a raw deal from the Junior Court. I won't admit you did, but le's us suppose so. Does that excuse you? Does that give you the right to go out and steal Dave Willkins' bike? If somebody holds me up on Superior Street and takes my money this evening, and I meet him tomorrow in front of the Indiana Theatre, and pull a gun and shoot him . . . is that O.K.? Is it? Come now, is it?"

"Naw . . . I guess not."

"Roy! Lemme ask you a question. You know how long it would take you to straighten out if they sent you up to reform school?" The boy looked at him sharply, shook his head. "Why, six to seven years, Roy."

"Now see here, I'm on the spot. You've really put me on the spot. This is your third offense, and automatically it's out of the hands of the Junior Court and goes to the police. The Junior Court no longer has any jurisdiction in your case. Now the chief and his crowd aren't in any too good humor with me right this minute. They want to send you to jail, or to a reform school, anyway. They think I've been soft; they can't see why on earth I spend all this time on you. Roy, you may force me to do what I don't want to do." He settled back in his chair, his arms behind his head. "Should I have put you in reform school back there last month when they advised me to? Did I make a mistake then? Did I?"

The boy looked at him. He didn't answer, but

various emotions struggled across his face, and it was plain that although he was still suspicious some of the rawness had gone—or was going. He was interested, if watchful.

"You see how 'tis, Roy; here's how things stand. I'm not a policeman, I'm a basketball coach; naturally they think differently from me. They've got authority, I haven't; but they've also got the responsibility now, too. They want you sent up, Roy, and I'm fighting 'em off."

Still no answer. No emotion whatever on the hard face; only the eyes betrayed the fact that the boy was gradually becoming more interested. Is this guy straight, his expression said. Or is he just another, just one more of 'em giving me this line of bull?

"Look, Roy, I know a little something about the trouble at home. I've been over there and talked to your grandmother. She's an old, old lady; she has no patience with kids. She doesn't understand youngsters; she'd be right pleased to have you sentenced to reform school for six years and off her hands. You realize that, don't you?"

He nodded eagerly. It was about the first spontaneous gesture he had made. Whatever his faults, he had no illusions.

Don came forward and leaned over the desk again. "Roy, I'm gonna try to do the best I can to help you, to keep you outa reform school this time, and outa jail, too."

Still that suspicious look about the eyes of the tough youngster opposite. "You feel as if you've had a raw deal in life, don't you, Roy? You feel as if everyone in Springfield was against you—the cops, the adults, the businessmen, the Junior Court, your own crowd, everyone. It takes a good man to lick that feeling, a darn good man. I don't hardly know whether you can or not. Now see here; no matter what the cops tell me, I feel there's good in you. And I intend to go to bat for you with the police, and try to have you put on probation. That'll mean another chance, one more chance." He hesitated a second. "Say, Roy, see here a sec. Tell me something, will you? Am I foolish to believe in you? How far can I trust you? Am I foolish, Roy, to believe in you?"

Slowly the boy raised his head and solemnly shook it. It was evident that he was serious and honest in the gesture. He looked hard at Don. This guy, maybe he's O.K.; maybe he is . . .

"Nope, I don't hardly think so, either. Now

lemme explain to you, Roy, just what this means. Lemme explain. Would you want to ruin some other boy's chances? If you let me down this time, Roy, I shan't trust the next kid who sits in that chair. I just can't. Understand?"

The boy nodded. He understood.

"But if you get into trouble again, just once more, I'm through, so help me. Am I a sap to believe in you? Roy . . . with the experience you've had, you should be helping other kids who are in trouble. Ever think of that?"

The boy looked down again, and once more there was silence. "If you were in my place, Roy—you see the spot I'm in, you see my job, having to handle these cops, having them on my neck—what would you do? What I'm doing, hey?"

At last the head came slowly up and stayed up. "Yes, I would, Don."

"O.K. That settles it. I'll have faith in you. You'll give me your word you won't do anything to get me into a jam. Right! Shake! No sermons, Roy, no preaching. But remember, this is your last chance. If you get into trouble or any more mix-ups, I'm through, so help me, I am. You've got me on the spot, you can see that, I guess. You know that crowd of cops at the City Hall;

those boys aren't so easy to handle once they've made their minds up about a case. And they've sure got 'em made up about you. I'll catch the dickens for this. But I'll go through with it, since you've given me your word."

Roy started to talk. Don waited. Then he hesitated, stammered, and was silent. Would he talk or not? Finally he burst out: "Look! I hate cops, all of 'em. They're stinkers, every one. But you . . . I guess you're O.K. I guess I had you pegged wrong. I hate cops, but you're a right guy."

Don stood up. He was exhausted.

"Thanks, Roy, I'll try to be, if you will, too. And I'll go the limit to get that job back for you in Maher's store, because whatever else you are, you aren't lazy. That's one reason I'm for you. Now let's us get over with Casey and see what we can do with Andy Anderson."

14

It was a wonderful morning in early July, bright and warm. Don felt pleased with the world, and only slightly less pleased with himself and his job. For things were moving. He was getting results. To do a job, to do it well, to get results. What more could a man ask?

That luncheon at the Rotary Club the previous day had succeeded better than he had anticipated. The crowd had listened to him with sympathy and approval. They were for him and his idea, and the pile of opened letters on the desk before him proved it. The summer sunshine filled the pleasant room and enhanced his high spirits. It all combined to give him a kind of glow. Possibly the glow was heightened by that column on the front page of the morning *Journal* describing the luncheon and his talk. Don had the pleasurable sensation which comes to a man reading favorable comments about himself in a daily newspaper.

The day before he had spoken at a joint luncheon of the Lions, Rotary, and Kiwanis Club, the three largest civic clubs in the city, to explain his new junior police. He wanted to get all the prominent businessmen in town together under one roof and sell them his idea, to show them what a junior police force could accomplish if backed by the entire town. For the present he needed their help and support, financial and otherwise.

The article in the *Journal* was both factual and accurate. As there were no funds in the city's budget for the organization and support of a junior police, he hoped to get funds from the businessmen in town. As the successful coach of the state's winning basketball team, he was listened to with attention and respect. When Don Henderson talked about the kids of Springfield, he could speak with authority. And the town would listen.

Once finished, he was questioned at some length and, thanks to his frank and complete answers, given full support from the three clubs right at the luncheon meeting. The Chamber of Commerce had already sanctioned the idea with a generous donation of funds. The civic clubs agreed, also, to help with money and in other ways.

So Don was happy. The further he read, the deeper became his glow.

This thing looks good, it looks mighty good. I'll have the *Journal*'s support to start, and that's important in this town. Peedad is sure to help all he can with the *Press*. The civic clubs are behind me, so's the Chamber of Commerce. Once I get the kids, and that's the easiest problem of all, I believe I can reduce juvenile trouble in this city to zero. Or just about.

At that moment his thoughts were interrupted by the sounds of his secretary coming into the outer office and slapping her gloves in the drawer of her desk. He started to call out and ask whether she'd read the morning paper, when he happened to turn over to the editorial page. The top editorial caught his eye. He was surprised to find it headed:

BOONDOGGLING UP TO DATE.
MORE WASTE OF MUNICIPAL FUNDS

Don flipped the paper open, folded it, laid it down flat on the desk and began to read. That would be old Frank Fager, the editor, who'd been round town ever since he came down from Fort Wayne more years ago than anyone could remember. Of course you'd expect him to be against the junior police; he was always against everything in town, no matter what it was. Don was amused as he started to read the editorial; but his amusement diminished the longer he read.

"A setup such as the proposed junior police would merely duplicate the work of the efficient Springfield Police Department and other agencies working with young people in town. Worst of all, it would be an additional expense to the city, and a drain on the municipal budget when many local improvements are badly needed. In some circles it would even be considered evidence of the growth of socialism so apparent elsewhere in the country today."

But . . . but . . . no . . . look . . . if you get kids working for their own city . . . if you ask them to perform duties . . . to take a part in running their own government . . . to have some responsibilities, why, that's not socialism, that's democracy. Isn't it? Sure! What's the old geezer talking about? What's biting him?

Now his amused attitude vanished. Don's glow was rapidly departing. He was thoroughly aroused. Instead of a glow, he was becoming strangely warm inside, and there was nothing glowing about that warmth. Nor did it have any relation to a pleasurable feeling, either.

"The Juvenile Aid Division, an excellent idea originally, was started at the suggestion of some of the more advanced thinkers in town, and without the entire approval of many of the solid citizens in the community, who perhaps allowed themselves to be persuaded into sanctioning the setup against their better judgment. The Division was placed in the hands of a very young man who has only been in this city a few years and can hardly be aware of the many problems existing here. Moreover, we were assured at its inception that the idea was a temporary one. That it was an experiment. That it would cost the taxpayers no money. Now look at the darn thing!

"The opening wedge was to secure a stenographer. Then it appeared there had to be a 'study' of each case; that meant records, that meant filing cases and cabinets; that meant more money. Files, desks, office equipment were secured. Then we were told that offices should not be in the police station; that the atmosphere was bad for the young rascals. Our doer-gooders believed this, and when it was suggested that if the Tuberculosis Association had rooms in the new County Courthouse, the Juvenile Aid should be quartered there also, no objection was made. This cost the municipality money, even though it wasn't visible to John Q. Public. We very much question whether there is any justification for spending taxpayers' money on a project of this kind.

"True, the necessary money is being raised by civic organizations located in town. Yet this regimentation of American youth can only mean one thing. We are being saddled with an octopus that is seizing power on every side, that feeds on power and will demand more power, and more funds, too. Where is the money coming from when the civic organizations can no longer shell out to support these newfangled ideas? The *Journal* believes the whole question of a Juvenile Aid Division to be a totally unwarranted interference in the rights of the individual, and considers it in line with the continued trend toward socialization of America, a trend which threatens . . ."

Don could read no more. The glow had long since left him and been replaced by a furious rage. He tossed the newspaper to the floor, grabbed his hat, and stalked from the room. The door shut savagely behind him. He was through the inner office and into the hall before his secretary could look up and say good morning.

To his surprise, and for the first time in his stay in Springfield, he did not find Peedad Wilson entirely sympathetic. The old man, his feet on his desk as usual, was taking the editorial with an equanimity Don found hard to understand.

"Unjust? Sure! Misrepresentation? Yep, of course. It's what you're up against in this town when you pioneer, when you start something new. You're waking folks up, Don, you're making 'em think. It hurts. Don't expect 'em to like it, boy."

"Yes, but, Peedad, the report of the luncheon on the front page by that young reporter is entirely different. It shows this will actually save the city dough; that it will first of all release the police for more important jobs. That it will . . ."

"I know, Don, I know all that. That's not the point."

"Y'see, Peedad, this was Tom Shaw's idea, really. We'd been having some trouble with some of those gangs out there, those tough kids in Shedtown, and he thought the whole darn thing up himself. He came to me with the plan just as it stands now. We figured to make boys between twelve and seventeen eligible for this junior police force. I think it's sound; I b'lieve kids can handle tough kids better'n grown-ups. Whenever I need to know what's what in some part of town, there's always a kid who tells me. We started out in a small way in the 6th District. Appointed Jay Hanwell the police chief, and Roy Miller the captain out in that district. He picked his own lieutenants. Know what? In the two weeks we've been operating, we cut down juvenile trouble in that district eighty-five percent. How's that!"

"So. Is that so! Good for you, Don."

"That's right. And the other day two kids patrolling out there along South Washington found a purse dropped in the road by a passing motorist. There was over two hundred bucks in it and some important papers. They brought it in to headquarters, and when the dame found out her loss and called up from Tipton, the purse was there in Andy's safe waiting for her. The kids got a twenty-dollar bill as reward. Know what? They turned it over to our junior police fund. So when I saw how things were working out, I went to Seth Newman, in the Chamber of Commerce, and the civic organizations, and they're backing me just fine. They understand. Now this . . ."

"I know. I realize, Don, what you're up against. Heck, haven't I been fighting it for years?"

"We're all set to operate. I've got the badges ready to order; here's the sample." He pulled a small gold badge from his pocket. It was a minor replica of a regular policeman's shield, with the inscription:

CAPTAIN

SPRINGFIELD

JUNIOR

POLICE

"Say! That's real nice!"

"You bet! We'll have a thousand members in this before we get through. Each kid gets a badge, see, and a certificate of membership in the junior police. Then he takes a pledge to be a law-abiding citizen and do his regular tours of duty on the force. Peedad, look here, you see how the Junior Court relieves the docket of the City Court. Now I believe our junior police can save the services of five patrolmen on traffic duty this year alone. In two months I'll have three hundred kids on street corners protecting school children. I'll have 'em out there in all kinds of weather, and I'll bet inside of six months I can cut injuries from traffic down at least sixty percent. I've got some of my best boys and some of my worst boys as captains, and they're all swell, they're all working together. Why, Peedad, we could really go places with this thing; we could do what you said last year, we could make this a city good enough for Lincoln."

Peedad felt his enthusiasm. "You will, Don, you will if you keep plugging, if you don't get discouraged."

"Discouraged! Shoot, when I see things like that editorial, and that old fella working behind the scenes to knife the idea, I think I'll go back to basketball."

"And walk out on the kids, hey! What kind of a thing is that to do? A fine guy you are! You want a better city. O.K., the way to have a better city is to have better youth. The way to have better youth is to work with 'em like you're doing. You set this thing up, you get it running, then you get peeved and quit because Frank Fager takes a poke at you and your Juvenile Aid Division. Why, boy, you haven't seen anything yet. Wait till you make a few enemies of important people in town. Now get back to your office and go to work and no more beefin', hear me! Chuck that newspaper away, do your job, and stop this talk of leaving your kids. Don't let me hear any more of that, Don. You never walked out on the Wildcats before, and you're not a-gonna start now."

"But, Peedad . . ."

"But nothing! You're just beginning to realize

what public life is. Now clear out. Get out and leave that man Fager to me. I'll take care of him in my Round-the-Town column this afternoon."

It was almost hot as Don came down the gloomy stairs and into the sunlight outside. The peonies round the white stone courthouse opposite were aglow, yet Don felt upset and unhappy. The unfairness of the attack stung, and he was unable to dismiss it as casually as Peedad did. The old man was callous about the whole thing. There was a trace even of bitterness in Don's feeling toward his oldest friend in Springfield.

15

Henry Remsen was generally regarded as one of the town's leading younger citizens. His modern jewelry store, on Buckeye west of Michigan, had developed from a small hole in the wall in little more than five years. In a highly competitive business, surrounded by others in the same profession on the same block, Henry held his own with something to spare. This was not so much due to the store with its wide, attractive entrance and up-to-date interior with large display cases on each side of the long room, nor yet to his stock, constantly renewed from the wholesale houses in Cincinnati and Chicago, as to Henry himself.

Henry had been born and brought up in Springfield, and he knew the place and the people where his entire life had been spent. As a youngster, Henry had always been industrious, always looking for jobs cutting grass, running the neighbors' errands, or doing chores in his spare time. His nearsightedness and his glasses prevented him from taking part in sports in school, consequently the pursuit of money became his sport. It was a game at which he was a champion. With his knowledge of the town and its inhabitants, he also possessed through luck or training—or a combination of the two—a faculty for remembering names and faces that was amazing. When folks entered his store for the first time, he greeted them as a friend. If he didn't know the customer's name, Etta, his clerk, usually did, and they had a system by which she wrote the name on a piece of paper and slipped it to him, so that he was soon speaking to Mr. Smith or Mrs. Jones. If Etta didn't know the client's name, Henry took trouble to find out from someone who did. Once he found out, he didn't forget it either.

No sale was too trivial, no job too unimportant for him. He would repair an ancient clock or a cheap wristwatch with the same concentration and courtesy that he devoted to adjusting Frank Shaw's elaborate Swiss chronometer. In a few years he had the jewelry trade of the schools sewed up; he went to great pains to design class rings, sold graduation gifts, and as the kids grew older, engagement rings and presents. It was natural that before long Henry was looked on as one of the coming men in town. Although a little too young to become a member of Rotary, he was the president of the Junior Chamber of Commerce, and every year he was asked to deliver a talk on Free Enterprise and the American Way of Life to the high school assembly. Henry did this with deftness and assurance.

When Carlene Benson came into the store that warm afternoon, Henry stepped forward. There was a smile, and yet not entirely a smile, on his face as he said, "Good afternoon, Miss Benson. Can I help you?"

Considering that none of the Benson family had ever entered his store, and that he no more expected her than Queen Mary, he felt pleased at his presence of mind. It was not wasted. For most storekeepers in town knew her as "Carlene," or "that Benson child," or "Wilf Benson's girl." Not Henry. To him she was a potential client and more—the first of the family to come into his store, and not, he hoped, the last.

The stock was attractive and well displayed. Indirect lighting of the latest design cast a glow over the showcases. Diamond rings sparkled in their plush settings. Precious stones of all kinds shone under the electricity. Wrist watches, polished with chamois skins by Henry and Etta at night when the store was closed, twinkled across the room. Over it hovered Henry, discreet, quiet, a man of the world who treated his customers like women of the world. Carlene's mother considered her a child not yet old enough to wear expensive jewelry, so Carlene liked Henry's manner.

Henry's first guess had been that she owned a broken-down wristwatch which no one else in town would bother to fix. That she had come to him as a last hope. When she mumbled that she wanted to look at bracelets, he was surprised. And pleased at the same time. He also was careful not to betray his feeling as he quickly pulled out one, two, three trays of bracelets. They were all prices, all designs. Carlene's taste was not cheap. Her eyes and her desires fastened upon the most expensive tray.

She fingered the stock longingly. Henry said little. Now and then he interjected a word to call attention to a design or point out some choice setting with a well-manicured little finger, suggesting, explaining, but leaving the choice entirely up to her. She was bewildered by the assortment, as older and more experienced women than Carlene Benson were often perplexed in the same situation. Carlene began to try on the bracelets, looking at them, admiring the gems that sparkled and glistened on her arm, taking one off and picking up another—and another.

As Etta went past them Henry spoke to her.

"Etta! See whether those emeralds went back to Silversteins, or if they're in the safe still. I'd like to show them to Miss Benson if they're here. Some bracelets we had sent down on consignment, the same thing Tiffany displays. A little expensive for Springfield perhaps, but I'd like you to see them," he said to Carlene tentatively.

Then the telephone rang. It rang and rang. Henry was annoyed.

"Excuse me, please, that's long distance. I've been trying to get Chicago all afternoon. Just a second." With quick, short steps he went back and into the office at the rear where he sat down. Carlene could just see his head and the back of his shoulders hunched over the telephone. She was alone in the front of the store.

She glanced round. The street was concealed by display counters, and there was no one visible except Henry, his head over the telephone in the back office. She had been trying the bracelets on her left arm. Quickly she took one from the heap on the counter, and thrust it well up her right arm, covered by the sleeve of her summer coat. As Henry returned, she was holding bracelets up and examining them at arm's length with her left hand. Her right hand was wrapped tightly around her purse which she held against her chest.

Etta returned full of apologies. The emeralds had gone back the previous afternoon. Henry nodded, frowned a second, and regarded Carlene. She declared that the things were beautiful, that they were lovely, but not precisely what she wanted. Indeed she admitted she didn't know what she wanted herself. She smiled charmingly and Henry was charmed. His head went down slightly in assent, he smiled also, though with a touch of grimness. As an amateur psychologist, he realized the spell was broken. Something had happened; what he didn't know. He cursed the long distance call, he cursed the Bell Telephone Company of Indiana, but he kept his curses to himself. Besides, she might be returning with her mother, in which case he could probably sell the old lady also. Outwardly he was grave and attentive as he followed Carlene to the front of the store and held the door open.

"A pleasure, Miss Benson, a pleasure; drop in again, please, anytime."

Carlene walked rapidly down the street. She felt the need of support, the need of something inside, and the first place offering sustenance was the Goody Shoppe, a few doors along. Entering, she found Dorothy June Barker alone in a booth. As she sat down beside her friend, she was not surprised to discover that her knees were shaking. The waitress came to take her order, and Carlene asked for a large coke. Then without a word she extended her right arm across the table and yanked up the sleeve of her coat.

"Oh . . . I thought your mother forbade you to wear jewelry like that, Carlene!"

"My mother!" Carlene was nervous and exasperated. "My mother just doesn't understand me!"

"Likewise. But how come she let you wear it?"

"She didn't. It isn't hers."

"It isn't! Where'd you get it? Why, it's brand-new, isn't it?"

"Yes, it's new. I just got it at Henry Remsen's."

"At Remsen's! You did! You did not! Carlene, where . . . Did your mother give it to you?"

"You know perfectly well she didn't; you know my mother; you know she doesn't understand me at all. Don't you remember she said I was too young to wear jewelry? You know all that. I have a date tonight, and I wasn't going out with Tom Shaw looking just like any old thing. I just wasn't, that's all. So I got this from Henry."

"Goodness! You mean you bought it?"

"Well . . . not exactly."

"Carlene! You didn't take it!"

"Shhhh. No, I borrowed it, stupid. I'm returning it tomorrow."

"Did you ask him? Does he know you borrowed it?"

Carlene looked at her pityingly. As a woman of the world she realized how much older she was than her best friend. "Henry'll never know the difference. It was easy. I walked in, tried on some bracelets, then when he was in the back of the store, I shoved it up my arm. But I'll return it tomorrow after my date . . . Don't worry."

Dorothy June was speechless. She fingered the bracelet. Then a voice above them spoke.

"Say! That's some dish. Your ma buy that for you, Carlene?"

They both glanced up. Anola Cray was standing over them, admiring the bracelet on Carlene's extended arm. The two girls seated in the booth were west siders; Anola lived out by the tracks near Warner Gear. She was a classmate of theirs, and if not a friend, at least an acquaintance they sometimes regarded with admiration. Her mother worked, and consequently Anola had the freedom they longed for. She had begun to have dates with boys months before they did, and she stayed out later, too. It was rumored, not without foundation, that once she had been picked up by the police at night and had spent two days in the town's jail. Moreover, it was well known that her brother Mike was a member of the Depot Street gang and a tough cookie. Carlene therefore felt like impressing her. She was anxious to show that you could live on Austin Avenue on the west side and yet be a woman of the world. Calmly she replied, "Like it?"

"You bet." Anola's admiration was real.

"Sit down." It was a command, and Anola promptly obeyed. "Guess how I got it." Anola, edging into the seat beside Dorothy June, was fingering the bracelet, touching it, turning it round and round on Carlene's pretty wrist.

"Gee," she said, "I dunno. I only wish I had a bracelet. Or a new dress, even. I got a date tonight and nothing to wear."

"Me, too," said Dorothy June, who understood Anola's feelings. "Know what my mother said? She had the nerve to tell me I'd better wear out some of my old things before I got new ones. And I'm going to the lake with Chester tonight, too."

"Yeah, that's where I'm going," remarked Anola, still fascinated by the bracelet.

"If you girls need dresses," suggested Carlene with some superiority in her tone, "why don't you borrow them for an evening, same's I did with this bracelet?"

"Borrow! How?" Anola was interested; she wasn't quite sure she understood, she leaned forward with attention. At that moment the waitress placed a double coke before Carlene.

"What's yours?" she said to Anola. But her eyes were upon the extended arm of the other girl, and especially upon the sparkling bracelet.

•

It was Etta who first noticed the disappearance of the bracelet. She told Henry just as they were shutting up shop for the night. At first he found it hard to believe. Then a check of the trays showed one bracelet gone from the tray Carlene had been inspecting. As she was the only person who had looked at bracelets all day, there seemed no choice but to take action.

Henry was upset. Taking action worried him far more than the loss of the bracelet. He was insured; he had no fear of losing money. What bothered him was having the police called in, as they surely would be if he notified the insurance company. Then a flash came to him. He remembered the Juvenile Aid Division and Don Henderson. There seemed a solution to the whole affair.

With quick steps that had anxiety in them, he walked down Buckeye to the County Court Building. Don's secretary was leaving as he reached the third floor, but Don was still at his desk. Hurriedly Henry told his story, watching the other's face with attention. He always watched faces, but now he was particularly eager to get Don's reaction. He answered a few questions. Don appeared less astonished by the incident than he had expected.

The telephone rang. "Excuse me, Henry. Hullo. Oh, hullo there, Andy. No, I hadn't . . . nope, not yet . . . hold on." He took up a pad and wrote down something. "What sort of dresses? I see. Katzmann's and the Bon Ton? When did it happen? This afternoon? Hold on a minute. What time? D'you know about what time exactly? H'm . . . O.K., I'll watch out."

He turned to Henry. "Some dresses and things were taken from Katzmann's and the Bon Ton this afternoon shortly after four. You remember what time it was when Carlene Benson came into your store?"

"Yes," said Henry. "I'd say it was about three, or a little earlier. Maybe a quarter till three."

"Good. There may be some connection. It might be some friends of Carlene's who took those dresses. Of course, again it might not. First of all, we must find out where she's at and what she is doing this evening. If she stays home, that'll be hard. Luckily I have some pipelines among the kids; I can usually locate anyone I want. If Tom Shaw isn't home this evening, chances are she's with him. Let's see now. It's too hot for bowling; the movies . . . no . . . they're either dancing at the lake or . . ."

"You'll be tactful, won't you, Don?"

Don stood up. "You want your bracelet back without any fuss, don't you?" he asked.

"Oh, yes, of course. I want to recover the bracelet. Only I don't want the police in on it."

"My department will handle the whole thing."

"Good. Nor the parents, either."

"That you'll have to leave to me, Henry. We have a regular procedure in these cases; we make no difference who the kid is; we act just the same for everyone. Now let me have time to ask a few questions. You go home and have your supper, and show up here at eight tonight."

Dave Freeman and His Six Singing Merrymacks were giving out at the lake that evening, and the dance pavilion was packed when they reached the place. They went up the steps, keeping close to the railing of the wide porch, standing as much as possible in the shadows, wound their way through groups of laughing couples, and walked around to the rear of the building, where through the open double doors they could see the throng within. It was not long before Tom Shaw's crew haircut was visible rising above the other dancers in the center of the room. He stayed in the center for quite some time, but at last came toward them. He had Carlene close to his chest, her left arm around his back and reaching toward his shoulder. Sparkling on her wrist was Henry's bracelet.

"That's it! That's it," he exclaimed.

"O.K., O.K. Now just sit tight, Henry. From what I gathered talking with a couple of kids after supper tonight, we'll see a few new dresses here if we're lucky. I was pretty sure there was a connection somewhere in all this; somebody has to start these things going."

16

The telephone jangled before Don had more than shut the door to his room the next morning. He heard his secretary's voice outside.

"Why, yes, Mr. Mason. Yes, he is; he just came in. Hold on, please."

"Good morning, Don, good morning, boy. How are you?" Harry Mason's hearty voice boomed over the wire. It carried with it a picture of the big man sitting at his desk in the main office of the Chrysler plant, and Don could almost see his handsome face. As president of the Springfield Chamber of Commerce, Harry was in on everything. "Don, 'bout that donation from the Chamber. I've told Seth to put it through this month. You're doing a grand job there, and we're behind you all the time. And, Don, say, I liked your talk the other day, liked what you said."

"Why, thanks, Harry, thanks lots."

"Yes, I feel you're really doing a public service. Just one thing, one more thing, Don. I'm all for your cleaning up these gangs of kids that have been rampaging round town, and making this a decent city. It's really a great work you're doing. But you gotta have tact, gotta be tactful, y'understand, boy?"

Don was silent a second. "Why, yes, Harry, I think I do. That's the reason I don't run about in a prowl car. I believe it's important the neighbors don't know when a youngster is picked up. If they do, most likely they say, 'Aha, they picked Mary up! She's a bad girl.' That's what we don't want; that's the reason I always go out in an unmarked car that attracts no attention."

"First rate. That's sensible, Don, that's really intelligent. I like your approach to the problem. I'm mighty happy you do things this way; especially since the Benson case is up today. I know you'll handle that right."

Don hesitated. The case was hardly more than twelve hours old, and here Harry Mason knew all about it. For a minute he said nothing. To be sure, Harry was one of the more prominent citizens in town. But how did he know of a case that hadn't even been certified to the Juvenile Aid Division yet? And what business was it of his?

"Just be tactful, that's all. Maybe you better call me on it later in the day when things get straightened out. I know we can count on your cooperation. I'm interested in the thing, and you can get me here at the plant all day. Tell you what, call me on my private wire—6564. Get it?"

Mechanically Don scribbled the figures on his pad. "6564. O.K., Harry." He put down his pad to see Casey standing in the doorway. The big officer had a woman's dress, a coat, and a box in his hand. Don knew the box contained Henry's bracelet. Before either could speak, the phone jingled again.

"Don! Been trying to get you all morning." The voice of the chief had a worried sound.

"We're kinda up against it, you'n me, with these girls."

"What's the matter, Andy? Seems an open and shut case to me."

"Yeah, I know. We got to go careful-like. One of the three is old Wilf Benson's girl."

"So! Who're the others?" He wondered whether the grapevine included the chief of police as well as the head of the Chamber of Commerce.

"Kid by the name of Cray. Anola Cray."

"Mike Cray's sister?"

"Think so. Know him?"

"Yep. That the lot?"

"No. Dorothy June Barker. Her old man's the insurance fella, president of the country club. Now look here, Don. We got all the stuff back, and I've sent it over to your office. . . ."

"Yeah, Casey just came in with it."

"O.K. Now here's what we're up against. We must be tactful on this, understand? I want you to go to work on these three girls and scare the hell out of 'em all. You do a wonderful job with kids; you're wonderful the way you handle 'em."

"You want I should scare 'em?"

"That's right." The anxiety was leaving the chief's voice. "Throw it into 'em, y'understand?"

"And then drop it, hey?" Don understood perfectly. What he found hard to understand was why the police department was stepping into his job. It soon became plainer.

"Now, Don, don't be hot-headed about this. You realize as well as I do we can't allow a thing of this sort to get into the Junior Court; we simply mustn't have any publicity about it in town; your job wouldn't be worth a nickel. Nor mine. I'd be reduced to patrolman in a week. No sense kidding ourselves."

Peedad's words came back to Don. Wait till you make a few enemies of important people in town. It was the same thing last year, he thought, the same thing when I offended Frank Shaw over the basketball tickets. Don's bitterness toward the old editor of the *Press* vanished.

"Could I be a bit tougher on that Cray girl, Andy?"

Quickly the other shot back. "Sure, by all means. Give her the works. I mean to say, she's not a first offender, is she? Or is she? Well, anyhow, you'd be quite justified in sending her off to the State School for a few years. She's a toughie, comes from Depot Street out by the Nickel Plate tracks, and frankly, Don, I'd say you'd be O.K. in sending her up. Seems to me the boys have picked her up before for hanging round downtown of an evening. I'll check on that. As for the other two, so long as we get the stuff back to the merchants, we can afford to frighten 'em, to let 'em go this time with a reprimand."

That's just it. We don't really want justice in Springfield. If we're after justice, if the Junior Court is set up to dispense justice to all alike, to young and old, strong and weak, why be tough on one girl and not on the others? These words were on his lips, but he managed to stifle them. Andy had a job to protect; Andy couldn't be blamed because folks in Springfield were the way they were.

"O.K., Andy. O.K., boy." He rang off. "That's right, Hank, lay that stuff on the table." He rose and, going over, inspected it. Inside the box was the bracelet he had seen the night before on Carlene's arm. He turned over the dresses. He whistled. "Can't see why girls like that want to take things . . . they have money. . . ."

"It's the danger and the excitement, Don, that's mostly the reason." The telephone rang and Don stepped back to his desk.

"Don! This is Wilf Benson!"

Here it comes, he thought. Wilf Benson, president of the Merchants National, was one of the town's most respected elder statesmen. It was the father of Carlene and not an elder statesman that was talking at the moment. Don felt sorry for him. His tone was sober. "Don, I understand you have my little girl over there."

"Why, she isn't actually here yet, Mr. Benson. She's due here shortly, though."

"I see. Well, I just wanted you to know this thing has hit me hard, Don. I can't understand why my little girl should do such a thing, just cannot understand it. She's always been a good girl, always, till she took to running around with that Cray girl at school. A bad lot."

Don determined to reserve judgment as to who was running around with whom. But the man's distress was apparent in his voice, and despite himself Don felt sympathy.

"Now then, Don, this is mighty hard on Mrs. Benson. Y'see, she hasn't been at all well this winter; she's been treated by a specialist in Indianapolis, and I . . . well . . . the fact is I haven't gone into it fully with her yet. Of course I want to make full and complete restitution of anything that's been taken. You realize that, don't you?"

"Yes, Mr. Benson, but I gather all the stolen articles were recovered last night." He looked at the big cop who nodded. "Yes, sir, it appears everything is here. Just what disposition we shall make of the case, of course I couldn't say off-hand."

"No . . . no . . . of course not. But on account of the girl's mother, Don, I'd be so grateful if you'd keep all this quiet. I mean, I'd appreciate your cooperation. In fact I'd be willing to give five thousand dollars to your department. I heard you speak at Rotary the other noon, and it's a grand job you're doing."

Five thousand dollars! A car of his own that he could get round in, another girl to work on office records, an assistant from the force, perhaps, to help with the increasing volume of detail. Don was tempted and he was annoyed. "Mr. Benson, would it be all right if we sent this Cray girl up? If we . . ."

Like Andy he bit immediately. He answered as eagerly as the police chief had done, and almost in the identical language. "I understand, Don, that she comes from over Depot Street by the tracks. I fear she's been a bad influence on Carlene and the other girl. You know how impressionable youngsters are at that age—oh, very."

"Yes, well, I'll have to talk to them and get to the bottom of all this, find out the exact facts, and see how things stand. You understand I can't judge the case in advance."

"Oh, no, quite. I understand that. But, Don, when you have the facts, I wish you'd call me back. Will you, please? Call me back, because I'm anxious about this. Carlene isn't a bad girl; she's always been a good girl, never given us any trouble. I can't think what got into her."

"Yes, I will, Mr. Benson, and thanks for calling." Thanks for nothing. He put down the telephone and stood thinking. What sort of justice is that! How's that square with real justice, the justice those kids dish out there in the Junior Court? Why, they'll crack down on their own friends, doing it almost every day. They don't care for anyone; they shoot straight.

Well, he doesn't know Mrs. Benson has been summoned in with Carlene. He'll find it out soon enough. The phone jangled again. This is how it's going to be all day long! He heard Marion, the secretary, speaking in the room outside.

"Oh, yes, he is. Yes, he is, Mr. Shaw. Just wait a minute, I'll put him right on for you."

Her honeyed, ingratiating tones jarred on Don's tangled nerves. He realized she was impressed merely by talking with the man who ran Springfield, Indiana. The buzzer sounded at his desk but he took no notice of it. Instead he opened the door and called out.

"Tell him I'm not in," he said in a voice that J. Frank could easily have heard. Don had just about reached the point where he was afraid J. Frank wouldn't hear.

17

No two kids, he thought, were alike. Each one was a problem, separate and distinct. Some you had to be frank and open with; with some you had to be sympathetic; some demanded time and more time, until finally they broke down and told what they had done. By now Don knew pretty well when to be a father and when to be the prosecuting attorney. But as he sat looking at the three girls before him, he realized this would be the toughest job of all.

The girls were in a circle on the stiff, hard chairs before his desk. On the table behind them were piled the spoils. Don said nothing; he was trying to recover from the shock that had hit him when he first saw the pretty, blonde girl. So that's Carlene Benson! Of course. It was the girl Tom Shaw was always walking with through the corridors at school; the one they were always kidding him about. More than once Don had seen them sauntering along Sycamore Street together after school.

Plain enough who was the ringleader. Carlene sat with her attractive legs crossed, tossing back her hair, unworried, sure of herself, far more at ease than Don. Next to her in a cheap coat and a thin dress, wearing no stockings and shoes that were scuffed and worn, was Anola Cray, sullen, defiant. At her right was Dorothy June, evidently the one to follow the others, and especially Carlene.

Well, someone has to start things going; we have to begin; this isn't getting anywhere fast. If they were only boys. Now boys—I can handle boys O.K. But these girls! This is my toughest assignment yet. I believe I'm far more scared than they are.

As he looked them over, postponing the moment when his mind and energy and intelligence would be thrown into conflict with theirs, he realized how true this was. He kept searching their eyes, hard eyes. Even Dorothy's eyes were hard. Only Anola kept her gaze toward the floor.

He shook his head slowly and tightened his lips. Here goes!

"What on earth possessed you girls to do this?"

No reply. Only Carlene responded with a shrug of her shoulders.

He continued. "You knew what you were doing; you're all old enough to know you were stealing. You girls aren't babies; you must have realized what this meant. Didn't you?"

Still no response, verbal or otherwise. It was like smacking a pillow. They were smarter than boys, and quicker, too. They were ahead of him each time he spoke. These girls would never break down; they would have to be broken down. "Come on, what possessed you? What on earth possessed you?"

Always that silence. No sign of their weakening.

"Which one of you took that bracelet?" No answer. "Carlene! I b'lieve you're the leader of this gang; I b'lieve you did. Girls, since Juvenile Aid Division was founded, that's three . . . nope, four months now, I've only lost three boys and one girl. A couple of hundred kids have come through here and I've only lost four. That's a pretty good record. Know what I mean when I say I lost 'em?"

They didn't know, and were hardly interested enough to show they didn't much care, either.

"I mean that the boy—or the girl—has to be sent out of town, to reform school or someplace. Now the only girl I've lost since we started was a second offender who stole a fur coat from Hallecks. Carlene, did you take that bracelet?"

He looked her in the eyes. She looked back at him. "I didn't say I did!" It was the first word from any of the three.

"Oh, I see! Then it wasn't you?"

The girl was far too quick for him. "I didn't say who it was." She showed by her triumphant look how pleased she was at her ability to outguess him. It was apparent the other two admired her ability also. With some considerable pleasure she looked at him, tossing her hair back on her shoulders, uncrossing and crossing her legs.

"Look here, Carlene. What say we cut out this funny business? Why not come clean? We know you took the bracelet; we have proof of it. Your people have money . . . What on earth possessed you to do a thing like that?" he added somewhat lamely.

Still no answer. He was baffled and they knew it perfectly well. No response, no dent in their defenses. "See here, this is stealing; this is a real crime, a crime that's punishable by several years in reform school; or worse, in state's prison. You girls think of that when you were doing this? I guess not." They were as firm and as unyielding as ever. It annoyed him, especially as perspiration was coming out on his forehead, and Carlene noticed it. With a gesture he took out his handkerchief, wiped his brow, then wished he hadn't. Never had such a barrier existed between his desk and the person seated before him. He would have given money for the hardest, toughest young boy in town to be sitting there.

"Look, girls," he appealed to them. "Look, I don't enjoy this. I don't like this sort of thing. I hate to scold you girls. . . ."

"Oh, Don . . ." Carlene looked at him with an amused expression, her face slightly on one side, and tossed her hair back. "Oh, Don." She was now speaking as the leader; that much was plain. "We don't mind you when you scold. We don't . . . we just don't pay any attention. We all think you're sweet, Don."

She flashed an attractive smile and tossed her hair again. The other girl, at the far end, tittered loudly. Only Anola Cray kept her face straight and her eyes toward the floor.

Don rose. He came round the desk and, sitting on the edge, leaned over toward them, toward the three citizens of Springfield, Indiana, accused of stealing. Leaned toward the daughter of the banker, the daughter of the president of the country club, and the girl from the other side of the tracks.

"I guess there's been some slight misunderstanding about this, girls. You don't seem to take this very seriously, do you? You don't seem to realize I'm trying to help you, and you don't care. Now, if I certify this to the court, and it's what I shall most probably do, what I feel should be done, you three girls . . . will go to reform school for a year or more. How would you like going without seeing your family or your boyfriends, day after day, month after month? Would you enjoy that? Nope, don't think you would."

He rose nervously and returned to the chair

behind the desk. At least he had succeeded in getting their attention and they were listening; before they hadn't even listened. "Now this is mighty darn serious for each one of you. If this goes up to the court, every one of you will have a criminal record. Wonder do you know what that means? It means you have a record on paper that follows you all through your life. If you're a boy, you can't get into the Army, the Navy, or the Air Force. If you're a girl, you can't become a nurse, can't do what you want to do. This record follows you everywhere you go; when you get a job in Chicago or Indianapolis your boss will be told about it. If you want to get married, your husband must know about it. That record is there, it stays with you all the rest of your life. D'ja think about all this when you stole those things?"

The girl at the far end was sober and wide-eyed at last. She was watching carefully, listening. Anola still sat with her gaze on the linoleum; he knew that because of her past record she was frightened. Only Carlene Benson remained aloof and challenging.

"Say! I wonder do you realize what this could do; where it could lead you, all of you, yes, every one of you. First, petty pilfering. Then shoplifting such as you've done. What next? Well, that's the way to start a criminal record."

"Oh! No!" The girl on the end uttered the two words involuntarily. He felt her slowly crumbling.

"Yes, 'tis, Dorothy, I've seen it happen to other girls. Girls quite as nice as you are, too. Let me get this one thing over with you all." He spoke to all three, but he was looking Carlene Benson in the eyes.

"There's been quite some pressure on me to drop this case, to forget the whole thing, to hush it up. Happens I'm not built that way . . . and . . . I don't intend . . . to drop it. You girls are the same's everyone else that comes into this room, and you'll take your punishment like the rest of 'em."

A quick spasm of fear dashed across the pretty face of the banker's daughter, and was as quickly gone. He knew what she was thinking. Could it be possible . . . does he really intend . . .

Don, having guessed her thoughts, hammered away at her. "Yes, I mean business on this. I don't intend to quit on you girls any more than I quit on any of the others. You girls will just have to stand up and take your medicine, same as they did."

Sound of sobs broke into his sentence. Dorothy June was weeping openly, without shame. But Carlene flashed a look of contempt along the row of chairs.

"This is gonna be hard for me. I'll most likely take the rap. But I can't do anything else. It'll be hard for you girls, too. But you stole, you took property that didn't belong to you, you thought it was cute and smart and a whole lotta fun. Now you're finding out different. You're gonna discover it's a good deal different before you're through with . . ."

Then with no warning, the hard-faced girl in the shabby coat put her handkerchief to her eyes. Her head was still lowered, but she was crying.

"Do you girls know what it's like inside of a jail? Do you know how it feels when you come out . . . when some particular boyfriend meets you on the street and doesn't ask where you've been? Why not? 'Cause he knows. He knows, everyone knows; it gets round town quickly. Yep, he knows perfectly well where you've been."

Carlene was weakening, she was going to crack; he could see the expression in her eyes slowly change, as it always did a few seconds beforehand.

"No, Don, no. Not that, Don . . . please, I

didn't . . . we didn't . . . it was my fault . . . but please, I couldn't stand that, I couldn't . . ."

She was crying at last—good, heavy, hearty sobs that filled the room. Once broken down, she let go; she cried worse than the other two. Tears poured down her cheeks as she fumbled in her purse for her handkerchief.

Don got up. He opened the window at the side, and instantly the room was filled with the fresh, clear air of an early summer morning. He went back to the chair behind the desk, sat down, yanked at a drawer, removed some blanks from a pile, and started slowly and deliberately to fill one out. This took some time. He was waiting for the storm to pass, and while he was waiting the trio cried. And cried.

"Now, girls, I think we understand each other. I believe you realize what you've done. That this isn't just a prank, and you aren't kids out on Halloween removing someone's fence post. If I'm right, it happened like this. Carlene, you feel your parents are stingy; they won't let you buy jewelry; so you just decided to take some. You went into Henry's store, and when he was in the rear telephoning, you slipped a bracelet in your purse. Anola, you went into Katzmann's with a tight-fitting coat or no coat at all. You slipped a coat on, and then when no one was looking you walked right out of the store. Dorothy June, you made the Bon Ton, didn't you? And you did about the same thing, only you took a dress instead of a coat. Now I want you girls to pay close attention. This merits severe punishment. I intend, first off, that we shall return all this stuff to the three stores, and you'll hand it over to the manager himself, tell him how sorry you are, and how you won't do it again. That's the first thing.

"Next, I'm gonna see you all get jobs this summer. Anola!" The girl's head came up at last. "Had you had a job these last few weeks after school ended, most likely you wouldn't be in this mess. What say?"

"Uhuh . . . I mean . . . nope."

"You know, Anola, inside you're good, I believe. I really do. But you're easy, you can't say no. Carlene! What I think about you and Dorothy is that you two girls are plain lazy."

The shoulders were heaving still. "Yeh . . . I guess . . ."

"Well, you're truthful, at least. Now then, we'll first visit the three stores and take back the things you stole. Next you'll all be put on probation for an indefinite period. What's that mean? Means you'll report here at ten o'clock every Saturday until further notice, each one of you. That means you show up. Third, you'll all have jobs, and you must hold 'em down, too. No excuses! If you fail to turn up a single morning, or if you don't do your job, or if you, Carlene, and you, Dorothy, fall down in any particular, I'll certify this to the Junior Court so quick you won't know what struck you. Believe me, girls, I mean business on this. And I think I know Tom Shaw well enough to know he won't play favorites."

Carlene was not looking his way now; she believed him.

"Keep straight. That's your first problem. Next, do what I ask. If you do, the only records of this whole affair will be right here in my files. They won't get any further. Slip once, any of you, and that's the end. This is a chance, but believe me it's your final chance. You've done a mighty serious thing, all of you.

"Anola, we'll arrange later about a job for you. Dorothy, you're to report to Mrs. Fentriss at the Tuberculosis Association here in this building in room 316. You report to her every morning and help her with her work. You'll be there same as on a regular job, 'cept you don't get paid, from nine to five, and you'll stay there until school opens in the fall. You, Carlene, are to work with Mrs. Gordon in the Settlement House on the east side, just the same. No funny business. Let one of those ladies tell me you've missed a day, or you haven't cooperated one hundred percent, and I'll be on your necks if it's the last thing I do in town. And if any of you think I don't keep my word, or that I'm reluctant to stick my neck out, ask the boys on my basketball team, my varsity who struck on me three years ago. You remember, Carlene. I think you knew all those boys.

"Is this all clear? Do I make myself understood? Don't come back here and say you were visiting in Fort Wayne over the weekend, or you didn't realize . . . or you had to go swimming with some boy. No excuses. This is an order." He looked round the circle, at the trio now crushed, red-eyed, and weeping slightly. They were defeated and they knew it.

"O.K. You can wait outside. I'd like to explain these things to your mothers so they won't misunderstand me, either. I want their cooperation, too." He rose and, opening the door, smiled at the three women sitting anxiously on the bench in the outer office.

Suddenly he noticed that his knees were trembling.

Boy! Does this take it out of you, this handling girls!

18

Curiously, they chose the same chairs their daughters had taken. The two stylish, well-dressed, plump women sat at each end and the fat lady with the cheap, crinkly hair wave was in the middle.

He tried hard to smile pleasantly but it was a thin and weary smile. "Mrs. Cray, you live on Depot Street?"

The big woman shifted and her chair creaked. "Yes, sir."

"That's right. I remember now, I was out to see you one night about Mike. How many children have you besides Mike and Anola?"

"Four."

"Are you . . . a widow?"

"Yes, sir."

"You work, don't you?"

"Yes. I work at Warner Gear. I been there ever since my husband died."

"Oh, yes, he was killed in France, I recall. Now these children of yours . . ."

"I've tried hard to make a good home for 'em. I've tried to see they had clothes and enough to eat, too. Sometimes . . . sometimes . . . My goodness, I don't know what-all's got into kids these days."

"I know, I know. I remember your place very well; it was comfortable and it was clean. You make a good home. Anola is always clean, too. By the way, have you had any trouble with Mike lately, Mrs. Cray?"

"No, sir. Mike's been a real good boy—ever since you got after him, since he joined that Scout Troop."

"Is he still working at Brogan's?"

"Yes, sir."

"What's he do with his money? Does he give you any of his pay?"

There was triumph in her tones. She looked at the other women. "Every week! Every week he gives it to me, all of it." Pride shone in her face. "The older one, too. They're both good boys. I can't complain." Then a trace of anxiety entered her voice. "So's Anola; she was a good girl, works hard round the house, gets the other kids' dinner at noon, never been in any trouble before, never . . . until . . ." Now it was indignation showing through. "Until she got to running round with those rich girls down at high school."

The chairs on each side of Mrs. Cray creaked loudly.

"Yes, yes, I see, I understand. What kind of marks does Anola get?" Don hastened to shift to other matters.

"She gets good marks. She's no dope, Anola isn't."

"Yes, I believe you're right there. Now, ladies, as you all know, this is a pretty serious affair. Stealing a bracelet isn't just a prank; it's a state's prison offense. It merits some stiff punishment, and I intend to see the three girls realize what they've done. I don't hardly think they did when they came in here this morning. I've given them some instructions, told them certain things they must do. First, they're on probation; while they are on probation they have to report in here to me every Saturday at ten o'clock. Next, they're all going to get jobs. I've told Anola I'll talk to her later about her job. Dorothy is to work with Mrs. Fentriss in the Tuberculosis Association, and Carlene will report at the Settlement House. If the girls do what I tell 'em, if they stay out of trouble from now on, the records in this case will never leave my office. They'll never be seen by anyone. At the end of a certain period, the girls will be taken off probation if, by their conduct, they deserve it. If not, if they break loose, any of them, I'll simply hafta certify this to the court, and they'll either be sent for a term to reform school or to the state prison. You ladies appreciate better than they do what that would mean."

They were worried now, all of them.

"Mrs. Cray, you have all you can do to keep that home together, and I sure remember, 's I say, how nice it was when I visited you about Mike last spring. But you two ladies, you others,

Mrs. Benson . . . and Mrs. Barker . . . tell me, please, Mrs. Barker, how many clubs do you belong to?"

She was surprised and a little hesitant. "Why . . . just the usual ones, Mr. Henderson."

"Well! I'm gonna tell you." He read from a slip in his hand. "Mrs. Barker . . . belongs to eleven clubs, including the Ladies Circle, the Springfield Club, the D.A.R., the country club, the two civic organizations, the Woman's Club, and the Friday Afternoon Club. Mrs. Benson, you belong to all of them besides two more bridge clubs that meet on Tuesday and Friday evenings.

"Hold on a minute!" He could hear the agitated movements of the chairs, and see anger rising in the women in the end chairs. "When a boy or a girl is brought in here, we look at their home life first off. It's obvious to me your girls aren't hungry; they have plenty of food and clothes. But somehow their home life isn't what it should be. They've been neglected or this would never have happened. I feel you have both helped the thing along; you've permitted your girls to get careless. Next they start running round town taking things from stores."

Now the two chairs creaked furiously. Sparks

of rage flashed from the eyes of the two stout matrons. "If you'll permit me to say so, ladies, it seems had you been in fewer bridge clubs and gone to fewer parties at nights, had you stayed home and kept your daughters home, well, if you'd done this, the whole thing might not have happened. I'm not saying it's your fault; I merely suggest you have some responsibility for it."

The banker's wife, with the expensive little hat of flowers and ribbons on one side of her head, rose angrily.

"Don Henderson, you're a fresh young man! You're an upstart. You won a basketball title, and you think you can run this city. You better go back to that farm at Center Township where you came from; you're too big for your boots right now. I'm leaving here this minute. I'm going to my husband's office straightaway, and I'll promise you that by six tonight you won't have any job."

"Yes, and *my* husband will hear of it, too, every word; don't think he won't. I shall tell him how I've been insulted by a young whipper-snapper, by a basketball coach. Why, he can make you or break you . . . you . . . you . . . you're only a basketball coach . . . you . . ."

Don waited. His tone was different when he

spoke. It was no longer casual and friendly. He rose.

"Ladies! One minute. I think you better leave this office and quick."

He leaned over his desk, reached for the door, and flung it open. The two infuriated matrons stalked into the anteroom where their daughters, still weeping, were sitting on the hard bench they had just vacated.

Mrs. Cray remained seated, open-mouthed. Her great frame shook. "Boy . . . I didn't think you had it in you. I thought them folks on the west side . . . I thought you was a stooge for them folks. Well, you really got what it takes. They'll never forgive you, Don, never." She raised her great bulk and came toward his desk and toward the door.

Don was trembling. She came closer, and moving toward him said in low tones, "Don Henderson, you done something for my girl. I ain't seen her cry since she was a baby!"

"Thanks. That helps, Mrs. Cray. Now . . . you girls there, you girls again, please."

He was still trembling as the three girls, red-eyed, returned to the room and sat down. "Now your first job this morning is to take back that stolen property. Fortunately it is all here, all undamaged. Each of you take something. No, Anola, you and Dorothy take the dress and the coat. Carlene will take the bracelet."

"But look, Don, someone may see us."

Once more tears flooded the faces of the three girls. "Pity you didn't think of that when you were taking these things. Too late now. We'll make the rounds in my car; if folks see you, they see you. This won't be fun for anybody."

They took the things from the table as he watched, standing behind the desk. Anola was the slowest and last of the three to leave the room. As she came past the desk by the door, she leaned over.

"Don, I'll work hard on that job."

Don looked down at her, at her swollen cheeks, her shabby, thin coat. He patted her on the back. "Thanks lots, Anola. That almost makes what I've been through this morning worthwhile."

In a few minutes they were standing in the modern interior of Henry's store, and Henry himself was walking toward them, quite as unhappy and embarrassed as they were.

Henry started to speak but Don gave him a sign. He wanted it all to come from the three girls, he wanted them to do the talking. For a minute no one said anything, and Etta, disturbed by the scene, vanished into the rear. Finally Carlene spoke.

"Mr. Remsen . . . here's the bracelet . . . I took . . . I stole yesterday. . . . I'm sorry about it. I didn't realize what I was doing. . . ."

Henry shot a hasty glance at her and took the little box. He stuffed it quickly into the side pocket of his immaculate double-breasted suit.

"Now that's fine of you, Carlene, that's just fine of you. I appreciate it . . . I really do, Don, I'm mighty obliged to you, I'm sure."

He meant it, too. The bracelet had been recovered without the help of the insurance company and the inevitable publicity that would have accompanied their entry into the picture. Shaking hands nervously all round, he ushered them into the street. Once again they were in the sunlight, Dorothy and Anola carrying the dress and the conspicuous coat.

The next stop was Katzmann's Chicago Store. Mr. Katzmann himself was in the back office. He looked up over his glasses at them as they came in, greeted them and heard them in silence. This time it was Dorothy who spoke for the trio. The manager listened carefully, and then turned to Don.

"I'd like to ask a question. May I ask a question, Don?"

"Why, sure, Sam, of course. Why not? Ask anything you like."

His bluntness was dismaying. There was a strange pause while he looked at them. "Which one . . . stole the coat?"

Dorothy looked at Carlene, and Carlene glanced at Anola, and Anola, frightened, looked at Dorothy. No one said a word. One of the three had stolen a coat from Katzmann's department store. Which one was it?

The silence continued, kept on, seemed everlasting. The girls eyed each other, Don watching them closely. Sam Katzmann, with his arms crossed, watched them, too.

"I did!"

The tears, still close to the surface, poured forth again. "I took it! These girls have everything . . . they have everything, clothes n'everything . . . and boyfriends. Anyone can have boyfriends . . . if you have clothes n'things. . . . I wanted a boyfriend. I took it."

Sam Katzmann walked slowly across to the

sobbing figure and put his arm round her shoulder. He turned toward Don. "I'd like to talk to her alone for a minute. Could I, Don?"

Don nodded and rose. The other two girls got up from their chairs with some eagerness, and he followed them into the hall, leaving Anola Cray alone with Sam Katzmann, owner and manager of the Chicago Store, "best values in Springfield."

"Anola, see here. I know something of what you felt. I've been poor, too. But I don't hardly believe you realized what you was doing when you took that there coat. It's a sixty-dollar garment. If you hadn't been caught, Anola, if that coat had never got back here, some salesgirl would have been in trouble; she might have been charged with it, and forced to work weeks and weeks to pay for it. Some innocent girl. Never thought of that, did you?"

"No, sir."

"You wouldn't want that, would you?"

She shook her head, unable to speak through her sobs.

"Don't cry anymore. I understand, I haven't forgotten how it is when you're young and poor. These other two, their dads have money, they can look out for 'em. But your ma's a widow lady. Tell you what; you want clothes for yourself. I'm going to give you a chance to earn them." He glanced down at the cheap coat, at the faded dress, at the shoes worn at the toes.

"You can't work in this store with what you have on. Here!" He drew a pen from his pocket and took out a pad, writing on it. Tearing off the sheet he handed it to her.

"This is an order for fifty dollars' worth of clothes. You can get fifty dollars' worth of clothes with this downstairs. You can fit yourself out with some new shoes, a new dress, and a nice new coat, too. Pick out what you want, and if that isn't enough, you come up and tell me. Then you show up to work on Monday morning, and I'll let you pay me something each week out of your salary. How's that? That's fair, hey?"

The girl broke down completely. Her sobs could even be heard outside where Don and the other two were waiting.

"Come, come, don't take on like that. You just show up, and first thing you know, one of these days, you'll have earned a brand-new outfit of your own."

19

Don was talking to the chief of police of Logansport. The crease in his forehead deepened as he continued. In the outer room his secretary listened to the conversation through the open door.

"Why, yes, Chief . . . yes, that's about the size of it. What's that? Well, yes, we had a situation in this town where the kids used to run down the nearest alley when they saw an officer coming. They all know me, they all call me Don;

they don't run when they see me. I can usually get to 'em.

"How's that? Well . . . we think so down here. You see before we had this Juvenile Division and our Junior Court setup, the only thing you could do was arrest a kid and sentence him in the City Court, or else release him. Now any boy or girl under 18 can be brought into Junior Court, and even if they are convicted, there's no official record to blot their names and go with them all through life."

There was a pause, then he spoke again. "Why, we did a lot of things, like controlling bicycle traffic. The first month after our junior police was organized, and started to hand out tickets, we had four hundred violations of traffic ordinances. Last month it fell away to a handful, maybe ten or a dozen. Yes, sir . . . yes, sir. . . . Yes, I handle all cases and I contact the school officials, of course. Wait a minute, Chief! Marion, get me those figures I made out last week."

She went over to the filing case in the outer office, took some papers from it, slipped them before him on the desk.

"Here 'tis. We've had a total of 204 cases since the 25th of March. Only seven cases were referred to the City Court. That's when the offense is serious, see, or when some citizen gets mad and insists on pressing charges. Now, several weeks ago, we had a bad situation, two prominent girls were caught shoplifting. The storekeepers got their property all back, however, so they didn't press charges. Let's see . . . let me see . . . 204 cases in all. Of those . . . only seven were referred to the City Court, and of those, only four were lost. That means we only had to send four away to an institution. One hundred and eighty-four have been put on probation and discharged. That means at present we have . . . we have thirteen cases on probation now. . . .

"Well, no, Chief, I'd hardly say that; I wouldn't exactly say that, either. No, it's not always the bad boys who get into trouble; we often find it's the good boys in a moment of weakness. I've learned in these few months that there really aren't any bad boys—oh, a few, but not enough to amount to anything. They all have more good than bad in 'em. You bet . . . how's that? Well, first off, you have to get the kid's confidence. That's the start. Then when the case is over, we check all the time. Who with? Their parents, their school, their church. We've cut our trouble here down to almost nothing . . . no, very few cases repeated, very few.

"O.K., Chief . . . O.K. . . . I'd be real glad to see you any time you come, any day. The Junior Court is sitting this afternoon for the last time until September, but it'll start up when school opens. That's when the Recreation Program closes in the parks, the kids get downtown again, going to school. You know how it is; kids are like dogs. Pen a boy up in school all day, and he's likely to break loose. That's why kids run home from school as hard as they can. Guess that's what most women don't understand. . . . Well, good-bye, Chief . . . thanks for calling . . . no, thank *you* for your interest. Let me know when you feel you want to come down."

He placed the phone back on the desk. "Well! They may not think much of our Division here in town; but it's certainly getting known outside in the state. The chief in Logansport wants to put in the same identical setup there. He's coming down to see how it works out. Marion, did the *Journal* carry our ad this morning?"

"Yes, it did, Don." She unfolded the paper

and brought it in. He glanced at the large advertisement in the lower corner of the page.

"ATTENTION
SPRINGFIELD
JUNIOR
POLICE

All captains will report to the Assistant Recreation Director in Jackson Park at four o'clock, sharp, this afternoon."

•

"Good." He handed the newspaper back to her. An idea came suddenly. This is the last session of the Junior Court until fall. I believe I'd like to see how they're handling those cases. I haven't been over for some time. Think I'll drop in for a few minutes.

Outside, the July day was warm and growing warmer. It was the kind of Indiana summer day when you worked without a coat and walked with care on the shady side of the street. But the County Building was cool, and the large courtroom was on the cool side of the street. Inside, the paneled room was dim and quiet. As usual, Tom, Mary Jo, and Earl sat on the raised dais before the American flag. Jay Hanwell with a gold police shield on his shirt was in a chair beside several defendants, while Ray Allen, a new boy, had become clerk of the court and sat at the desk beside the door. On the bench the three judges were listening so closely to Chester that they failed to notice Don. The clerk beckoned to him to come inside the railing, but he shook his head and sat down on a bench in the rear. It was warming to see the large crowd of parents and boys and girls present, and especially to note the attention with which they regarded proceedings.

Don glanced round. At the dais were the two boys and the girl judging their equals. Below was Chester, earnestly questioning a boy in the witness chair. Behind Chester were several boys waiting to testify; at one side was Red Crosby, head down, taking the testimony. Last of all, Don looked at the crowd on the benches beside him, listening with respect to the whole thing.

Why, this works! This really works. I never coached 'em or told 'em what to do; I just threw it into their laps, and let 'em handle it the best way they could. Give kids responsibility, and they'll come through for you, every time. I've always believed that; I've always felt if we could do it in basketball, we could do it in other things, too. Now, here's the proof in this room. Anyone can see it before their eyes.

He watched the case, hearing Chester address the black-haired boy of about fourteen in the witness chair. What struck him was Chester's ease and fluency, and the difference in his handling of the problem, the way he had changed and grown in a few short months. Now there was authority and sureness in his tones. He knew his job, he was on top of it, he was master of the task before him.

"First off, you trespassed, didn't you?"

"Yes, sir."

Don smiled at the idea of a fourteen-year-old boy calling a sixteen-year-old boy "sir." Yet somehow, in that room, at that moment, it was not in the least out of place.

"Yes, you trespassed. Second, you undid those locks, and made trainmen risk their lives. You took the locks off the signal boxes, and trainmen risked their lives, and we could have a bad accident when the fast freight goes through town. Would you want trainmen to get killed?"

The boy shook his head solemnly. This was no joke, it wasn't fun. Two other boys, apparently waiting to be examined or who had been examined, stared at Chester.

Now he turned to the judges. "This is an example of what trespassing can do. These here kids had played along the railroad spur, hooking rides on freight cars; otherwise they wouldn't have known how to uncouple a train. They had trespassed, so they knew how to pull levers and cut the trains. Well, that'll be all." He turned to the chair. "You want to ask him any questions, Jay? Nope? If not, I'll call Mr. Hanson, the railroad detective."

A smartly dressed young man with big shoulders stepped to the chair and was sworn in. Don was less interested now. He listened for a while, then he went over to the rail and leaned on the clerk's desk. "What's next, Ray?"

"Well, le's see . . . We got three kids next. Seems they chipped in to buy a watch together, an' they was each one to wear it a week an' pass it on, and now . . . one busted it . . . and we're making him take a job and get some money to repair it. Then there's the two Evans twins, the ones that stole their grandmother's bridge an' hid it, and got the reward for finding it. Jay brought that case in last week."

Don wanted to laugh and he didn't want to laugh. You couldn't laugh. "You been on this some time?"

"Yep. They've all been examined. I guess the judges will consider the case as soon as Chester gets through with the detective."

Chester seemed likely to continue a while, so Don slipped through the swinging doors. He wanted to get away, to get into the square below; he wanted suddenly to tell people about it, to shout to the folks crowding the stores across the way, to call to them, to drag them in to watch for themselves, to see what the young citizens of Springfield, Indiana, could do alone. If only they were given a chance.

He walked slowly down the steps in the dim coolness of the building, thinking with pride of that scene in the courtroom above. I guess maybe we're an all-right people, way down. I guess we are. We know we're a scrappy race, and we know if folks gang up on us and want a scrap, we'll oblige 'em. But maybe we're even good enough to solve this problem of peace; the problem of living together. Isn't that what makes a nation great? Not a lot of cars and machines and refrigerators, and radios and things, but the willingness to work together, to help each other do things for the state. That's us, the state.

Peedad says it better. He can always say things better, Peedad can.

The heat and the sunshine smacked him in the face as he crossed the square. He was turning to old Peedad, not only because the editor understood, but because he had been the one to fight for Don ever since his arrival in town as basketball coach. Most of all, because Peedad loved Springfield and the kids of Springfield. And believed in 'em, too.

Someone spoke, someone else called his name, and he waved back as he edged through the cars parked diagonally against the curb, and went across the square to the old-fashioned brick block where the old-fashioned man ran his newspaper. Don was joyful, he was full of lightness and exhilaration, and he wanted to share it with the man who had helped give it to him.

The wooden stairs creaked. Peedad would be in the dingy office to the left at the top. His feet as usual would be on that never-diminishing pile of stuff on the desk, that mass of papers and material that seemed never to get smaller.

The room was dingy and hot, the sun poured through the windows and baked the place. But the chair was empty. Peedad wasn't in.

Don felt let down. Of all people in town, of all people in the world, the old man was the person he most wanted to see right then. He stood there, disappointed. Then he turned, went slowly across the hall to the presses. Sam, the operator, came from behind a machine, wiping his hand on his dirty apron. There was a strange look in those familiar eyes, a peering, intent look behind the spectacles.

"Where's Peedad?"

"Why . . . Don . . . he's at the mayor's office . . . I expect. That is . . . if they'll let him in . . . he's upset . . . he's burned . . . he's mad, oh, he's really mad about it, Don!"

Don felt perspiration on his forehead. Was it the intense heat of the crowded, low-ceiling room, or words he had heard several weeks previously and half remembered? Something is wrong. He went out with no delay, down the creaking stairs, and across the square again.

Inside, the courthouse was dim and refreshingly cool. The elevator was upstairs as he passed the door, so he climbed the stone steps two at a time. Reaching the third floor, he heard the voice of Mattie, the elevator operator. She was talking to a couple of men who were shoving and banging chairs into the elevator, while he rounded the corner and flew past.

"It's a danged shame . . . a danged shame," Mattie was saying.

Queer sounds came from the corridor to his office. Outside his door were several city employees, men he recognized as belonging to the Department of Public Works. They were carrying out furniture.

He suddenly saw it was his. Those chairs in the elevator were his, too!

"Hey! What is this?"

Then he caught sight of Marion, her handkerchief to her face, inside the room, crying. Now his desk chair was being carried past by two men.

"Say! What the . . . What goes on here?"

They put down the heavy chair and looked at him. Someone he knew—a friendly hand touched his arm.

"Sorry, Don. We got orders. Looks like they're closing up shop on you, boy."

He jumped to his desk and grabbed the phone.

Nervously he stabbed at the dial. "Police headquarters?"

"Jim, this is Don, at Juvenile Aid. Lemme talk to Andy."

"Why, Don, Andy's gone to Bedford for that Patrolman's Protective Association meeting, you know. He won't be back here until Thursday."

He saw; he realized instantly what was taking place. No use wasting time. He rang off and dialed City Hall.

"Mayor's office, please . . . Miss Casey? This is Don Henderson over at Juvenile Aid. I'd like to speak to the mayor."

"Why, Don, he's in South Bend at the Elks' Convention. He'll be there all week."

"Oh, sure. Is the police commissioner in his office by any chance?"

"No, he isn't, Don. He left town for Chicago yesterday."

That's it. That's the way. The old run-around. Clever, these people. They gave the orders and then ran for cover. "I see. Well, thanks." He put down the phone.

His head buzzed. The men in the two small rooms were standing round awkwardly, with embarrassment, disliking their job. Now they began to haul the big table out the door. Why, that's part of me, that table. That's the table where I talked to so many kids, the table where we piled up the stuff those girls stole from the Bon Ton and the Chicago Store.

He stood trying to think. Who else was there he could call? Harry Mason? No, Harry would say it served him good and right. Gotta have tact, gotta be tactful, y'understand, boy. Frank Shaw! Frank would be pleased; Frank must have been in on the deal, must have helped put the thing over. The Chamber of Commerce? No, that's Harry and Frank under another name and in a different office. Who then?

Why, Peedad, of course. But his heart fell as he realized Peedad was quite as helpless as he was.

Now the big table was being shoved and edged through the door. Don felt he was being cut in two.

"Mighty sorry about this, Don. It's orders we had from the mayor's office. Nope, he didn't exactly give them himself; someone phoned the boss and told us we should come up and dismantle your office today, that's all. We sure hate to do it, we hate to. You was good to my kids,

Don, that time you caught 'em hooking rides on freight cars; we sure hate . . . we sure do. . . ."

"O.K., boys, O.K." He perched on the end of the desk, as he had so often done before, for the last time. In a minute they'd be back. Leaning over, he cleaned a few personal things out of the drawers; a knife, a special pencil someone had given him, a leather wallet sent as an advertisement. Now the filing case was thump-thumping through the door.

There goes part of me in those files; that's part of me, there. It's my time for the last months, all of it night and day, and my thought and energy, and my efforts, and my life. My heart, too, part of it's in those files.

Outside Marion was sobbing. He yanked things from his drawers. A mimeographed copy of a speech someone had sent him, the speech of a college president in Chicago. He had underlined one sentence, and his eyes fell upon it. "Democracy in the end depends on the virtue of the individual, and a democracy that is corrupt is doomed."

He tossed it to the ground. Then he stooped over and picked it up and stuffed it in his pocket. It's not the kids who are delinquents in this town;

it's the adults. The adults who have ceased to grow everywhere except around the middle. We ought to have an Adult Aid Division in this city; that's what we really need.

Bitterness conquered him; he was submerged in defeat. It was like nothing he had ever experienced before, a complete and overwhelming disaster. Then he recalled the words. Not Mrs. Benson's words nor those of Mrs. Barker; but hard words, acid words, words spoken by a boy in a worn leather jacket and frayed trousers, a boy fingering a cap, who looked up at him in anger.

"I hate this town. It's unfair. Everyone's unfair; everyone's against me in Springfield. I hate it!"

20

The electric fan buzzed and hummed. That and the creak of Peedad's rocker were the only sounds in the hot room.

The old man and the young man were too close in disappointment to need words; too bitter even to say much to each other. They sat under the fan in the terrible heat of the July evening, Don leaning over, his arms on his knees, his head down; Peedad lighting and relighting his pipe. Over and over it went round in Don's head; the start of it all, the first night in the police station with Perry Taylor, the slow growth of the Division, the Junior Court, the junior police. Then disaster. And the wreck of everything.

What next? He'd have to go back and finish the summer as Recreation Director, for he was only lent to the Juvenile Aid Division, and was under contract to the city until September. Then it was over, he was through, he could leave on the first train, somewhere, anywhere to get away from Springfield, Indiana.

I hate it. I hate the place . . . and yet . . .

Peedad's wife entered the room, preceded by the pleasurable sound of ice tinkling in glasses. "I put a lime in it, Don; Peedad always likes a lime in his."

"Why, that's real nice of you, Mrs. Wilson. That's good." The taste of the cool drink in the steaming night was soothing.

She went to the mantelpiece and wound the large ormolu clock with a huge key. The timepiece was like the owner of the house, in tune with everything in the room, the rocker, the desk where he worked occasionally of an evening, and the square-framed, old-fashioned davenport. The whole place resembled the man himself; it was simple and unpretentious, and also, Don noticed, slightly worn and run down. As he looked up, he observed that one of the editor's shoes needed soling, and the cuff of his shirt sleeve was frayed.

She finished winding the clock and, turning round, faced them. "Don't stay up late now, Peedad Wilson. Hear me! Don't keep him up, Don. You boys have both had a hard time today; you both need sleep. I put Rex out, Peedad. Will you watch and don't let him scratch the screen door when he wants to come in or he'll have another hole through there. And mind now, don't you boys stay up talking half the night."

There was something funny about anyone calling Peedad a boy, and yet not entirely funny either. He was younger than some of the men in town who were much his junior, some of the men like Harry Mason at Chrysler. What was it? What kept him like that? Because he was always fighting, perhaps. Harry didn't fight; he was always on the right side, always tactful. Yet compared to Peedad he was fixed and set and an older person. And Don felt sure that Harry's shirts were unfrayed and that his shoes needed no re-soling.

She left the room and they could hear her going slowly up the stairs.

"I'd better be going."

"Don't leave yet. I shan't sleep."

"Me, either."

There was a longish silence while they sipped their cokes. Overhead Mrs. Wilson moved around in the small bedroom above. A faint scratching came from the screen door in front, and Peedad hastily rose to let his Airedale in. The dog came inside, and immediately lay down in the path of the electric fan at his master's feet.

The two citizens of Springfield sat thinking, without saying much.

"Well, Peedad, we had it coming."

"Sooner or later, we had it coming. You had to find out, same's you found out in basketball, that as soon as you step on other folks' toes, they holler."

"I guess Springfield's no different. . . ."

"Hell, no. There's J. Frank Shaws in lots of other towns in this state."

"Peedad, last year I used to think the kids were O.K. and the adults were the ones who gummed the works in this town. In a way, I still do. I haven't lost my faith in the kids, not one bit. But since last fall I've met lots of good folks here. There's so many wonderful people in this city. At first, today, I hated Springfield; I hated it like I never hated anything in my life before. Now . . . I dunno."

"I understand. A thing like this cuts a man mighty deep; it's the injustice of it. Try to remember it isn't the town, it's our society that's done this, done it first of all to Frank Shaw—then he turns round on you."

"That's right. You know, Peedad, I never realized there were so many wonderful folks here in town until I got into juvenile work. Like . . . well . . . like Miss Rockwell, the probation officer; and George Spencer, the principal out in that Roosevelt School in the tough district by the tracks; and old Mrs. Crane on South Mulberry. Know what? She lived with that gang of kids there, crowd of young hell-raisers, and she saw they needed food first off, saw there was a relation between food and behavior. So she had 'em in once a week for a big feed. Why, they just love that woman now; they'd do anything for her. When they got to letting air out of the tires of the parked cars at the steel mill, I called her up. She spoke to 'em one day, and we never had any trouble from then on."

"Yes, you're dead right. There's plenty of good folks in this town."

"Like, for instance, Doc Jordan. Now you take Doc Jordan. I had that boy, kid by the name of Perry Taylor. He was a mean one, he was the meanest kid in town. Well, sir, right away I saw he was skinny and undersized, so I hauled him off to the Doc for an examination. Kid ought to have his tonsils out, says the Doc. His folks, they don't have any dough; O.K., who's gonna pay for it?"

"Well, who was paying for his visit to the Doc?"

"Why, I kinda took him over on my own responsibility; but I didn't know's I could afford an operation of that kind. So I asked the Doc, and he said, 'Don, don't you worry about the bill.' Know what, Peedad? He did the operation and just never sent any bill. Moment the boy was operated on, he began to fill out and broaden out, and now he's one of the most responsible kids in school. He's the manager of the team, and next year . . ."

"Doc Jordan's a great, good man. He's not the only one in town."

"That's just it. This afternoon I felt like I hated Springfield. Then I get to thinking of all these people who helped me, the good folks, the ones I've known and worked with . . . When a thing of this sort happens, you hate the town at first, but you can't help remembering there's a lot of folks in Springfield besides J. Frank Shaw."

"Yes, sir. There's mighty fine folks in this little town."

"And some stinkers, too. I wonder what makes the J. Frank Shaws! Now you take Tom . . . I suppose the old man was like Tom once."

"Certainly. Once he was like Tom. Then he got his dad's money, and the power came with it. That's the thing which corrupts folks. They like to be known up and down the state as the man who runs Springfield. They don't really want to be mayor, they don't want to hold office, they dislike the responsibility that goes with it, they'd hate to be up there to be shot at by everyone, they just enjoy laying low and pulling wires."

"Like he pulled them on me." The bitterness flooded back again, as if every time he really thought of it he was opening a raw wound. What would happen to the setup now; to the Junior Court, and the junior police . . . and the Division?

"Seems like there's so many fine folks like Doc Jordan in town. Take Joe Beckley; you remember him—fella that runs Joe's Lunch on Superior Street. Joe's kinda no-account, but nobody knows how many down-and-out kids he has fed in his lunchroom there. Seems as if with folks like Doc and Joe Beckley we ought to make this a better city."

"We could, Don, we could." The old man slapped his hand on the arm of his rocker. "We could if we only got together. This town belongs to the people; to Doc and Joe and . . ."

"To Mrs. Cray who works at Warner Gear and brings up six children, and Sam Katzmann at the Chicago Store, and Miss Perry down at the high school, and Jackson Piper's folks, and the kids; Tom and Carlene and Mary Jo and Red and Anola. Yes, sir, this place belongs to the people, not to J. Frank Shaw. Why can't we get together; why can't we take it away from him and give it to the folks to whom it really belongs?"

The old man leaned over and picked up the

glass on the floor beside his chair. There was no tinkle of ice now, for the ice had melted in the heat.

"If we could . . . if we could only get together. By Heaven, someday we will, too."

21

When Peedad brought him into the rustic office of the Director of Recreation in Jackson Park, Don immediately felt he knew the little man. Or at least had seen him somewhere before.

"Don, I want you should meet Harvey Patterson."

"Glad to see you. How are you, Harvey?"

"Just fine, Don. How're you?"

"Sit down, sit down, both of you." The little

chap was almost elegant compared to Peedad. He wore a thin summer suit and had a small well-trimmed mustache. In fact, he could be a banker or an insurance man along Superior Street. Most likely someone who's been on me for tickets or a man I've met at Rotary, thought Don. I've sure seen him before.

"Don, Harvey works out at Delco. He's the president of the biggest CIO local in town, and pretty influential in labor circles. Isn't that so, Harvey?"

Don gasped. A labor leader! I've seen his photo in the *Journal*, I guess, but he sure doesn't look the part.

"Why, I dunno, Peedad. I imagine I'm acquainted with most of the boys." The little fellow smiled. He certainly failed to measure up to the cartoons of grasping labor barons with rotund stomachs who were vividly pictured nearly every morning in the *Journal*. Something's wrong somewhere, thought Don, as the visitor spoke again. "Yep, I've been round this town quite some time. Came to work at Chrysler when they first brought the plant here years ago, and then . . ."

The name Chrysler brought sudden bitterness

into Don's heart. "Ha! You must know my friend Harry Wilson out there. I bet he's something to handle."

"Brother, you ain't humming. He's a dilly, that man!" Harvey Patterson shook his head reflectively and took a cigar from his pocket. He bit the end off with a quick gesture and then struck a match. To Don's dismay he seemed prepared to stay for some time. It was the end of a long and steaming day and Don was exhausted. This interview was unexpected, and he thought to himself: Well, what's cooking here?

"Don, Harvey and I were just going by, and we dropped off so's you could meet each other. There's a situation here in town maybe you could give us some advice on. The election this fall will determine the future of the town of Springfield for a long time. It's likely to settle whether J. Frank Shaw and his crowd, the Plunder Boys as I call 'em, get in to stay. Y'see there's a movement on to buy the Central Valley Power plant. They're against it—naturally enough."

Don frowned. Yes, and so'm I, too, he thought.

He disliked the idea, had disliked it from the start. Government in business, even municipal government in business, was something from which he recoiled. As a Hoosier, he had an independence and a liking for efficient management that made any such silly idea as an electric light plant run by the city, repellent. It was another one of those wild, socialistic schemes of which he thoroughly disapproved, and just thinking of it brought a frown to his forehead.

"What we'd like to do is take over the Valley Power Company's plant, lock, stock and barrel. We'd give the employees the same jobs at the same salaries, if they want to stick. Roscoe Stallings, the lawyer, thinks we can condemn the property."

"Roscoe Stallings! I'd hate to take his advice, Peedad. He hasn't had a successful case in town for goodness knows how long."

There was a moment's silence, and the old fellow looked up with that queer, quizzical glance of his. Don knew something was coming. "And I haven't had a successful newspaper, either, according to that line of thought. Maybe we need a few unsuccessful people in town, Don, to counteract Frank Shaw and the successful men."

Hang it, the old man's right. Roscoe's a good person, only . . . "What's he say about it, Peedad?"

"Why, he's made a study of municipal plants in this state. He thinks we can condemn the property and force them to sell at a fair price. If we can do it, if we can get the town behind us, we can cut the tax rate, pay off the bonded indebtedness . . ."

"Hold on a sec, Peedad." As usual the old man's enthusiasm was carrying him away; he had mounted his hobby and was off in pursuit of the dragon without stopping to think. "Hold on now. Why should we, at this particular time?" It was the side of the man, the weakness of his friend, he had heard most criticized in town, and the side he himself most distrusted. Of all the crazy, hare-brained schemes—buying out Central Valley Power! Why, they give good service, they furnish cheap electricity. What's the idea? The whole thing's another one of Peedad's visions; the kind of thing that makes folks laugh and call him impractical. Imagine! Springfield running its own power plant! Imagine the politics, the graft, the mess we'd be in. No, sir; we have enough of that already in this town.

Then before Peedad spoke, Harvey Patterson took the cigar from his mouth. "Don, d'you think, would you guess, the folks hereabouts are any dumber—or any more crooked—than folks in Logansport? Or Peru? Or Richmond?"

"Why . . . no . . . I s'pose not."

"Or any less patriotic or capable? You wouldn't, would you? No. Well, *they* have their municipal power plants and they run O.K."

By George, so they do. He's right. But anyhow I'm against the idea; it's socialistic. Besides, it's impractical. "But see here, Peedad, why do it now? What's the hurry about it?"

"Well, the point is the franchise has to be renewed this fall for a term of years. Here's our chance to refuse to renew it and buy the plant. Now you take those other towns; they've all done it at one time or another. They've got lower tax rates than we have. Some of 'em haven't any tax at all. They give mighty good electric service, too. Why can't we . . ."

"I'll tell you why not." Harvey Patterson flicked his cigar ashes to the floor. "On account of your friends uptown, Frank Shaw and Harry Wilson and the rest." The little man never raised his voice; he talked evenly, but he impressed you. He knew Springfield. You paid attention when he spoke. "Both those boys are heavy stockholders in the Company; they'll stand to lose if this goes through. Frank Shaw will fight it; so will the Chamber of Commerce. He dominates it, as you found out, Don. So will the *Journal*; he owns it. So will Station WSWP; he has a controlling interest. So will the merchants along Superior because they're told to; they all owe the banks money, and Frank is the banks. But if we could get to the people . . ."

"Tell the people the truth, tell 'em the facts, and they'll always do the right thing. That's the strength of America." Peedad was off again, mounting his horse, galloping Pegasus through the clouds. But Harvey Patterson was realistic and sure of himself.

"Yes, we must tell 'em. Then if we had a strong candidate for mayor, I believe we'd win. We could break the grip of that crowd on this city; we could bust it once and for all; we could condemn the power plant, pay off the bonded indebtedness, and then be in a position to go places."

H'm. A labor leader, a radical, a rabble-rouser, a red. Yet somehow Don wasn't so sure of his own position. He recalled hearing well-informed people speak of Harvey Patterson as a dangerous person. He didn't look dangerous; in fact he looked exactly like Henry Remsen, the jeweler on Superior, the president of the Junior Chamber of Commerce who made a speech at high school every winter on private enterprise. No, Harvey hardly looked dangerous. But you could never tell.

"I don't see . . . I don't hardly get it."

The little man continued calmly. "Let me explain. Here's what Lebanon did. They bought the Company out; same thing. O.K., they've paid off most of the dough they borrowed in Chicago to buy the plant. Then when they do pay it off, they can turn that surplus every year which went to the Company in Indianapolis—and the stockholders like J. Frank Shaw here in town—back into the municipality. See? They can wipe out taxes, or build new schools, roads . . . why, no end of things. No telling what that town will be. If Lebanon with seven thousand folks can do it, why can't Springfield with forty thousand? There's fifty thousand dollars a year the Company takes out of this town. What say we give it back to the people?"

Don squirmed in his seat. He felt on the spot; he didn't know the facts; they might be putting something over; these socialistic schemes were dangerous . . . the opening wedge to communism.

"We only need one thing. A strong candidate to run for mayor on the Democratic ticket on a platform of buying the power plant. Someone who can take on J. Frank's man."

"Like who?" said Don, innocently.

"Like you, Don," they said together.

He looked at them, frowning. Me! Me run for mayor? Why, they're nuts!

"You must be crazy, both of you. Don't make with jokes. I'm a basketball coach, not a politician."

"Just so," said Harvey Patterson. "That's why we want you."

They came at him from both sides, first one and then the other.

"What's it matter if you were a coach? Coaches have become mayors before in this state; remember Paul Lostutter in Bedford, and that chap in Lebanon, and . . ."

"Nor you weren't a Juvenile Aid man when you took that job, either! But you put it over right enough. You cut our trouble here down to nothing. Don, you're the most influential person in town, more'n the police chief, more'n Andy

Anderson, more'n any editor, more'n the mayor even, or anyone. Everybody in town knows you and likes you, too; that is, nearly everyone."

"Yeah! Nearly everyone!"

Peedad leaned forward. He was his most persuasive, and Don knew from experience that when he was his most persuasive he was his most dangerous. "I've had this in mind over a year now. Remember that game against Fort Wayne in the Semifinals at Muncie a year ago last March? Remember? I sat at home that evening listening to Buck Hannon. 'What on earth do you want to listen to that basketball for?' asks the wife. 'Account of Don Henderson,' says I. 'If he wins tonight, he can be mayor of this here town.' Then to myself I thinks, thinks I, say, maybe that isn't such a bad idea at that! So I watched you. I saw you put down that riot in the spring. I knew you had the stuff then; you sure showed it the way you handled the Juvenile Aid Division this year. Made everyone in the whole state anxious to know about it and why it was successful."

"You got enemies in town; why, sure, Don, we all have. I have enemies right in my own crowd, in my own local. But the boys at the plant have talked it over quite considerable, and they're for you. There's hardly a man there whose kids haven't come in contact with you one way or another. The CIO will support you pretty near one hundred percent, too. Labor'll back you, labor'll be behind you in this town, Don, because they've seen you stand up to J. Frank; they know you won't play ball with those people."

Despite the intense heat, Don shuddered. Hastily he protested. "Why, you must be crazy, both of you. I know nothing about this . . . this power and light stuff . . . and all. I'm no politician."

"Tell you we don't want one. We want a scrapper. Of course, any good guy could do it. But we think you're the one because you believe in something and you proved it. You made things work, you set up the Court and made it stick, you organized . . ."

"Yeah, I understand. But, Peedad . . . this town . . . I wouldn't want to stay . . . I don't hardly believe . . ."

"Still hurts, doesn't it, boy? Still hurts. Well, I understand that. Look, Don, if you were mayor you could reinstate that Juvenile Aid Division; you could put in some youngster like this new secretary at the Y, this man McHale, and really go places. That's only the start."

Don rose and turned away. Peedad was quite bad enough; almost everyone in town considered the editor mad and predicted a dire end for him. But to tie oneself up with a bunch of reds like the CIO and the radical labor element; no, thanks. "Nope, Peedad, I don't really hate the place anymore; but I'd just as soon not stay on. Even if I could be mayor. It would be better all round if you got someone else."

"This place is a headache—at least it would be if you stayed and went through with it?"

"Yes, I believe it would be."

"Don, remember last spring when the *Journal* ran that editorial about the junior police, and you were all burned up, and I told you that you hadn't seen anything yet? Remember? Now they got you, and you're sore, and you're gonna leave just when we need you most. You want a better city, as I told you that morning, and the way to have a better city is to have better youth. The way to have better youth is to work with 'em; like you were doing. Nope, you get poked in the jaw, the Plunder Boys hang one on your chin, and once is enough. You're sore; so you're quitting when there's nobody in all Springfield to take your place."

The frown deepened on Don's forehead. He tried to speak, but the little man jumped in. "No one," he echoed, "no one to take your place." The cigar was out now. "Don, we need you the worst way. Stay here and lick this thing. If everyone gets behind you, we can win, and I promise my gang will." He rose. "Think it over; we sure need you, Don. I must go. Have to work on the early shift tonight."

This last remark was a shock to Don, who imagined labor leaders never worked; at least in the *Journal* they didn't. They were leeches who sucked the blood of honest workingmen without ever turning a hand to honest toil themselves.

Don was surprised. He was surprised, he was annoyed with Peedad, and most of all he was confused. Very confused.

Peedad walked over and took him by the arm. The editor was weary from the long day in the hot, sunny office on the square. He seemed older and frailer than ever. Yet there was still fire in his eyes; a kind of flame that Don had never seen in the eyes of Harry Wilson or J. Frank or the men of the Chamber of Commerce who were all so much younger. What was it he called them? The Plunder Boys. A good name, too.

The fiery eyes held him in their intensity; some of the flame seemed to penetrate his being. He was held against his will, ready to say no, anxious to refuse, fully intending to do so, quite unwilling to tie himself up with the CIO and the radicals from the Chrysler plant and Warner Gear and the steel mills, the troublemakers of town; determined to avoid the struggle ahead.

Yet Peedad held him there, battered him down against his will, made escape hard, harder every second, difficult, impossible.

"It's a chance, Don, that's all, for we'll have every force in town ganged up against us. The odds are against us, no matter what Harvey says. It's a battle and a tough one. But we have something to fight for, and you're the man to lead us. Look, you didn't quit on the Wildcats last year; you've never walked out on them yet. They need you now more than ever. Not for me, not for Harvey here, not for the grown folks in this town. For the Wildcats of Springfield, Indiana. Help us make this a city good enough for your Wildcats, a city good enough for Lincoln. What say, Don? Will you take a chance? Will you fight the thing through with us? Will you?"

They watched, the older man at Don's side, the younger standing anxiously across the room. He looked down at Peedad, hating him, yes, and loving him also at the same time.

You put it that way, you rascal, you put it like that; you know me; you know you can always get me. What can I say to him?

"Yes, of course I will, Peedad!"

22

Don walked slowly through the park a few days later, reading as he walked the editorial in the morning *Journal* which had been handed to him on leaving his office in the Recreation Building. He had missed it that morning, and this was his first chance to see it, although a dozen people had mentioned it during the day. The sun was still powerful, and it was hot even under the trees in the park, but there was something beside the summer warmth which heated him within as he read down the page.

The editorial was headed:

GROPING AT STRAWS

"The Democratic party, which has long been weak locally with little or no influence in civic affairs, is groping at straws. We refer to the purported nomination of our good friend and neighbor, Don Henderson. It appears he will be the Democratic candidate for mayor in the city primaries next week. The Democratic bosses must have called on everyone in town before resorting in desperation to an unknown young man with no political training whatever, a man who has only been a citizen of our city for the past three years. Don Henderson, who came here from Center Township to coach the high school basketball team several years ago, has the respect of everyone. But he is so completely lacking in experience and ability for the position he is said to be seeking, that we foresee another landslide for sound government such as happened in the last municipal election four years ago. We therefore expect with confidence the adherence of all right-thinking voters to the Republican nominee, Dale Pennington, a man with conspicuous ability as well as a long and distinguished business record in Springfield."

•

The column continued at length, extolling the virtues of the rival candidate. Don stuffed the newspaper in the pocket of his coat. Discounting the verbiage of Frank Fager, the editor, he realized there was truth in those remarks. Of course they had asked every prominent Democrat to run; nobody wanted to take on a hopeless cause. The whole thing was absurd, ridiculous, not to be considered. Without the fire in Peedad's eye to sway him, Don clearly saw that running for mayor was something he should never have considered. Slowly he walked along Michigan, planting his feet firmly, determined to see Peedad, to face up to him that very evening and stop this nonsense before it went further. That sort of thing wasn't for him! It's not too late now. Tonight I shall be firm. I just cannot get myself into any such mess. What's more, I won't.

The sound of rushing, charging feet broke into his thoughts. Looking round he saw a small, excited, breathless colored boy charging down upon him. That eager look in the boy's face told Don that he ought to know him.

It was Norman Hanscomb.

That's it, that's the way it is; you work with a boy, you try to solve his problem, you help him if you can, and then you promptly forget him in the mass of work, in the dozens of others needing attention. But he never forgets you.

"Hullo, Norman." Thank goodness I remember his name. "How're you?"

"Just fine, Don." His face was beaming; he was panting loudly. In one hand he had a piece of white paper. "I wanted to come . . . to show you . . . to give you . . . this . . . and I wanted to see it, too."

To see what? What's this about? He took the folded white paper that Norman extended. It was a letter.

"You want I should read this?"

The boy nodded vigorously, still panting. The letter was addressed to Norman Hanscomb, 561 S. Water St., Springfield. It was from Dave Harrison, the manager of the Woolworth Store.

"DEAR NORMAN:

"This is to acknowledge final payment of twenty-five cents due on the total of $1.50 for the six pairs of gloves taken from this store during the months of January and February, last. You have now paid the entire debt, and I feel you deserve credit for your faithful work, and for meeting the responsibility as promised. I would also like to congratulate you, and at the same time say that should you want a job, be sure and look me up here at the store. I can always find a place for you. Kindly give the enclosed receipt to Don Henderson, and show him this letter. With best wishes,

"Sincerely yours,

"DAVID M. HARRISON, *Mgr*."

"Say! Gee! I've lost it!"

The boy stood still, an anguished look on his round face. He turned about, looked back, took a few steps, felt carefully in each pocket. "I've lost it."

"Lost what?"

"The receipt. Mr. Harrison sent me a receipt. He said I was to give it to you. Now I've done gone and lost it. And . . . I'll have to earn that money all over again."

His face was twisted in misery; he stood still, hesitating, not knowing what to do.

Don placed his hand on the boy's shoulder. "Why, you won't need that receipt, Norman. This letter's just as good as a receipt; it's the same thing, it proves you paid your debt. It tells me you did the job, that you don't owe anything to the Five and Ten; that's all I need to know. And I'm mighty proud of you, too. As for the receipt, forget it."

"Is it O.K., Don? Is it O.K. without the receipt? I had it, I had it this morning, in my pocket with the letter."

"No matter. If you find it, turn it in to me. Otherwise I'll keep this letter as receipt. You've done everything that was asked of you. Have you been a good boy otherwise? Have you been all right at home? Have you still been helping your mother?"

"Yes, sir, yes, Don. I've drawn the water, and lugged coal, and done everything what she asked me. Oh, say! Say! Look! There it is now! There they are!"

He pointed down the street. The two were nearing Don's boarding house, and from the distance he could hear a band practicing. But he saw nothing. Looking down, he perceived Norman's intense excitement, watched his steps quicken. The boy was ahead of him now, skipping, running.

"Hey! What is this? What's up?" But Norman couldn't wait. He was running rapidly ahead, covering the ground at an amazing speed. Whatever it was, Norman was excited. Don approached the corner of Michigan and West Walnut, about to turn the corner to his house. Then he saw.

What he saw was the band, all of them, in uniform. The entire high school band, and the Wildcats, Heaven knows how many. They filled the street as far as he could see. There were faces at every window as he passed along, and from every porch housewives were watching. The trees already were black with kids seeking vantage points from which to see the fun, and others were shinnying up fences, telegraph posts, and even the tops of parked cars.

He stood amazed, ready to turn and run. They saw him first.

A dozen of them swooped down, hustled him toward his house, where his landlady was waiting on the porch, watching with a broad smile. She began to appreciate that she was sheltering more than just the high school basketball coach, famous as that individual might be in Springfield.

The crowd yelled as he appeared, the band began to play the Wildcat song—the old Wildcat song of basketball days.

There was Tom Shaw. The big fellow pushed and edged through the crowd with authority, shoving up to him. Quite plainly Tom was managing the whole affair. And wait until J. Frank hears about this, thought Don.

Well, he'll have to take it. So'll I. It's too late for either of us to cut and run now.

Then they closed in on Don. The band was still playing the Wildcat song, and the kids took it up.

"Fight . . . fight . . . Wildcats . . ."

Why! There's Red. Hi there, Red, hi, boy! And there's Mike Cray. Why, Mike! And Perry and Roy Miller; just about all my tough cases. Funny, when you see 'em like this, they're just the same as any other kids.

"Fight, fight . . . Wildcats . . ."

Maybe Peedad's right at that. Doggone, he *is* right; the old fella's always right; he knows, Peedad does. I was intending to leave 'em. There's Anola now, and the Evans twins who pinched their grandmother's bridge . . . and . . . yes . . . yes, sir . . . there's Jackson Piper . . . and my whole ball club . . . well, now . . . what d'you think of that . . . the whole darn team! Hang it, they're here, all of 'em. There's the Morgan boy, and Russ Spitler, and Chet and Dave and . . . goodness knows who all.

Now he was being pushed and forced up to the stoop, and someone had placed a box on the top step, and he was standing on the box, looking down at that ocean of faces, every face a familiar one, moving, twisting, edging closer.

He glanced about while they yelled, at Norman Hanscomb, now perched dangerously on the overhanging bough of a tree stretching across the street, at the dozens of other kids whose faces he knew, some in the branches, some swaying precariously from telegraph poles, singing, all of them, as hard as they could.

"Fight . . . fight . . . Wildcats . . . we will . . . score."

This is bad. When Storey down at the high school finds they've called out the band, he'll be hopping mad. But what can he do?

Then Don noticed the banners. There were seven or eight of them, homemade, kids' banners.

WE WANT DON
HENDERSON FOR MAYOR

VOTE FOR DON HENDERSON
HENDERSON—THE WILDCATS' CHOICE

Now the band finished. All, that is, except the trumpeter, who invariably squeaked on long after everyone else had ended. Tom Shaw worked through the crowd and up toward the top step, until he stood at Don's side. From the box, Don was about on a level with the giant center's chin.

The street below was black with kids, they jammed it from curb to curb as far up and down as you could see. Cars full of workers returning from offices in town were now unable to get past, and lined up to watch the fun. At the end of Michigan, a man sat with a friend in a large Cadillac, watching the scene closely. He could have turned round and gone home by another street, but he was interested.

"Quite a crowd," said one of them.

"Yeah. Lucky, kids don't vote," replied J. Frank Shaw.

Meanwhile from every window in the vicinity a face peered. The boys and girls were now yelling and waving at the figure on the stoop, all of them, the ones like Roy and Perry he knew well, the boys on the team he had worked and suffered and won with, the ones he only knew slightly, the kids who were merely familiar figures passing through the corridors down at school. He stood there, silently watching, a serious expression in his face, because his thoughts were serious.

Gosh! Just ten minutes ago I was ready to walk out.

Tom was talking now. His voice was high-pitched and squeaky, so different from the appearance of his huge frame. The excitement in his tones made his voice even more high-pitched and shrill.

"Kids . . . we came here this afternoon . . . so's Don could see we're behind him." The cheers broke out. For a long minute the boy was unable to continue. "This is a great day for us, because, for the first time, there's gonna be a candidate for mayor of this town that we all know. We all know him, and we all love Don Henderson. He's gonna make his first campaign speech right here, now, this afternoon, to us. That's the way it should be, 'cause he's our man."

They wouldn't quiet down. They refused to stop. From the branches of trees, from the roofs of porches, from the telegraph poles, from the tops of cars and from far down the street they yelled, that sea of upturned faces below called to him. Then they broke into the familiar yell.

"Yea! Wildcats! Yea! Wildcats! Yea! Wildcats! . . . Don . . . Don . . . Don!"

And to think that only ten minutes ago I was ready to leave town. Thank Heaven they don't know; no one knows; no one's going to know, either.

He looked at them, waiting until the noise finished. It took a long, long while to die away. There was quiet at last.

Here goes! My first campaign speech. My first one. It better be good, too.

"Wildcats, friends, citizens of Springfield, Indiana . . ."

23

The office of Roscoe Stallings was the office of the small-time Indiana lawyer. You could tell by one glance that its occupant was not an attorney for the town's larger corporations, and never tried cases for the principal citizens. The office, in a word, resembled that of the editor of the *Evening Press*. As did the owner.

The room was largish, with two cubbyholes at the end, one for the boss, another for his girl. In the big room was a mass of furniture, apparently placed there for no other reason than to store it. By the wall stood an old-fashioned grandfather clock, long since silenced; there were four or five green-covered rockers; a number of ancient bookcases filled with reports and law books; half a dozen antique filing cases; a tattered cane settee; and some stiff, hard-bottomed chairs. On the wall were faded photographs of picnics and conventions. At the side hung a dim picture of Theodore Roosevelt. Opposite was one of F.D.R.

The room was jammed. Boys and girls were squatting cross-legged on the floor; men, their shirts open at the neck, leaned on the hard chairs; women sat in the green-covered rockers. Beside the closed door stood Peedad, looking over the staff of his little army. At his feet were Tom and Carlene Benson and Jackson and the boys on the basketball team.

Harvey Patterson from Delco was there, Earl Hasler from Chevrolet, and Murray Swanson from Warner Gear. Standing behind Jackson's father was Roscoe, next to him, Jim McHale, the secretary at the Y, and on the settee were Miss Perry from the high school and Anola Cray's mother. Sam Katzmann and his wife were present; so were Whitey Moore who lived in the housing project at the south end of town, George Munroe who owned a small haberdashery shop on Buckeye, and Gus Maher, the grocer.

Peedad Wilson was speaking and they watched him closely, listening with care. Why, thought Don, it's like a team before a game. That's what it is, really, the first game of the season.

"That about takes care of it. Roscoe here knows politics in this town. He'll handle the political angle, he and Harvey. So if you have any questions, and most likely you'll have plenty, get in touch with them. Our headquarters will open tomorrow at 505 South Superior. The phone isn't listed; you call Democratic headquarters. The number is 4156. Now everyone here knows what the job is, what we have to do. We've won in the primaries, but we still have to buck the organized faction in control of this town. To do that with any hope of success, we must organize, too. Isn't much time; only coupla months or less. Folks are saying it can't be done. I don't hardly believe that, do you, Don?"

Don was brought up suddenly. Faces turned toward him, friendly, inquiring, anxious, worried, tired faces. Some young, eager faces on the floor, also.

He waited a minute as they searched his countenance. His lips were tight. He said what he felt. "I never went into a game I felt I was going to lose; guess I'm a little old to begin."

A murmur of approval swept the room as Peedad continued. "That's it, that's the kind of stuff we'll have to have. If we have it, we can beat these—well, I call 'em the Plunder Boys. You all know who they are, everyone in Springfield knows 'em, no need to call names. They've got this town in their grip; we intend to shake it loose; by Christopher, I believe we can, too!" Once again the ripple of approval swept the room. His enthusiasm captured them completely; it was contagious; he had no illusions and yet no defeatism in his heart, either.

" 'S I say, we must organize. To win in politics, you gotta organize. That goes for us all, boys and girls like you young folks here, the same as everyone else. Because we need you; you can help; you're part of this town, you're part of America. You can be of use. After organization, and in fact to help it along, we need money. Money to organize and to conduct the campaign. If we don't get us some money and become organized, these boys'll pass us like the Southwestern going through Chesterfield."

He paused a minute and looked them over carefully. "There's one rich man here tonight. But I'm not asking him to make this a success, this campaign. He's promised me a large sum; 'tain't enough. Even if it was, I wouldn't take it. The money must come from us all. From everyone in this town who wants to make Springfield a better city.

"So, first off, everybody here tonight has pledged two things. They've pledged to give a dollar, and then they've pledged himself or herself to call a group meeting of fifteen other folks in the neighborhood, to get as many people as possible into this thing. Each of those fifteen is to bring a dollar, and agree to hold a meeting in turn. We can't ask Don to speak at all these private gatherings, but he'll attend some. Harvey will come, so'll I, so will Roscoe. Remember, we want a dollar from each individual who attends the group meetings.

"What for do we need money? For organization and campaign purposes. The opposition has the *Journal*, and the radio station, the Chamber of Commerce, and the Merchants Bank behind them. To win, we must get the people of Springfield behind us. They're sympathetic, lots of 'em, they feel Don has had a mighty raw deal; they know the work he's done with the young folks here in town. But we have to get our story across. That takes money. We need cash to pay the rent of that store which will be our headquarters, we need money for promotion, for printing, for mailing costs, for time on the air. All the printing will be done in my shop without profit, and any advertising in the *Evening Press* I'll donate free. But we'll need to answer some tough ones in the *Journal*, unless I miss my guess. That costs money.

"There's certain groups to be handled by some people here tonight. Harvey, you've got the CIO. Murray, your job is the A.F. of L. Mr. Piper, you'll be the leader and you'll be responsible for your side of town. Whitey, you've got to do a door-to-door job on the folks in the Springfield Gardens. If we can carry Piper's precinct and yours by big majorities, we'll have a chance. Once again, there isn't much time. We've got a terrific job on our hands, every human being here, young and old . . ."

Don listened with respect mingled with admiration as Peedad went on, explaining, outlining plans, arranging strategy, discussing personalities who could be counted up to help, advising this man, replying to a woman's questions, suggesting who could be useful on the south side or the west side of town. His knowledge of the city and its people was colossal. He was an editor, an impractical geezer, old Peedad Wilson, the man everyone loved—and laughed at, also. Yet here he was marshaling that conglomerate crowd of people of all kinds, of every age and both sexes, of different races and color, fusing them into a team, inspiring them with a common cause, blue-printing an organization he hoped would be strong enough to take on the toughest political machine the town had ever known. His fiery eyes, and the flame in his face, held them. Every person.

The flow of questions increased, and Don edged toward the door, followed by Harvey Patterson. He was due at his first regular rally since his nomination, to be held in the Lincoln School on the north side. It was early when the two men reached the building, and only a few youngsters playing basketball were in the empty gymnasium where it was to be held. Zeke, the janitor, came forward to shake hands.

"Hullo, Zeke. How are you?"

"Tolerable, Don, tolerable. Guess I'll live till I die. How're you?"

"Just fine, Zeke. Say, you gonna vote for me?"

The old man looked him in the eye. This old man couldn't be fooled. This was the first time Don had asked the question, in fact the first time it had occurred to him to ask it. There was something significant in the old fellow who knew the school, the school system, and politics in the town from way back. "Don, I 'low as how I will." And he shuffled off downstairs without another word.

Harvey looked at Don and Don glanced at Harvey, without saying a word. If all the Zekes in town feel that way, or even a lot of them, we can win. By George, we can; yessir, we can lick 'em. He paced up and down beside the edge of the floor, watching the kids, hardly seeing them. But suddenly something caught his eye, the eye of the trained expert.

"Hey! Hey there! You in the red and white jersey. Don't hook that boy! You hooked him. What's the matter? You know the rules, don't you? Can't get anywhere in basketball that way."

The boys all stopped, listened with respect, and then went on as Don came toward them on the floor, watching. He followed them a minute, then spoke up. "No . . . no . . . you're not together . . . you aren't a team. You in the blue, move in there . . . move in front . . . worry him . . . get your hands up . . . there, that's more like it! Not that way . . . watch it . . . watch it when you throw . . . like this . . . here . . . gimme."

He extended his hands, and someone tossed the ball to him. He came jogging down the floor, zigzagging among them, through them and under the basket. Jumping up, he lofted it deftly into the net.

"See! See what I mean? D'ja notice how I was watching it all the time. Now try it yourself, and mind you keep your eyes on it."

The boys responded with alacrity, imitating him with earnestness. "That's good . . . that's more like it . . . now then, le's go . . . pivot . . . go on . . . good . . ."

They were hard at it. Don removed his jacket and tossed it to Harvey, for he was moving rapidly up and down the floor, following their pattern, and the room was hot. "Look! Le's get together on this. Le's see if we can't work that ball . . . don't hold it . . . pass it . . . basketball's a team game . . . and get your hands up, you . . . you in the green pants . . . hold your position, kid . . . don't let him knife you there . . . don't let him go in."

He grabbed the ball again and showed them how to do it. Then he handed it to one boy, and stood dancing before him, arms extended. A few people had entered from the other end of the gymnasium by this time. They were Hoosiers, so they understood the scene perfectly, and leaving the chairs set up under the far basket for the rally, they came down the floor to watch. Soon a line of adults had formed completely across the court. Don Henderson as basketball coach was quite as interesting as Don Henderson the candidate for mayor. Possibly more so.

"Now then . . . pass that ball! Remember, all of you, basketball's a team game. O.K. now, the score is close, we're pressing 'em, it's outa bounds here . . . now, sharpen it up a bit . . . sharpen it up . . . that's more like it . . . that's better . . . now you're beginning to get it . . . now you're a team . . . that's it . . . don't let him run either way, you in the blue . . . come on . . . come on . . . put out . . . extra hard . . . harder!"

The crowd grew larger as the boys went to

work more furiously. Time for the rally came at last, went by, with Don forgetting everything except the game. The adults in turn forgot the rally, too, as they watched him hammer away at the youngsters with the basketball. They were on the inside, they were behind the scenes, they were watching the coach of a winning State team teach a gang of unformed kids. Far from being restive or annoyed, they enjoyed the spectacle; in fact they seemed willing to settle for an entire evening of basketball. Occasionally as he passed up and down, Don could hear comments, usually shrewd ones.

"He can shoot, that boy . . . can hit, too . . . the one in the striped jersey. That's my lad . . . the lefty . . . yes, he's a mighty smart little player, I've been watching him . . . big boy can shoot with either hand . . . see him in there . . . see?"

Finally Harvey could stand it no more. He was one of the few adults present more interested in politics than basketball. Stepping onto the floor, he seized Don by the arm firmly. At first Don paid no attention, but he couldn't break Harvey's grasp.

"My goodness!" He glanced up at the clock

covered by a wire netting on the wall behind the basket. Then he looked at his wristwatch. "My goodness! Well, boys . . . that's about all, that's about all this evening, fellas."

Groans, cries, protests came from the two teams. "Oh, no, Don . . . don't stop now . . . please don't quit, Don . . . jus's we're going places . . . oh, gee!"

"I must. I have to stop, boys. Sharpen up that defense a mite, sharpen it up there, and you'll be O.K. Here, gimme my coat, Harvey! Sorry, folks, sorry to have kept you all waiting. I plumb forgot what I was here for when I caught sight of that basketball."

He yanked at his jacket, and edged through the crowd, mopping his perspiring face. Past the rows of chairs and up to the table under the far basket, where Zeke had placed a pitcher and a glass of water. It tasted good. He drank one and then another large glass, while the crowd turned and settled slowly into the seats. The boys, curious, stood on the sides, watching. One of them had the basketball under his arm.

It was a crowd far larger than any adult audience he had ever addressed, and ordinarily he would have been nervous. In fact he had been dreading this moment for days. Because he knew they were interested enough to come out, that they all wanted to size him up as a candidate for mayor, that they would be anxious to see whether he was sore and disappointed at the events of the summer. He also realized that his first organized meeting could make or break the campaign. But there was no time to be nervous. He was hot, panting, sweat on his forehead, and he stood mopping his face while they settled into their seats, expectant and politely interested.

This Don Henderson's having a rally tonight over in the Lincoln School gym. 'Pears like he got kind of a raw deal in that Juvenile Aid work last summer. Let's us drop over and hear what he has to say.

They were friendly faces, but shrewd and skeptical ones, too. He yanked his typewritten speech from his pocket. Now the speech seemed stale, unreal and formal in the mood of closeness and unity he had felt with the youngsters on the basketball court.

"Folks, most of you have been waiting some time for this meeting to begin, quite some time, and I rather guess I owe you an apology. But you all know basketball, so I imagine you'll understand how it is. When I saw that ball and those kids there . . . I just . . . seemed like I just had to get into the game. Now, I've got a speech here I'd written out. Spent some considerable time and effort on it, too. But I don't intend to use it. I'm gonna chuck it away, and tell you all how I feel about things in this town, so's everyone here, even these kids, can understand."

He tossed the folded manuscript onto the table. There was a sudden silence in the room, the scraping of the chairs stopped, the coughing died away. Heads came up, people who had settled back leaned forward. They were watching closely.

Say, this fella Henderson, he's smart . . . can't ever tell about him.

"Folks, I'm happy you were all able to follow our little practice session for a few minutes this evening. Because it must have been pretty plain to you . . . to everyone here . . . the difference between the boys, between this bunch of kids when you first came in . . . and just now . . . when we stopped." He paused, mopping his brow with a damp handkerchief, seeking words to express his feeling. This can be good, if only I can say what I feel. Or it can be . . . Well, it's sure a funny campaign speech. But maybe I can say it best in terms of basketball, 'cause that's what I know best, and so do they.

"Yes, sir, that's exactly the way it is here in this town. There's been some people in Springfield . . . I don't care to name names and I don't say that some of 'em aren't mighty fine people, but they've been running things by themselves. All alone. No team play. No, sir, no team play; everyone for himself, and the . . . the blazes with the community. They've been kinda working at cross purposes with the public good, so to speak. They weren't . . . well, let's put it this way, they weren't working for the team. What my party wants, is to make a team. We want a team in which everyone is in there, in which everybody is working for the town of Springfield, Indiana. Even these kids here, on the sidelines. We think they're important. We want team play. That simply means we want a team on which everyone gets a chance. Not just a few of us.

"Now we feel that one way to accomplish this is for the town to buy the Central Valley Power Company's plant. There's been some funny things said, and quite some confusion about this idea, so I'll just outline how we propose to do it. First off . . ."

People were watching him. They were listening. Even the folks who had just come out of curiosity, who had merely come to see what Don Henderson would have to say for himself.

24

The early shift was coming off work at the Chrysler plant. Hundreds of men streaming out to lanes of cars parked beside the factory, hundreds of motors starting, roaring, moving off as the owners went home after the day's work. One man in a checked shirt, open at the neck, who was standing beside his car, called to a driver going past.

"Hey there, Jack! Hey there!" The car slowed up and he stepped over. "I wanna speak to you."

"Hello, Smoky. What's cookin'?"

"Look! You wasn't to the meeting last night, was you?"

"Nope, I couldn't get there; my wife wasn't well."

"Thought so. The Union elected me chairman of the plant registration committee. You've gotta help."

"Me? Nuts! Naw, I can't. . . . I'm not . . ."

"Nuts, nothing! You gotta help on this. We intend to see that every eligible voter in this here plant registers—and votes, too. I'm coming round to your place with Joe and Ralph at seven; give you the dope then."

A horn honked behind them. He stepped back. "Seven. See you then."

•

Whitey Moore sat at the telephone in the front room of his small apartment in the housing project at Springfield Gardens.

"I do wish you'd come and eat, Whitey," his wife called from the kitchen. "Your supper'll spoil."

"Just this one call, Mother, one more call. This is the last."

"My goodness, you're at the telephone all day

and night. I believe I'll be glad when this election is over."

"Believe I will, too. Hullo? That you, Sandy? This is Whitey, Whitey Moore. Say, you registered yet? You haven't? Well, kid, you better had. How's 'at? Yeah, four more days; that's correct. I know, I know you been sick, but lemme ask you a question. D'ja register last year?"

There was a long silence. Then he broke in, impatience in his tone. "That's just the point. That's the way it is with all you guys; you won't take the trouble to register. It's raining outside the last night, or you don't feel so good, or you hafta bowl, or something, and then you can't vote; then you kick about the government we have in this town, and wonder how J. Frank Shaw gets away with it. Now see here, you and your missus get down to . . . wait a sec . . . you're in Precinct . . . 18 . . . that's the hose house on Sycamore at Bedford. You get down there tonight; otherwise I'll come out in my car and drag you down. You will? O.K., Sandy, I'm checking on ya!"

The stout lady wheezed as she climbed the steps to the porch and rang the bell of the lower apartment in the little two-family house. She had a black book in her hand, and opening it, peered carefully at the list on the written page.

A woman came to the door wiping her hands with her apron. On her face was a sorry-we-aren't-interested look. The expression changed when she saw her visitor.

"Why, good evenin', Mrs. Cray. Come in, step right inside."

"Good evenin', Mrs. Mac. I can't come in; I wish I could; my feet seem like they'll give out on me. But I have the rest of this street to work. I'm checking tonight. Have you and Mac registered yet?" She held an accusing pencil against the book in her hand.

"Why, goodness sakes alive! I was talking to Mac about it at breakfast this morning; funny you should ask. You know, we been meaning to. We will though . . . one of these days."

"One of these days isn't good enough. It's this week or not at all. If you don't register this week you can't vote in November. We gotta register; we gotta vote. Now the committee, they'll send a car round for you if you like."

"Mercy, no! It's just round the corner in Fath's grocery. We will tonight, when Mac gets home from work I'll tell him; we'll do it tonight I promise you."

"Mind you do. And I'm a-gonna check; I'm sending Anola round to check this street tomorrow or Thursday. I have to turn in my report to headquarters Friday morning, so mind you do, Mrs. Mac. Now let . . . me see." She looked at the book. "Who is it lives over you? The Finnegans, don't they? That's right." She pressed the bell firmly.

•

The Venetian blinds were drawn, and the indirect light above cast a pleasant glow over the smoky room. A large vase filled with red autumn chrysanthemums was on the empty, glass-topped desk. The room was modern, elegant, with a thick carpet on the floor and a few prints on the wall. A luxurious leather couch was along one wall, and there were some comfortable chairs, all well filled by copious gentlemen smoking cigars. The office plainly belonged to a man of taste and means. The only jarring note in the taste and elegance, the only reminder of the world outside, was a large white map pinned on the back of a door. It showed Springfield divided off into its twenty-eight separate election precincts, with the Wildcat River cutting the town in two.

J. Frank Shaw sat with his feet on the half-opened drawer of the desk, listening with interest to the conversation but taking little part. He seemed to be busy offering a box of cigars to those nearest.

"I tell you, J. Frank." A little man in a large chair in the corner spoke. "I tell you, they're really getting 'em out. They're really registering 'em this time."

"I understand the CIO has Warner Gear and Chrysler pretty well organized; they even have committees out there," said a voice.

An elderly, gray-haired man in a double-breasted suit leaned over and tapped his cigar against an ashtray. He cleared his throat. "That's the trouble. That's the whole trouble; you put your finger right on it, Max. Once we had first-class native workingmen in this town, good, solid American stock. Then those big plants came here, and they brought this outside element in. The troublemakers . . . bah!"

"Want the plants; must have labor for 'em," remarked someone philosophically.

"Yeah," the old man responded instantly. "But

it's a foreign element, Dave. That's what I object to. These fellas bossed by Russians and Jews from Detroit and New York and goodness knows where-all. Springfield was a good town until these agitators got in. D'ja see my editorial on that today, Frank?"

The man at the desk slapped the box of cigars down. He answered briefly. "I expect I did. Joe, tell me, how you think things stand?"

The little chap in the corner replied.

"J. Frank, I confess I don't like the look of things any too much. These boys are getting organized. They're registering voters right and left."

"They're registering our people, too, aren't they?"

"Why, sure. But a large vote, well, I'm afraid of a large vote. I don't like a large vote."

"The boys here in this town are O.K." The man on the couch tapped his cigar again on the ashtray. "It's the gang from outside, the radical element, that crowd from Toledo and Detroit that have come to work in Springfield who make the trouble."

The man behind the glass-topped desk yawned. "Well, we've had reform movements in this town before, and licked 'em, too. I recall my dad telling about the fights he used to have. Peedad Wilson and these fellas today are a bunch of amateurs."

Echoes around the room approved his last sentence. "Starry-eyed idealists." "Bunch of visionaries."

"Why, sure, they've even come out openly as Democrats, instead of playing foxy and waging a non-partisan campaign. If you fellas do the work, it'll be easy. So long as this town is sixty-five percent Republican, we're sitting pretty."

"Sixty-five percent Republican, yes," said the little man in the corner. "That's all right, but what about the newcomers? How'll they vote?"

"They'll vote right. Especially the way Wilson is pushing this crazy, wild-eyed socialistic scheme of the Municipal Power Company. And running that chap—that basketball coach. In the old days, in my dad's time, they had candidates, not some young squirt who isn't dry behind the ears."

Again the echoes of approval. "Must have tried just about everyone in town before they . . ."

"I know they went after Jack Rodman. And I understand Judge James refused to run."

"And Cassidy and Hank Bleyer, too."

"Just the same," the little man said, "just the same, they're really getting the voters out, they really are."

•

The boys and girls were waiting on the sidewalk outside headquarters. Their bicycles, dozens of them, were lined up at the curb or leaning against the front of the store. The boys wore checked shirts or sweaters. The majority had on faded corduroy pants, often well marked with inscriptions in red or blue crayon. A few wore short, fawn-colored coats. Most were hatless, one or two had on cloth caps with flaps buttoned over the top. The girls were all stockingless. Nearly all were adorned with a round celluloid disc, four inches in diameter. It carried three letters in red on a white background.

D O N

The gentleman whose name they wore came suddenly through the door. He, too, was hatless. In one hand he had a fistful of papers. Instantly the shoving and pushing, the calling and yelling stopped. They crowded about him.

"Tom! Oh, there he is! Are we all here now?

All the captains here? Roy! Where's Roy? Anyone seen Roy?"

They were packing in closely around him now, making a tight circle. "Dunno," said Tom Shaw, looking over the mob from his superior height. "Haven't seen him."

"Here he is! Here comes Roy."

Roy Miller rode hastily up on his bike, dismounted, flung it down and joined them.

"Right! Now we're all here. You captains . . . do all you kids understand what this is about? Why it's important? Because as captains, you'll each be responsible for your particular precinct. Get this, Roy . . . and you, too, Jackson, and you, Buck. You'll receive your leaflets in a minute; they'll be in bundles of a hundred. Take plenty for your precinct, then distribute them to the kids. Get this if you can, it's vital. Have them shove the leaflets in the mailbox in each house. Be sure you don't miss any."

"Suppose there ain't no mailbox."

"I'm coming to that, Stanley. In that case, you push 'em under the door. Don't let your kids sit on their bikes at the curb and chuck 'em at the porch; whatever happens, watch that. The wind just blows 'em away. You'll have to circulate and see things are O.K., check your kids, watch 'em. If you pass anyone on the street, or they do, hand out a leaflet. That's important, too. Remember, you girls, it's just as necessary to have the women register as the men.

"Next, these buttons. You'll all have a supply of these little buttons marked R. That means if a man or lady you talk to has registered already, he gets one to wear. You ask folks are they registered. If they say yes, O.K., hand 'em a button. Otherwise don't give 'em out. Remember, today we aren't working as Democrats or for any particular candidate. We aren't worrying how the folks are going to vote. We want to get the vote out. Our only chance is a heavy vote. But we aren't working as party people today, so I'm going to ask you to take off my badges there, and see your kids do."

There was a hasty unpinning of the large celluloid discs. They went into pockets and purses.

"Now, what all's the idea of this registration business? It's a good idea. The town uses the lists on election day, to check, to see the voters really are the folks listed as citizens of Springfield. So's there can't be any frauds. I'm gonna read this leaflet, Tom, and if any of you don't understand, stop me.

" 'Citizens of Springfield. If you don't register this week, you cannot vote in November. At the last election for mayor, less than thirty percent of the qualified voters went to the polls. Register this week. Full information as to the registry place in your precinct from the office of the registrar of voters, in City Hall. Phone 3846.'

"Everyone understand? O.K. then, get busy."

There was a whoop, a shout, and they surged round a man at the door who was laden with paper bundles. Taking them, they mounted their bikes and charged off down South Superior. The road each way was black with them.

25

Autumn. The barns full and bursting through the flat, rich countryside. Corn stacked in the fields, yellow triangles of gold. County fairs all over the state; huge cows in the stalls, great hogs in the pens, rows and rows of bottled vegetables on the shelves, trotting races on the tracks, friendly faces swarming through the gates.

Autumn. And politics. Everywhere politics, after basketball the Hoosier's greatest sport. Politics in every town and city in Indiana.

Autumn, and the harvest moon above Springfield. Peedad Wilson walked across the square with Judge James in the warm, mellow October evening. The sounds from the auditorium in the County Building across the street, where the rally was being held, grew louder as they approached.

"Frankly, Peedad, I dislike the thing. The whole idea is radical—it's un-American."

"Judge, there's only one answer to that and you know it. If a municipal power plant is all right for Peru and Richmond, why is it un-American for Springfield?"

"Well, 'tis. This foreign element in town wants it; I don't like that. There! Listen to 'em howling inside." The roar from the auditorium came to them plainly as the two men rounded the corner of the building and drew near the entrance to the hall. The soft evening had necessitated the opening of all doors and windows, so the commotion and uproar from within surrounded them.

"Hear that! Hear that yelling! Peedad, it's fascism!"

The old chap stopped still on the concrete walk. He grabbed the other by the arm. "Nonsense, Judge, that just ain't so. Fascism and these isms they've had abroad only come when the electorate is apathetic, when people don't give a damn. It never comes when they get out and argue, when they're fighting mad, like our good folks in there. Why, that's a healthy sign; don't you ever forget it."

They were at the door now. They were inside. The scene within was complete confusion. People were standing up, rising all over the audience to shout something at the chair, sitting down, standing again. On the platform, Harvey Patterson was pounding the rostrum with a gavel. Then in the midst of the pandemonium a figure leapt from a chair at the back of the stage and stepped up front. It was Don. The noise died away.

"I think I can answer that question. If Peru can do it, if Lebanon can do it, if Richmond can do it, if other American cities can do it, by George, we can do it here in Springfield!"

Applause crackled over the hall. Peedad and Judge James worked their way through to the rear, to the only empty seats left in the large hall. Whatever else happened, it was plain that the townspeople were interested in this election.

Down front a pretty blonde girl rose. Peedad

adjusted his spectacles and peered ahead. He leaned over.

"That's Rheba Benson—Wilf Benson's daughter."

"Oh, is that so? That's the one Don had on the spot last summer, isn't it?"

"No . . . no . . . that was Carlene, her younger sister. This one is dead against us. She hates Don. Listen . . . get this!" He leaned forward, straining to catch her words. A silence fell over the crowd.

Don stood on the platform with his feet apart, his hands on his hips. There were murmurs from the rear of the hall from people who could not hear what the girl was saying. Don held up one hand for quiet. Finally she finished. He spoke.

"Lady . . . here . . . says I've been doing quite some talking in this campaign about Americans. She says there's a lot of foreigners come to Springfield in recent years from Kentucky, from Detroit, from Toledo, and other places. She wants me to define that term—American. O.K. I'll just do that." He took a couple of quick, nervous steps across the platform and came to the center.

What he needs, thought Peedad, is a basketball in his hands.

"Here's what I mean by an American. First of all, he's either a foreigner, or the son of a foreigner, or the descendant of one. He thinks, on the whole, this thing we like to call democracy is pretty good. He believes in education for all. He believes in the right of workingmen to organize; in freedom of speech, of religion, of the press. Lastly, he believes in a government of the people, by the people, and . . . most important of all . . . for the people. Which is exactly what we haven't had in this town lately," he added, almost savagely.

The roar that greeted his last sentence was tremendous. The judge turned to Peedad and raised his eyebrows. Peedad cocked his head and glanced at the judge.

They looked back to the platform. Don was fighting mad now, and the crowd knew it, liked it.

"Then there's two more things that make an American. He won't ever believe a thing can't be done merely because it hasn't been done before. That isn't the way we made this nation. We made the U.S.A. by believing nothing was impossible. Finally, when an American sees something, when he sees injustice, by golly, it hurts . . . he gets angry. He wants to do something about it."

A man way down front rose, clapping. Another stood; then more and more, until over half the audience was on their feet. Still Don stood up front on the platform, his jaw out. Then all at once he swung around and went back to his chair. The crowd seated itself.

The judge turned to his friend.

"He's pretty good, Peedad. He makes sense."

"Well, he ain't exactly what you call a speaker; but he believes, Judge. He believes in America."

The judge nodded. Harvey Patterson was standing in front again, now pointing down toward the floor.

"The gentleman in the brown suit." A small, bespectacled man rose not far from the pair in the back. Peedad nudged his friend. "That's Lawyer Richards. He's mixed up with the Power Company, he's their attorney in town."

"You telling me." The judge was listening with attention to the question.

"Will the speaker be so kind as to tell us, so's everyone can understand, what the advantage would be to the average citizen of this town if our power company, which gives first class service at cheap rates, were turned over to politics and to the machinations of political appointees and grafters?"

Applause broke into the end of his query. Don came down front again, waited for the noise to die away. Now the whole packed hall was listening.

He started slowly. "Seems to me . . . folks . . . there's been quite some confusion about this question of the town buying the Power and Light Company's plant. Some of the statements I've seen in print, anyway, don't exactly jibe with the facts. I'd like to say a few words. Last year, the Richmond Municipal Gas and Electric Company turned back the sum of $456,318 to the taxpayers of that town. Peru turned back $454,890, and Longansport over $50,000. Lebanon in their first year of operation figured to clear $14,000. Actually they cleared $34,000. These, ladies and gentlemen, are savings to the taxpayers of the respective towns. . . ."

Instantly the little man was on his feet. "Is the gentleman aware that in making these comparisons, he's forgetting that the Federal Government does not tax municipal light plants. It's unfair. . . ."

"I'm not forgetting anything. I'm merely stating facts. Those are the actual sums turned back to the town, sums earned by municipal power plants. Now I believe the original question was this: What would be the advantage to the average citizen of this town if we bought the electric light company?

"The advantages are many. There are three main ones. You pay here $.385 for 100 kilowatt hours of electricity. If you lived in Richmond, you'd pay $.251; if you lived in Peru, you'd pay $.297. If we bought this company, we could reduce rates as these towns have done, do it for industrial as well as home consumption. We could make the town more attractive to new industries. That means more jobs for all you folks here; that means prosperity to the town.

"Second. If we didn't care to reduce the power rates, we could redeem the bonds and own the property outright in twelve and a half years.

"Third, we could bring the ownership and management of the property back to Springfield where it belongs, instead of the way it is now, being owned and run by people with offices in a New York skyscraper. Does that answer the question?"

The little man rose instantly, but his words were lost in a storm of jeers. There were others in the audience beside the two friends in the rear who were aware of his connection. Don raised his hand for quiet. His voice could be heard above the roar.

"Let's have the question; le's us give everyone here a chance to be heard."

Finally the questioner's tones conquered the din. "How can you assure us that the management and personnel of the utility plant when owned by the town will be free from political interference and abuse?"

Again there was silence. Politics once more. Politics, the whipping horse, the despised and yet seductive profession that everyone in Indiana laughed at and indulged in. Politics which dragged everything down, which meant corruption, graft, inefficiency. Politics in Indiana.

Don stood there, his arms folded. "I can't guarantee anything. No one can. Only maybe, Mr. Richards, I have more confidence in the people of Springfield than you have."

Applause. Cheers. Laughter. Heads turned

toward the lawyer. The meeting broke up in a burst of noise.

Peedad and the judge edged up front. "Why, the boy surprised me, he really did. He's a scrapper, ain't he, Peedad? Where'd he get his stuff on the power plants? I never heard those figures before."

"I'll tell you just where he got 'em. He went and dug 'em out himself. He's been round to those places, to Lebanon and Peru and Richmond. It was his own idea, Judge. For the last two weeks he's been studying their plants, consulting with the managers and the mayors and controllers. He must have spent the best part of last week over at Lebanon with their city attorney, going over the figures, checking up on that fight they had with the Power Company. You know it went up to the Supreme Court."

"Yes, I recall it did, twice, I believe. Well now, good for Don, good for him! He means business, doesn't he?"

"You bet he does! At first he didn't know anything about municipal ownership; in fact he was a mite afraid of it; but he went out and learned fast. That's the kind of a boy he is." They stood watching him as he bent toward the circle of people standing below the platform explaining some point, answering a question, replying to the doubts of someone else. They listened, interested.

Funny, thought the old man as he watched, he's not the same. He's not the same Don Henderson as the diffident kid who took over basketball here three years ago. Nope, he's not, he's different; he's plenty different; he looks different and he is, too. That crease in his forehead is deeper now and sort of fixed. It's defeat that did it, and the struggle he's been through ever since he came to town. But it has given him something—confidence and authority. Why, he could no more have handled this crowd two years ago, or even last year, no more'n nothing.

Then Rheba Benson burst in the side door, flushed, annoyed, determined. She pushed into the dwindling circle at Don's feet; now she was up front and close to him, yet her voice was penetrating and carried through the emptying hall.

"Don Henderson! You might like to know what those young roughnecks of yours did this evening. They let the air out of the tires of my car and every car parked round the square, too."

He stood looking down at her, upset, disturbed. "That's what happens," she went on, as the knot of people turned in surprise, watching her with open mouths, "that's what happens when grown folks put kids to their own uses. Seems to me you must be pretty hard up when you have to depend on kids to help win an election."

His mouth formed words, but they didn't come. He stood looking down grimly, changed his mind, hesitated. A dozen questions came to his mind. How could anyone know it was my crowd? How could you know? Most of them were here at the rally. Suppose it was, suppose two or three did; that's a kid's trick; it's silly, but it's a kid's trick.

Then he made up his mind how to act. Ignoring the girl, he glanced round the hall. "Tom! Where are you, boy?" His voice was low but it carried.

Tom spoke from the side of the platform where with another boy he was rolling up an American flag. In the middle of doing it they had hesitated, watching the scene.

"How many captains you got here?"

"Don, they were all here earlier. Most of 'em are round, I guess; Jay Hanwell is here, and Jackson is round some place, and Buck . . . and Red."

"Get 'em all together. One of you borrow a

26

Doggone, if it isn't more exciting than basketball!

That says something in Springfield, Indiana.

It *was* exciting, too. Never had the city been so torn by a mere election. Everyone had an opinion as in basketball, and as in basketball everyone expressed it freely. Usually elections came and went, with hardly more than half the population of the town voting. This time from the start it was plain by the large registration, by the general intensity as the campaign progressed, that the vote would be heavy. People were not only interested, they were stirred, moved, often antagonized and annoyed. Every store in the downtown district was decorated with posters—mostly pictures of Dale Pennington taken some ten years before. Or else they carried large white placards that said: VOTE REPUBLICAN. Every car had an enormous YES or NO pasted to the windshield. People had made up their minds now about how they would vote on the purchase of the power plant. As the campaign continued, the Buicks and Cadillacs were adorned with increasing appeals to

"SAVE SPRINGFIELD"
OR
"SAVE SPRINGFIELD FROM COMMUNISM"

Yes, people were annoyed. They were frightened also, many of them.

For the town was divided into two camps; the majority, the right-thinking citizens, the solid, substantial crowd, the people from the west side and along Austin Avenue, were on one side. On the other were the Wildcats or most of them, the unthinking younger element, plus certain less articulate sections of the community who as a rule were not greatly interested in politics. Strangely, few merchants in the business section displayed Don's photograph in their windows. They knew him, they called him by his first name, they shook hands cordially and wished him well when they met. They meant it, too. But it appeared that they supported Pennington.

Don's backing didn't come from downtown. Nor from the *Journal* and the business element. It came from strange sections of the city; from Shedtown and the people along Water Street by the railroad tracks; it came from the colored families in the north end. Those were the places where you found his face in the windows. There and in the little unpainted and unpretentious wooden houses on the west of town. And along the lines of parked cars in the rear of the steel mills or beside the Chrysler plant. There, also, you saw the YES stickers on the windshields.

One morning in early October Don sat in Peedad's office. The old man was looking over the early edition of the *Journal* with practiced eyes, something he had been doing regularly every day

"Vote NO on election.

"CENTRAL VALLEY POWER CO."

Don threw the newspaper down. He was incensed.

"But, Peedad, look! Peedad, look! That just isn't so! I mean . . . we know . . . we've shown . . . we can prove our figures."

The old man swung round on him angrily. "Course it isn't! We know they've cleared a profit averaging close to sixty thousand for the past ten years. We know they paid taxes every year to the U.S. Government of twenty thousand, which as a city we wouldn't have to pay."

"O.K. . . . there's eighty thousand!"

"Right. We can either use that to cut rates or reduce taxes. If other towns can we can. Anderson has no city levy; its government is operated entirely from revenue from the municipal power plant. Shucks, Don!"

"Look, you'll answer this in the *Press* tonight, Peedad?"

"I'll answer him O.K. Who'll read it? It'll be read by eight men and a dog."

Don hesitated. He was in despair. "Can't we go into the *Journal*, too?"

"I only wish we could. Money, my boy."

"How do we stand now?"

"Scraping on bottom. Sam's done a wonderful job keeping us afloat. He's getting funds, and the dollars are rolling in from all over town; yes, sir, I mean it, all over town. Only it costs to campaign for mayor. Everything costs, nothing comes free."

"Shoot!" Don turned on a radio at his elbow. A smooth voice pattered persuasively.

". . . And, folks, if you want representative government in this city—that means the kind of government on which this nation was founded—if you're against socialism and things of that kind, support Dale Pennington, won't you? Support him and the whole ticket. Experience counts, remember. You wouldn't hire a boy to run your business. Why put one in charge of the city's business?"

He switched it off. "We ought to get on the radio if we only could. We ought to tell people the facts."

"Sure. That's what I've always believed, tell the people the facts and they'll think straight and act the same way. But you know Buck Hannon."

"You mean he owes J. Frank dough?"

"Certainly not. It isn't as simple as that. He owes the Merchants Bank for dough he borrowed to take over the station. Frank has a controlling interest in the Merchants, that's all. Besides there's Jentzen's Bread; Frank owns that; it's one of Buck's big accounts. And Cary's Furniture Store has been his since the last depression. But maybe I'm doing Buck an injustice; fact is, he's afraid of public ownership. Might come to radio. That's why he's giving all this time to Pennington and the Repub. Committee."

"See here, if he gives it to them, he should give us a chance to reply. That's fair play. Freedom of speech, both sides get a chance, you know."

"Sure, I know. But it's like the ads in the *Journal*. If we have the money, we can buy space to reply to them. If we haven't, too bad. He'd tell you Pennington and the Repub. Committee buy their time and he'd be glad to sell us time if we can pay the price."

Don glanced out the window across the busy square to the cars parked diagonally against the curb before the County Building. He thought of his office on the third floor, remembered the afternoon they cleaned him out, the tears of the girl in the outer room, the feeling in his heart as he saw the files and the table and the desk being carried through the door. There was the same sudden bitterness he had felt that afternoon. Something's wrong here, something's all wrong.

"Where you speaking tonight?"

"Shedtown. And in the African M. E. Church."

"Don, you ought to save yourself. This thing is peaking up; you'll be worn out before the end. Besides, you've been in Shedtown before. I don't believe any candidate ever went out there once, let alone twice. Or the colored district either."

"They're all citizens. They ought to know what it's about. Besides, lots of the boys work on the night shift one week and the day shift the next week. They want me. Old Piper wants me, too, he wants me again. Says I don't talk down to them."

Yet Don's most active supporters and the hardest workers were the Wildcats. Several things brought this about. In Don they had a friend. For once they had a candidate they knew, not someone who was merely a name to them. Many of the Wildcats who were Republicans were for him, too. Some of the parents tried to interfere without success.

"If I were you, Jane, I wouldn't have much to do with those reds down at Democratic headquarters."

"Oh, Dad, Don Henderson's not a red; he's a basketball coach."

"So . . . maybe . . . but his crowd is. Those CIO boys at Warner Gear are a bunch of communists, and you can't tell me any different. Better stay away from them."

But the high school boys and girls held daily rallies; they flooded headquarters spoiling for work. Every day before school a committee of girls spent an hour cleaning the place up. They swept the whole office, straightened out the mess in the inner room, arranged things on the desks and tables, piled up the campaign literature and material which had spilled to the floor, and generally got the room ready for the regular workers who did not arrive until afternoon. Nor was that all.

They jumped on their bikes after school and ran errands. They spent hours addressing envelopes in large, clumsy handwriting. They checked voting lists. They distributed posters, stickers, and placards all over town. They talked more than one merchant from whom they bought sweaters or class pins into placing Don's photograph in the window beside Dale Pennington's. The more daring carried bunches of small cards with his picture and the words VOTE YES on them. These they handed out on street corners, often to people who discarded them immediately. Others grinned and stuffed them in their pockets.

Sometimes cars were actually parked beside the dingy headquarters on South Superior bearing signs on the windshields: "VOTE RIGHT—VOTE REPUBLICAN;" or "VOTE NO! SAVE SPRINGFIELD FROM COMMUNISM." The owners of the automobiles were not the boys and girls working until all hours of the night inside. As Wilf Benson said one evening at Republican headquarters in the Springfield House: "No use; I've done everything. I've pleaded, threatened, argued with Carlene; can't do a thing. Y'know, I went down to fetch her last night about eleven. Why, say, it isn't a political campaign with those folks, it's a crusade."

Meanwhile Sam Katzmann and Roscoe Stallings, realizing the importance of getting their story across to the people of Springfield, waited on Buck Hannon in his office on the top floor of the Merchants Bank Building. The entire twelfth floor was given over to Station WSWP. You stepped out of the elevator into an elegant waiting hall, with tinted walls, flowers, and an elegant blonde girl sitting as receptionist at a desk in the center. Easy chairs were grouped at the sides. She smiled expectantly.

"Mr. Hannon . . . why, yes, of course. Mr. . . . Mr.? Oh, yes, Mr. Katzmann.

"Won't you go in? This lady will take you to Mr. Hannon's office." Another goddess appeared at a door to escort them down a long hall, past rooms with men working, past other rooms where teletype machines were clattering, into the sanctum where Buck awaited them.

He was a real radio executive, with a double-breasted gray suit, a red carnation in his buttonhole. His blonde hair was pasted straight back from his forehead, his glance was friendly, so was his handshake. His attitude was non-committal, however; if he knew what they wanted, he gave no sign. Although there was some slight nervousness in the quick gesture with which he shoved out the chairs.

"Buck, we were wondering what we could do to persuade you to let Don go on the air."

The big man's glance behind the glasses was bland. His head moved rapidly from side to side.

"No persuasion necessary, Roscoe. The air is free to everyone in this country. And this station here that I run is a public servant. We're open to all the people. I'd guess we actually do more public service in Springfield than any other organization."

"Time on the air costs money. If you haven't got money, you don't get on. It isn't as free as all that, Buck."

Buck's blandness was not punctured. He was in no way upset. "Public service," he said, slowly and distinctly. "We give away more free time than any station in the state. Last year we even gave away more than Fort Wayne or Indianapolis."

Sam interrupted him. "Does the Republican committee pay for all Pennington's time, for those spot announcements, too?"

Buck's expression changed to one of firmness and dignity. "Absolutely. We're under no obligation to give time to a political party. If we did we wouldn't eat. We'd have every crank in town up here. I'm anxious to make this station a public servant, however. Now in the last twelve months . . ."

"Then we must have dough on the line! So? A hundred bucks for a fifteen-minute spot, that's it, isn't it?"

"Why, yes, those are our rates."

"Listen, Buck, we intend to buy time later in the campaign. Right now, we haven't got any too much dough. But I'd like to ask you one question. According to my figures, friend Pennington has had seven talks, the Republican committee has been on the air with the Congressman and four outside speakers, besides a couple of dozen of those spot announcements every day. Think that's fair? Is that giving both sides a chance to be heard?"

His blandness vanished. He squirmed in his chair. "If you folks cannot raise the money, it's not my funeral." His shoulders went up, his head moved to one side, his hands were extended. "However, tell you what! I want to be fair, I want WSWP to be a public servant. So I'll just *give* you the time, yessir, by George, I will. I'll donate a spot to you. There! What could be fairer'n that?" He swung round to the desk and flipped open with practiced fingers a black, loose-leaf notebook ruled off into squares with figures on them. Some of the figures were in red.

"Now then . . . lemme see . . . here's a spot for you. Here we are . . . tomorrow, nope, hold on a sec . . . Wednesday. Wednesday night at eleven forty-five. How's that! Won't cost you a penny either, not one red cent."

The two men went down in the elevator without a word. As they stepped out on the street, Sam looked at his companion. "Never used to understand what old Peedad meant exactly when he talked about the Plunder Boys. Think I do, now; they've got this town in their grip."

"I'll say. Eleven forty-five at night! Imagine! Eleven forty-five at night when most of the town is abed."

"Generous buzzard, public-spirited bloke, ain't he!"

Meanwhile the campaign in the press was just as one-sided. Every day advertisements were smacked over the inner pages of the *Morning Journal.* Daily the citizens of Springfield grabbed their paper from the front porch to read something like this:

"POLITICIANS WRONG, AS USUAL

"Politicians talk about a popular demand for municipal ownership of the light and power plant. There isn't any such bird. Because long ago Indiana folks discovered that municipal ownership and industrial development are like oil and water. They do not mix.

"We hope Springfield people will ask for the facts about the electric company before voting for municipal ownership. If voters believe the unfounded talk of lower rates and lower taxes under municipal ownership, they will vote the city into debt and heavy taxes.

"We, the undersigned, are selfish in our viewpoint. We work for the Central Valley Power Co. The story is that if the city takes over the electric plant, we will lose our jobs. That will be because we are not politicians. Do you want friends and neighbors thrown out of work to satisfy the socialistic schemes of dreamers and impractical idealists?

"Vote NO on election."

•

Then followed a list of twenty-two names of employees of the company, all citizens and voters of the town. Peedad and the little group met to consider the advertisement. The old man was angry. Roscoe was angry; so was Don, so was Sam Katzmann. "Twenty-two names, that means at least forty-four votes. We've got to answer this one right away. We must buy space in the *Journal* tomorrow, and I'll find the money to pay for it," Katzmann said.

The next morning the first advertisement of the campaign on the other side appeared.

"TO THE CITIZENS OF SPRINGFIELD

"For your consideration we present the following facts. Central Valley Power Company has taken an average of $60,000 a year from this town for electric power furnished in Springfield. We believe this money should be spent at home and not distributed to stockholders in other parts of the country.

"We propose to acquire the electric light plant for a fair sum to be determined by arbitration, to continue the services of EVERY employee who wishes to work here at the same pay they are now receiving. And to furnish power to the municipality and private citizens at the same rate as previously.

"Can municipal ownership succeed in Springfield? Why not? It has in Crawfordsville, in Lebanon, in Peru, in Anderson and other towns. What they can do, we can do. Central Valley Power has never lost money here. Last year their net earnings were $64,746.36. This company weathered the depression and even made money doing it. That's why they are spending large sums to convince you not to take possession.

"Friends, don't be misled by false arguments. Don't be afraid of your government. It's you.

"Vote YES."

"DEMOCRATS FOR HENDERSON, INC."

Late that evening, Don left headquarters after a tiring day, a day that included four addresses, numerous conferences with different groups of citizens, and work on the dozens of details needing his attention. His voice was tired and raspy, and he left to get some rest for another long day ahead. As he closed the outside door, a car drew up at the curb and a woman leaned out.

"Is my sister in there, Mr. Henderson?"

At first he didn't recognize her. But not many people in town called him Mr. Henderson, so he knew she wasn't a supporter. Then he saw her face. Rheba Benson.

"Just a minute." He turned back, opened the door, and called to the girl in the rear behind the railing who was banging a typewriter. "Your sister wants you, Carlene."

"She's coming," Don said to Rheba Benson; "she'll be out in a minute."

"She'd better be. Dad's just about sick of this, every night, every single night."

"I've repeatedly told her not to stay here after nine, Miss Benson. There seems to be so much to do. . . ."

"I should think you people would be ashamed. You must be hard up to use kids like my sister. At Republican headquarters we have trained workers, not kids."

Now he was angry. "Look, Miss Benson, don't you think it's kind of a good thing for these kids to take an interest in their own government, to get some training in how it works?"

"No, I don't; not from a bunch of foreigners, not from the gang of reds in there."

"What gang of reds? Sam Katzmann's no red; he always voted Repub. till this fall."

"I mean those CIO people; those foreigners."

"What foreigners? I hear lots of folks hereabouts talking of foreigners. These boys are from this region. Harvey Patterson lived in town all his life. Whitney Moore comes from Centerville. Pat Springer was brought up on a farm at Moorestown."

At that moment Carlene appeared, crossing the sidewalk, her body stiff. Instead of getting in front beside her sister, she carefully opened the door and got in the rear of the car.

"Good night, Don! See you tomorrow," she called out from the back seat.

Don was uncomfortable. "Oh . . . g'night, good night, Carlene." The car moved away.

Thank goodness I'm not in that car between those two this evening, he thought, as he turned up Superior Street toward home.

27

The door to headquarters opened and a white-haired man came slowly down the long room toward the railing. Don, alone at a desk checking reports from the various precincts that had just come in on the morning mail, did not recognize him at first. Then he saw the reddish face, the thick eyebrows, the jaw, and at once remembered the old chap.

Long ago Joe Cassidy had been Springfield, Indiana. Politically, he was the town. As Democratic boss, he ran things, and it was said that he could elect or defeat any man for any office he chose. For years now he had been a legend. Because all this had happened some twenty years ago, before the reform movement when young Frank Shaw, keen, intelligent, idealistic, came from the university to grapple with Joe and eventually overthrow him in an election they still discussed whenever politics were mentioned. Joe retired from the game thereafter, devoting himself to a growing and profitable business.

"Don, I just dropped by to shake hands and wish you luck, boy. Is there any way I can be of use to you?"

Don rose, kicking over the chair by mistake, glancing hastily around the empty room, hoping that a *Journal* reporter wouldn't drop in and find him talking with old Joe Cassidy. It could so easily be misconstrued. "Why, thanks lots, Joe; that's mighty fine of you. Nope, I guess there's nothing much . . . just now."

"Don, I'd like to give you some suggestions—that is, if you wouldn't mind them coming from an old-timer who's been out of harness a long while."

"Of course not, Joe, of course not. I'd sure

appreciate it." Politics and basketball—same thing; everyone wants to coach from the sidelines. Well, I'm used to it. "Go ahead, shoot!" Yet his words were empty. He glanced over the old man's shoulder, trusting no one was peering through the enormous plate glass window that gave onto South Superior. The Shaw crowd would be delighted to discover him in conference with Joe Cassidy.

"Don, see here, I like the way you've run your campaign. You talk plain, and in politics plain-speaking individuals are apt to come out on top. I like the way you've campaigned, too, out there in Shedtown and round the south side and in the colored district. That's smart, hasn't been any of that in this town for goodness knows how long. Folks like the personal touch, they like to have a little link with the candidates who are running for office. That's fine; this enthusiasm you've stirred up, all these youngsters working for you, we need this. You've woken everyone up. But don't go and fool yourself, Don. Enthusiasm won't get votes at the polls."

"Why not?"

"It won't. You are bucking one of the strongest machines in one of the most conservative towns in this conservative state; it's over sixty percent

Republican. To lick it, you have to get to a lot of folks you just aren't reaching now. Many of 'em are frightened by the municipal power issue."

"Good grief, Joe, that surely doesn't scare you. You weren't worried by that ad in this morning's *Journal*, were you?"

"Me? Ah, no. I know Frank Fager too well. Nope, I ain't scared, but lots of the good folks are. Then you made a mistake right at present to call yourself a Democrat. Frank Shaw taught me that lesson years ago; he called his crowd the Reform Party. 'Course, I know he built up a machine that'd make mine look sick. That's all right, that's the way we run things in this country; if you don't like the gang in power, you work to throw 'em out. Only, see, boy, I'm talking to you as a politician, and, Don, when men get behind closed doors in politics, they get mighty realistic; they talk votes, not enthusiasms."

Don wished heartily he was behind closed doors in the back room. Anyone might enter at any moment. Yet he respected the old man's opinion, and the longer he talked with him, the less the name Joe Cassidy seemed to fit the tag it was given in town.

Anyhow, here's a chance to learn something;

this old fella's been round a long while. "What would you suggest, Joe?"

"First, why don't you try to reach the folks I'm thinking about, the good, solid people who usually vote Repub.?"

"How?"

"By forming a non-partisan citizen's committee. I like Harvey and his crowd; they're all good lads, but some folks are frightened of them."

"You tellin' me!"

"Sure! Then why don't you form a non-partisan citizen's committee? Get some of the old line Democrats to join, too—men like Frank James."

"The judge! He's against us. Peedad told me."

"Nope, you're wrong there. He was at first; he isn't now. Guess he's been reading those ads of theirs in the paper. Get a good doctor, get the judge, get that young minister down by the steel mills; his people are all workingmen, he'll stick his neck out."

"Why, sure, but . . ." He looked hard at the old man. This was the person folks talked about, the former town boss, Joe Cassidy who ran Springfield for years and years. Rooked it, too, people said.

"I know what you're thinking, Don. This seems

a funny idea coming from me, man who used to be the Democratic boss. Aren't you?" He leaned over, stretched across the railing, and took Don by the arm. "Listen, boy, I'm a rich man. Every cent came out of trucking, clean money, it is. My old dad came here from Ireland in '83, Don, and settled in this town. He worked with a pick and shovel most of his life, and left me a small livery stable. I ended up by electing the mayor of Springfield and leaving my boy a trucking business worth over a hundred thousand. Now, Don, look at me. Wouldn't I be a heel to chisel on a country like this? Wouldn't I?"

Don looked. He saw a worn old face. He also saw fire in the eyes, that strange fire Peedad had when aroused.

The old man wanted to be believed. Don believed him.

Unknown to them both, unseen, the door opened and a man entered. Don stood there motionless, the old Irishman gripping his arm tightly. Then there was a sudden, unexpected flame, a flash, a noise, and the smell of burning powder.

They turned round. Earl Reynolds, the photographer for the *Journal*, had stopped by on the chance of picking up something for his paper.

Without waiting to be asked, with no invitation to shoot, he acted as every smart cameraman acts when he meets a picture ready and screaming to be taken.

•

That evening before the big rally they sat in the little back room on the hard stiff chairs, Don and Peedad; Harvey Patterson, Roscoe, and Katzmann.

"Personally, I like the idea. I'm for it."

"Me, too."

"And me. But we'd have to work fast; there's only a few weeks left."

"This is the right moment, toward the end of the campaign. It'll have more effect now. We could do the whole thing from here tonight by telephone. Ask, say, twenty, no, say, ten people. Have each person suggest one more. The twenty would be enough. It ought to be nonpartisan, as Don says. All ages, both sexes. Then we could answer that lousy ad in this morning's *Journal* and sign it Citizen's Committee for Henderson."

"Don should answer that at the rally this evening."

"So I will. That ad was something, wasn't it?"

"Yes, but loads of folks won't be there. We can't broadcast it, therefore we can't reach everyone. How're we doing for funds, Sam?"

"We have almost five hundred on hand, and bills for three sixty. Then Bennet gave me a check for a hundred and fifty this morning."

"Roger Bennet! Why, he's a registered Republican."

"Sure he is. He doesn't want anyone to know he gave the money, either. Let me tell you, he isn't the first merchant in town to slip me some dough on the side."

"Say! What do you know about that! O.K., let's see where we stand. Who could we get to head this up? Someone to be chairman who's well known in town, a man everyone knows and respects."

"I know one guy who is all out for Don and isn't afraid to say so, either. He's a Republican, too."

"Who?"

"Doc Jordan. He thinks Don is about one hundred percent."

"That's our man!"

"Doc Jordan, swell!"

"Doc Jordan would be great. He saw the work

you were doing at Juvenile Aid, Don. He was plenty sore when they shut down on you."

"Suppose we start with the Doc as chairman. Who then?"

"Harvey, you ought to be there. Labor should be represented."

"I'd like Dave to be on; the A.F. of L. would want to come along."

"O.K., who else?"

"Jackson Piper's dad."

"And some good woman who's with us. What about Miss Perry at the high school?"

"Right, and the judge. Judge James."

"The judge! Don't believe he would."

"I b'lieve he would. I have reason to think he would."

"All right, what about Mr. Goetz, the minister of the Methodist Church on the south side?"

"Yep, he'll stick his neck out. And Gus Maher, the grocer, he's for Don all the time and doesn't give a damn who knows it."

"I'd like to make one suggestion."

The circle turned toward Don. "This may startle you all a little, but I think we should consider him. And I think he'd help us out lots. Old Joe Cassidy."

They looked at him for a moment in silence. There was a frown on Harvey's face, and Peedad alone nodded. The rest kept still. Finally someone spoke. "What for do you want him on the committee, Don?"

"Because I think he's a good American."

Silence again. Then Sam Katzmann said, "That's the best reason I can think of. Maybe you're right. From what I know of this town, I'd say Joe's all right."

Later that evening Don stood on the platform of the hall in the County Building reading from a slip of paper in his hand. The crowd jamming the room listened with attention. It was surely true that the election was arousing attention in town. Again, after many years, Springfield was getting politically-minded.

"Folks . . . I refer to the advertisement in this morning's *Journal*—'Vote NO and save Springfield.' Now, there are a few facts printed there that need explanation. First of all, it's stated that the cost of buying the Central Valley Power Company's plant might be $300,000, and might be $750,000. That someone is asking you to sign a blank check. This isn't true. City auditors and experts from outside have studied the assets of the company and believe that a fair valuation would not exceed $150,000. This cannot be paid by taxes, nor can one cent be levied against your property.

"Next! That Springfield will lose business if the town takes over the company. Untrue. The employees of the power plant have all been requested in writing to remain at the same rate of pay, if we purchase it. They've been assured of their jobs; we need them badly, we don't want them to leave town. Next! This ad is signed by some twenty workers of Furman Press, on Buckeye Street. They do all the printing for the power company. I'd like to read you the last paragraph of the advertisement as it appeared today. 'Over the past ten years, Central Valley Power has turned some $60,000 into our pay envelopes, all of which has been spent by us in this city. Now we are asked to embark as a municipality in the power business, consequently we will lose this sum. Naturally we're against the idea. Vote NO on Election Day and help save Springfield.' "

A storm of applause rippled over the hall, showing that the meeting had both sides in attendance. He waited until it ended.

"These arguments will be fully answered in

tomorrow's *Journal*; but I'd like to say one thing. There is no intention whatever of taking any business away from the Furman Press or anyone else. No other printing plant in town is equipped with multiple presses to handle this work, and no other concern wants it!"

This time the interruption was as sudden and the noise was louder.

"Just one more thing. The advertisement in my hand states that the city of Peru recently tried to borrow $100,000 from Washington to make up a deficit in their municipal light and power works. This is incorrect. I called the mayor of Peru to check this morning, and he assures me they have never attempted to borrow or borrowed any money from the federal government. Further, within the last few years, the municipal plant in Peru has built a new city building at a cost of $75,000; a city garage which cost $50,000; and a new generator for the water works at a cost of $165,000. Last year the plant showed a profit of $126,000."

The applause was tremendous. But the opponents of the measure were not silenced. A man rose down front.

"I'd like to ask, in view of the uncertain business conditions ahead, aren't you asking us to pledge the credit of our city with little or no security should we be unable to run the electric plant at a profit?"

People leaned forward. Small businessmen from Superior Street; farmers in boots from the surrounding country; young married couples listened intently, watching him.

The hall was quiet. How would he answer? Nice fella, that Don Henderson, but no experience. Kinda impractical sort of chap, ain't he?

"I'll answer that question . . . by going back a little in history, to one of our great men. A man who believed in the people. His name was James F.D. Lanier, and when this state was on the verge of bankruptcy in the Civil War, he lent money to our government without security to save Indiana. Credit? He hadn't any. He relied on the Hoosiers. That's what I'm doing today."

28

Late afternoon. The November sun was setting in a blaze of red. Bad day tomorrow, folks said, looking at the western sky. Slowly the streets grew dimmer, fog settled in over the Wildcat River; it was dusk, it was dark. Men rustled home through the leaves. The time for food, for supper, the time when they poured back from the offices downtown, from the factories and plants, the time for rest. Few citizens of Springfield had time for rest or a regular meal even, that night.

The boys had constructed a small platform on the edge of the sidewalk before headquarters. Not a large one, a small, homemade carpentry job of planks and boards nailed together on the top of several boxes. Strong enough to hold Don, to raise him above the heads on the sidewalk, so the marchers could see him when they went past.

Promptly, as the advertisement in the *Press* had announced that evening, the column started. They went up Buckeye and down Indiana Avenue, through West Walnut to Superior, thus touching or going through almost every precinct in town, and passing headquarters on South Superior Street where Don was to review them. Thence to Forest Park, the scene of the final rally of the campaign held by the Citizen's Committee.

Up front was the high school band. The high school band and yet not the high school band, either. So many protests had been made since they turned out for the celebration weeks before, that the boys and girls were obliged to appear without uniforms. Their instruments, however, belonged to them, and were their own to use as they pleased. So although it was not the entire band, the majority paraded that night.

Directly behind the band was Doc Jordan carrying an enormous white placard.

CITIZEN'S COMMITTEE FOR HENDERSON

He was followed by dozens of people Don had known or seen round town. He caught glimpses of them as they flashed by: Gus Maher, the grocer; George Spencer, the principal at Roosevelt Junior High; Dave Harrison from the Woolworth Store. Next came Whitey Moore heading a crowd of marchers from the housing district. He carried a banner: SPRINGFIELD GARDENS 100% FOR HENDERSON.

After that Harvey's CIO local from the Delco plant who yelled and shouted at Don as they went past; then the boys from Warner Gear, with the steel workers last. They all wore large celluloid buttons. Some of the buttons simply said DON. Others also had the word YES.

Music again. A boy with an accordion rounded the far corner. Song broke into the night air, clear sharp voices could be heard. They had a poignancy that made the little group around the stand glance up. The accordion player was nearing them; behind him, another boy walked backward. He had a stick in both hands, beating time to the music. It seemed as if every colored kid in town was there, singing:

"Let's elect Don Henderson . . .
Henderson . . . Henderson . . .
Let's elect Don Henderson . . .
HE'S . . . OUR . . . MAN. . . ."

They turned and shrieked when they came up to headquarters, and as Don waved back they yelled louder than ever. Over the noise he heard a familiar voice shouting his name. It was Norman Hanscomb in the rows of marchers, waving his hand.

"Hey, Don . . . hey there, Don."

Now he was gone, now they were all gone, vanished into the blackness of the distance. Still he could hear their voices as they faded away.

"He's . . . Our . . . Man . . ."

Then they were upon him. His Wildcats, rank after rank, row upon row. Up front, Jay Hanwell carried a huge sign: HENDERSON FOR MAYOR.

Directly behind, a special group apart, were the ten boys of the team, the championship team, the team that had won the State, his team, all of them. Next, the rest of the Wildcats, divided into precincts, with a junior police captain complete with badge at the head of each precinct.

They carried dozens of familiar, homemade signs.

WE WANT DON
HENDERSON—THE WILDCATS' CHOICE
VOTE YES FOR DON

There's Red, too. Hi there, Red, hi, boy. And the Evans twins, and Russ Spitler, and Chet and Dave and Mary Jo and goodness knows who-all.

Hang it, they're here, they're with me, every single one!

YEA! WILDCATS! YEA! WILDCATS!
HENDERSON—HENDERSON—HENDERSON!

They stood cheering, then they re-formed, yelled again, waved and moved along, cheering as they went between the crowded sidewalks downtown, along Superior. Past Republican headquarters in the Springfield House—that would be Peedad's idea—past the Merchants Bank Building where the lights were on and the

Venetian blinds drawn in Frank Shaw's suite, and so on to Forest Park.

To the park, where he and Perry had gone the night of the State, the night they'd won the Finals, the night Andy was sure the boy would run away north, and they'd pick him up the next morning in Logansport.

Don jumped down. It was over, and the knot of people around the platform turned inside, talking. Sam Katzmann was there, and Roscoe and Harvey and half a dozen others. Don was due at the rally in the park, but there was work to be done, so the volunteers stepped within to begin.

The long, narrow room, an empty store, filled up slowly. At the far end was a low railing dividing the place from side to side, a swinging gate giving access to the rear. The walls were a dingy white trimmed with red. There were campaign posters and stickers and photographs of Don, and maps everywhere, maps of the city, maps of precincts, the same large map that hung in Frank Shaw's office showing Springfield divided off into the twenty-eight separate election precincts, with the Wildcat River cutting the town in two. Wooden chairs, hard, uninviting, were scattered about. Behind the railing, typewriters were banging at half a dozen tables. Carlene and a corps of girls from school had come in and were working intently, heads down, unconscious of the men moving back and forth, of the increasing hubbub, pausing only occasionally to answer the ringing telephones.

"Henderson headquarters . . . Henderson headquarters . . ."

The street door kept slamming. Voices echoed greetings. "G'd evening, Earl! . . . Hullo there, Harry. . . . How are you, Sandy? . . . How are you, boy? . . . Roscoe, I'd like for you to know Jerry Moore, works out to Warner Gear. . . . Bill, how are you tonight? . . . Why, sure's yer a foot high . . . Where's Jack? Has Jack showed yet? . . . Who's covering 14? Jack is! I thought so. That's what I figgered. . . . He worked in our office. I thought he was a Republican. . . . Here's Jack, here comes Jack now. . . ."

More men entered. Short men, tall men, men in sweaters and windbreakers, men with their shirts open at the neck, men in corduroy pants, in leather jackets, men wearing caps and overalls who had come straight from the assembly lines in the plants; women with them, too, women in sheer dresses with cheap hair-dos, girls from school and from the downtown offices, people from the housing project, from the colored district on the south side, from Water Street and Shedtown across the tracks; almost every part of Springfield was represented. They were all talking together; confusion hovered over the smoke-filled room; order seemed an impossibility as they poured in.

Harvey Patterson walked inside the rail, stood at a table up front, and looked the room over. At the sides the different precinct captains were showing their men the boundaries over which they were to work the next day. The faces about him were tired and drawn; many of them, he realized, had been standing all day on the assembly lines and would stand all day in the damp and cold tomorrow outside the polls. He rapped thoughtfully on the table with the end of this pencil. They looked up; he tapped again.

"O.K., everybody. All of you folks grab yourselves a chair."

His spectacles shone in the light above as his head bent over his notes, then came up again.

"Now, boys, all you precinct captains, you

appreciate how important you are in this setup. We've got a tough job tomorrow, a tough job, and we can't win unless we get out every single vote. That means unless you hustle. Each captain has two helpers at the polls. If he hasn't, if they ain't here or they don't show by tomorrow morning at six, get in touch with us right away.

"We've got to see our friends come to the polls and vote. All of 'em. I think we have the organization to do it. The city is divided into four sections, with seven precincts in each section. There's a captain over each section, someone who knows the ropes; his job is to help you out in case of trouble. But should anything unusual happen, let us know immediately.

"No use kidding ourselves, Dale Pennington's a vote-getter. We know why; he's done lots of favors for folks here in town; we all know about the beer racket in town, and the slot machines; we understand why he's fighting the municipal power plant. We know he has the Shaw machine back of him, too. He has plenty of friends in town. O.K., so has Don, plenty, and most of you saw 'em this evening. It'll be close, awful close; and they're smart, so if they think they're likely to be beaten they'll pull anything. We must be prepared for any last minute tricks. Be ready for that, all of you. Realize the importance of this election; let's make sure we get our message across to the voters."

A cough, another cough, resounded in the packed room. "Don't start hauling people to the polls until after seven. Get your invalids out of the way by noon. Should you need legal advice, Roscoe will be at his office with a staff to help; call four sevens. That's seven-seven-seven-seven. Four sevens if you need legal advice. Don't insult anybody out there. Be courteous. Some of 'em 'll say: 'Hey, folks, you gonna let those CIO boys take over your precinct?' They'll try to get you mad; pay no attention.

"Oh . . . one more thing. I've smelt liquor on two men here this evening. That's . . . absolutely . . . out. That's no good . . . at all. If you can't work without that we don't want you.

"Now, the Junior Voters for Henderson. They've done one swell job, and only those of us here at headquarters can appreciate it. I'd like to thank Tom Shaw and his gang; we simply couldn't have functioned without them. These kids have been wonderful. As to their setup and how it'll work out tomorrow—well, guess I'll let Tom tell you himself. Tom! Stand up, boy!"

The tall lad with the crew haircut uncoiled himself from a chair in the rear, and rose, slightly uneasy before the crowd, realizing his position here in Democratic headquarters, surrounded by men his father had fought for years. Heads turned, men stretched to see the All-State center, the son of J. Frank Shaw, Republican committeeman from Indiana. All the time he was speaking or Harvey was talking, the phone jangled. And Carlene or Anola answered: "Henderson headquarters . . . Henderson headquarters . . ."

"Well, Harvey, the gang is ready, I believe. We've got things organized; four cars for each precinct to haul voters, and ten kids on bikes as messengers. There's three girls attached to each precinct to sit with kids while their mothers vote. Then we have a pool of five cars and twenty messengers who'll be here at headquarters on call from five-thirty in the morning. Should your kids not report, please call me here. But . . . they will."

A burst of applause, quick, hearty, broke out. Heads moved together along the rows of chairs. Eyes were raised approvingly. Kid's different from J. Frank, ain't he! Say, you know, he's not the same kettle of fish as his dad.

Harvey rose again. "Now we'll check the precinct captains and their helpers. Want you all to stay till we finish, 'cause Don is coming in after the rally at the park to say a few words. O.K., Precinct One. I'll call out the captain's name and his workers. If they ain't here, sing out. Sing out good and loud, so's I can hear you. Number One! Earl Hasler . . . Paul Douglas . . . and Herman Bencke."

"Check!"

"Number Two. Harry Preston . . . Hazel McRoberts . . . and Dennis Divine."

"Check!"

All the time and continually the smoke settled lower in the room, the air became heavier, the phone jangled, and the girls, their voices strained now, replied.

"Henderson headquarters . . . Henderson headquarters."

Ten-thirty. Eleven. Eleven-thirty. It was nearly midnight before the checking was finally complete.

Harvey spoke to the rear of the room. "What time is it . . . quarter till twelve? Has he come yet? He is! Don, come up front, boy, and say a word to the fellas, will ya? Just a word before we send 'em home." A figure moved from the dimness beside Tom Shaw, and came toward the railing, through the gate, and stood facing them. There was no noise or applause. They were exhausted, and this was only the beginning. They knew it, too.

"Now before Don speaks, you understand, don't you, I want every one of you here at five-thirty for final instructions. Want you to be at the polls when they open at six; we'll take you out in cars from here. Don't forget; it depends on us all tomorrow, each one of us. We want to work together, we want harmony, we want help. One more thing. Sam Katzmann says the finance committee is to meet in the back room directly we finish here."

He sat down, a list in his hand, and started checking it. Don came to the table under the light. The crease in his forehead was deeper, and his eyes were reddening. In his hand was a small, white piece of paper, several inches square.

It was like the last few minutes before the Finals of the State, when you were all set and ready to go, when you'd told them everything you could, when words weren't really much use anymore, when the team was there before you, when you felt them as a team, as a unit of which you were a living part.

"I want first off to thank you, each and every one, for this . . . for what you've done. I want to thank Harvey for his great organizing work all fall, and Sam Katzmann who collected the money to keep us going, lots of it from merchants along Indiana Avenue who gave to Sam when they wouldn't to anyone else in town. I want to thank all you folks who gave dollar bills and quarters; and Roscoe, and Tom Shaw for his wonderful hard-hitting outfit. All of you, every single man and woman. Believe me, it's something to see you, to work with you, to be one of you.

"Now I have no idea how we'll come out tomorrow. I know we have 'em scared. I know if we put up the kind of a scrap we can, we'll be in there or thereabouts at the end. In basketball there's only one play that counts; putting the ball through the hoop. In politics it's getting out the vote. Let's us get our folks to the polls. If we do, we'll win, and if we win it'll be on account of the support you people here, you men and women, put out with this fall."

The outburst was real. They cheered and they meant it, too. "Whatever happens, this organization, win, lose or draw, will continue. The Citizen's Committee is not going to wind things up tomorrow night; no, sir, it's too important for that. We're going on, fighting for this town, for Springfield, for you folks here and your kids. There's a lot of things I'd like to say about it, and so forth, but I'm going to end up with a few words, 'cause I know you're pretty near done in. So'm I." He coughed twice. His voice was going fast. "I'd just like to read you good people some of the stuff our friends over across the way are sending to the voters. Many thousand of these have been distributed. It's made me pretty sick. Here 'tis."

He held up the little white sheet. The men close to the front saw it was six or seven inches long and four or five wide. They could read the top lines.

" 'Wake up, Americans!' " His voice was hoarse. Or was it grimness?

" 'Join the crusade to save America from communism and foreign domination. Make no mistake. It's either Dale Pennington or Russians and Communists who want to run our lives, tell us what to do, and saddle our city with socialistic schemes for municipally-owned power plants. This is the opening wedge.

" 'Rally! Help save the homes of America and your personal freedom.

" 'Vote Pennington and Republican for God and Country. Your ballot is secret. Only God and you will know how you vote.' "

He stopped, and his head came up in the light. Silence over the room. Someone in the rear coughed; otherwise there was no sound, no movement among the weary crowd. Only tight lips, anger on the drawn, white faces of the men in windbreakers and leather jackets.

"Boys, there's no signature and no way of knowing who wrote this. Most likely we can guess. There's just one thing I'd like to say. I believe in America. I believe America belongs to the people. But . . . there . . . is . . . no room . . . in America . . . for these kind of people.

"Let's us go and knock the hell out of 'em tomorrow!"

They rose, every man, every woman, every

kid, yelling, fighting mad as they turned toward the door. Chairs banged together, scraped against the floor; a dozen, a hundred hot voices mingled while they squeezed through the door into the cool, damp morning air without.

29

Four twenty-eight A.M. The little group slouched out into the damp morning air, drawing coats around their throats, and across the street to the lunch wagon, almost the only place open in Springfield at that hour. The red sign, EATS, hanging out over the sidewalk and visible far up and down the street, glowed in the misty blackness.

They slumped inside, quiet, tired, exhausted, and sat in two booths. It was the first food Don had taken since luncheon the previous day.

By the time they crossed back to headquarters, the clock out by the Merchants Bank Building at the corner showed almost five. Several cars were parked at the curb beside headquarters. They were covered with colored paper streamers, banners and posters of all sorts. Around the corner of Indiana Avenue another car came toward them, then another rumbled down the silent stretches of Superior Street. Somewhere a church bell sounded five times.

Harvey stood with Peedad by the door. They were checking the men arriving, on the large city map which showed the various precincts. "Bill, you take Earl and Claude. Mac, you're in 22, aren't you? You go west, take Virgil and Sam. Carl, you're south . . . in 6 . . . that's right. Tom! Where's Tom! Tom, will you run Sam and Mrs. Shuler and Wilbur Reed out to South Jackson, and then stop at the Willard School and pick up Victor Jones and his brother; they're on 14."

Don stood watching the two weary men. And others, equally weary, who shuffled through the door—the workers at the polls, privates in the army, men on whom victory depended. They would do the work, the dirty work, like all privates, and take little of the glory. Many of them had been standing all the previous day on the assembly lines in the plants; they would be on their feet in damp and cold and perhaps in pouring rain until eight that evening. What for? Not for fun nor yet for money, either. Not for jobs nor for reward. For nothing. And not for nothing. They were doing it for America.

Who said you couldn't get folks interested in politics? Who said you couldn't get folks to work for something in which they believed, for their country?

Don went from one to another, shaking hands, saying a word of thanks, of encouragement, of support, only to find each man was concerned with him.

"Don, we have that precinct all sewed up. Don-boy, don't you fret 'bout 12. . . . We'll put it over, boy. You get yourself some rest. . . . You're beat. Looks like you're all tuckered out, Don. Go get yourself some sleep. When you wake up, you'll be mayor of this here town!"

A car started through the black silence outside. Then another. Two girls came through the door and without a word went to the back of the room, took off their coats, and sat down to work. A telephone jangled, and one answered.

"Citizen's Committee for Henderson."

"Don!" It was Harvey, shaking him by the arm. He was almost asleep on his feet. "Don, what say you and I and Peedad take a swing round and check up just to see everything is O.K. The captains are on the job, but I'd like to follow up a little." The three men climbed into Harvey's ancient Chevrolet and the car swung down Superior to the nearest polling place, the Lincoln School. It was still dark and cold, an early morning, piercing cold. On the concrete walk leading to the front entrance, two men and a woman were stomping their feet, trying hard to keep warm as they waited for the first voters. Inside the basement a light showed; people were moving round a long table; it looked warm and cozy.

Don and Harvey and Peedad came slowly up the walk. They exchanged words with the men, their hands stuffed into their overcoat pockets. Vaguely Don heard them through his fatigue. "Don't start hauling for another hour yet . . . get your invalids out of the way by noon, Chester."

Leaves fluttered down on the concrete in a sudden gust. Far down the street a car came toward them, its motor loud in the stillness of the moment. Don thought of his country, and the cities all over the country like Springfield, and the villages and towns where men and women were doing the same thing at this same moment. He felt America. He felt democracy.

Cold, silent, they piled back into the car, turned the nearest corner, drove a few blocks to the next voting place, a hose house. Here a fire of wood and boxes was burning, and the watchers were standing round cheerfully. They greeted Harvey with enthusiasm. These boys were sure of themselves and their precinct.

"Don, don't you worry about this precinct. Run along, Harvey, run along and leave us take care of it."

"Got any Repubs. here, boys?"

"Why, yes, Peedad, a few."

"How many?"

"'Bout enough to spit on."

So to 12, to 16, to 3, to 2. To the Roosevelt School; to Shedtown, where Mike Cray was standing beside his bike, and rushed up quickly to Don. "We're gonna win today, Don. We're gonna lick 'em, you wait and see!" Then on to 19, to 5, to 4 where the polling booth was in a grocery store.

It was not quite so dark now; the faint glimmer of morning was in the air, the polls were open, men and women were lining up outside the lighted interiors. Don noticed them carefully. They were all serious; no one was joking or laughing; no one was even talking. They felt it. They felt America as he did.

Daybreak was nearly on them when they returned to headquarters. By this time the room was a confused mass going and coming; cars were driving up outside and moving away; kids were grabbing their bikes parked on the curb and rushing off, or were returning with messages and packages; workers in corduroy pants and leather jackets shoved inside. Behind the railing at the far end the ringing of the telephone continued.

"24? Yep, we'll get someone right over."

"Hello. Citizen's Committee for Henderson. At 18? He didn't show! He didn't? O.K., right away." Carlene put down the phone and looked up. "Harvey! 18 is short a man."

"18! That's the Willard School. That's Skinner. We just came from there. He can wait; he has that one under control."

"Mary Jo, the 15th precinct has no captain. Jake is sick, his wife says."

"Citizen's Committee for Henderson."

Don's head buzzed. He had a bad headache, and retired to the quiet of the small room in the rear, where he collapsed on a chair. The *Journal* was on the desk at his side, as well as a special morning edition of the *Press*, out early because of election. The ballot was printed on the front page of both papers.

"SAMPLE BALLOT

"Shall the city of Springfield, Howard County, Indiana, purchase, acquire or condemn and operate the public utility located in the serving said city, used and useful in furnishing electric utility service to the City of Springfield, which said electric utility is now owned by the Central Valley Power Company, Inc.

"YES. To vote in favor, mark an X in this square.

"NO. To vote against, mark an X in this square."

He turned to the editorial in the *Press*. It was Peedad himself, that editorial, for more than once Don had heard him say things of the sort. Characteristically, on Election Day he did not mention candidates but things in which he believed—that he felt were more important than candidates or local issues.

"This paper has always been run on two principles. They were Lincoln's principles. The first is that the people should be told the truth; and that if you tell them the truth they'll make the right decision every time. The second is not original either. But lots of Americans had to die for it in the last 170 years. If they hadn't, we wouldn't be here now. It's this: Springfield belongs to the people."

Not to the J. Frank Shaws, thought Don, adding the phrase Peedad always used in this connection. The editorial ended:

"And this newspaper believes that if the people of this town know the truth, we can have a city good enough for Lincoln."

By Heaven, we can, too. And if I have anything to say about it, we will.

He picked up the *Journal*. There was a large advertisement splashed half across the page.

" 'NO' WILL SAVE SPRINGFIELD

"Your vote of 'No' will save the city of Springfield from:

"1. A blank check to be filled in later at your expense by the politicians.

"2. Costly litigation, which you will pay for, covering perhaps years and years.

"3. Higher taxes for you to pay.
"4. Higher power rates for you to pay, also."
"5. 6. 7. 8. Politics; politics; politics."

Shoot! Why can't they play fair? What's the matter with those folks, anyhow! He tossed the paper to the floor. They must be scared to give out like that. Rising, he walked out into the big room. Confusion and clamor assailed his aching head. The ringing phones, the noisy typewriters, the milling, chattering crowd hurt. A man in a checked mackinaw came toward the rail.

"Hey there, you fellas, I just heard this Benton, this commentator Buck has, give out with a special broadcast. He called us folks commies. Says the CIO is communist. I was going out to Royertown hunting; I ain't now. Anything I can do to help here?"

Harvey was instantly at his side. What did Benton say? Exactly what did he say?

"Don! Where's Don? Don, we should crack down on that hard before too many people get to the polls. Mary Jo! See if you can find Buck Hannon on the phone. If he's not at his office, try his home. Sure, wake him up. We must answer that, Don; it can do us plenty of harm round town." He grabbed the telephone. His lips were tight. "Buck! G'd morning. This is Harvey Patterson. Buck, we'd like five minutes of time this morning to answer your man Benton. . . . No time. . . . You haven't any? What's that? Commitments! Boy, you better find time, this is Election Day. . . . I say you better find time. . . . I'm not threatening you, I'm telling you. . . . Ever hear of the Federal Communications Commission? You have! O.K., think they'd like to know we couldn't get five measly minutes on your station . . . that we were refused time this morning because of your commitments with Janzen's Bakery and Carey's Furniture Store? Do you? O.K., O.K., Buck, you call me back here in ten minutes."

He was angry as he rang off. "We'll get you on, or we'll all go up there and take Buck Hannon and throw him out."

"But, Harvey . . . five minutes, even, that's dough! That's thirty or forty bucks! Where'll we get the money? We're scraping on rock bottom now. And we'll have to put it on the line; he won't trust us today or send any bills."

Harvey took a battered billfold from his pocket. "Here's six bucks. All I got." He smacked it down on the table.

"My local'll give five bucks."

"And mine, too. Here 'tis."

A girl shoved a dollar out. Someone else threw a bill on the table; now they were a small pile, growing higher, higher, as angry men closed in, tossing out coins, emptying purses.

An hour later, Don and Harvey and Peedad walked down Superior to the Merchants Bank Building. Cars flashed past carrying large posters, many decorated with colored streamers of ribbon or paper; others honked loudly as they noticed Don on the sidewalk. There was a holiday atmosphere, the shops and taverns and stores were shut as on Sunday, but an un-Sabbath-like excitement spread over everything. People spoke to them as they went past, and Hank, the traffic cop on the corner, said, "G'd morning, Don."

A sound came toward them. It issued from a highly decorative truck with an enormous picture of Dale Pennington covering the front. Under the photograph was a large sign.

"VOTE NO! SAVE SPRINGFIELD!"

Sounds came closer, a voice assaulted the trio as the truck drew nearer. It was a smooth, oleaginous voice, odiously persuasive or meant to be.

" . . . So, folks, if you really want democratic government in your city . . . that means the kind of government on which our nation was founded . . . if you're against socialism and other things of that kind, and I know you are, support Dale Pennington and the whole Republican ticket. Don't forget to vote NO, either. And remember, experience counts. You wouldn't hire a boy to run your business, would you? No, of course not. Well, folks, why put one in charge of the city's business?"

The noise disappeared as they went in the door and stepped inside the elevator. Old Matt, the janitor, sitting on a stool, looked up from the morning *Journal*.

"Why, Don! Good luck to you, boy, good luck. We're behind you in this, yes, sir."

The beautiful receptionist was missing from the outer room of Station WSWP on the top floor. They wandered unescorted down the hall, to find a far from bland Buck Hannon. His face was worried. He took them into a large empty studio, with a piano and some musical instruments against the wall. Behind a glass partition along one side of the room were two engineers who waved at them cordially. The three sat round a table over which a microphone was suspended.

Buck hovered about them. "Do you . . . Shall

I bill you for this, Peedad . . . Harvey? Or how do you want . . ."

Harvey looked across the table at Don, and pulled a roll of bills tied with an elastic from his pocket. "Guess you'll find it all there, Buck." He turned back to Don.

Now they were alone. In a few minutes one of the men behind the glass partition nodded approvingly and smiled. He raised his head. Then his arm went up. It came down suddenly, one finger pointing at Don.

In a husky, tired voice Don began.

"Friends, voters of the city of Springfield. The Citizen's Committee has bought this five minutes so I could remove some misconceptions that seem to have sprung up over the issues in these last few minutes of the campaign. One of them is about the members of the CIO who have steadily supported the Democratic candidate in this election.

"Folks, these people have been called a good many names, and today, only a short while ago, they were called communists. They don't like it; neither do I; it hurts them and it hurts me. I'd like to say that as basketball coach here I knew most of their kids, and never thought about 'em one way or the other, 'cept as Americans. I didn't know their parents. But since this campaign started three months ago, I've got to know the fathers and mothers of these same kids, men and women who work in our town; who work, well, in Delco and Warner Gear and Chrysler, maybe alongside some of you people. Folks . . . why, they're no more communists than you are!

"Some of 'em have been called foreigners in my hearing. Well, a few of 'em were born in Europe, if that makes a man a foreigner. Pete Wyzanski, for instance. Lots of you on the south side know Pete. And Sam Katzmann, I guess nearly everyone in town's acquainted with Sam, and Dave Wolchuk. These men, seems like, were born abroad. So were our ancestors—all of 'em. What of it? Can't foreigners be patriotic, too?

"Now I've only got a few minutes left, and I'd like to read the program for America sent out from CIO headquarters to all the locals, a program to which these people subscribe. They believe in it. They think it's good for our country. So do I. Here it is . . . and I'm quoting now.

" 'We are for:

" 'A job for everyone who wants to work.

" 'Fair wages for every worker.

" 'The protection of the rights of labor.

" 'A good home for every family.

" 'Medical care for all who need it.

" 'A chance for everyone to become educated.

" 'Insurance for the sick; aged; crippled.

" 'Fair play with all nations.

" 'If you are for these things, you are with us.'

"That's the end of the quotes, folks. That's the end. And I'd like to say I'm with 'em, too." He paused. His time was up now, and Buck Hannon was running furiously round the control room, fussing, stewing, but the two engineers pretended not to notice him and they didn't shut Don off.

"Folks, what's un-American about that program? If we had all those things here in Springfield, we might have . . . a city good enough for Lincoln."

30

Three P.M. Still cold and damp, still no rain falling. The antique Chevrolet swung up to the Frederick Douglass School and stopped at the curb. Harvey got out and went up the walk.

"Hello, Jackson. How's things going—and where's your dad? Oh, hello, Mr. Piper, how's it going?"

"First rate, looks fine. Them fellas killed any chance they had in this precinct this morning. They sent half a dozen cars through scattering these kind of things round." He handed Harvey a sheet of paper with the words:

VOTE REPUBLICAN
VOTE REPUBLICAN IF YOU KNOW
WHAT'S GOOD FOR YOU!

"We'll run up a big plurality, Harvey, a big one."

"Looks O.K. here. I only wish it was like this everywhere round town. I'm mighty worried about 16." He walked back and climbed into the car. "Let's us have a look at 16, Don."

Along the way they passed one of their own cars buried in colored streamers, prowling slowly along the street, stopping here and there to pick up voters on the sidewalk and drive them to the polls. A man at the wheel yelled to a passer-by:

"You voted, Sam? We'll vote you. Jump in; we'll vote you and bring you back home."

"That was Smoky, wasn't it? He's sure on the job, Smoky is."

"I expect that was him." A boy on a bicycle whizzed past, waving to Don and shouting at him. The boy's face was familiar, but Don was too tired to remember him. They drew up, parked the car and got out. The polling place was the basement of a small church on the corner, and a line of people were standing patiently before a table on the sidewalk, having their names checked off. The man in charge of the workers came forward.

"Hullo there, Harvey. Hi, Don."

"Hullo, Bill. Know anything new?"

"There's about eighty or ninety gone in so far."

"H'm. Not voting fast, are they?"

"No, they ain't." His face had a troubled expression. Harvey nodded.

"Think we'll send you a couple of cars and two extra helpers, Bill. This is a busy precinct and it's running behind out here. C'mon, Don, let's us take a look at 5."

Precinct 5 was the Roosevelt School where they had stopped in the early darkness of the morning. Now everything was changed; the workers were no longer stomping their feet on the concrete walk, there was life and movement all around, and a gang of boys standing in a circle was ribbing an elderly cop whom they knew to be a Republican. He pretended not to notice them and greeted Don affably. But he wasn't enjoying himself.

A familiar face detached itself from the people

round the entrance to the school, and came toward them with a long, white voting list in one hand.

"Harvey, say, what can I do about this? We've had a lot of our good voters thrown out 'cause it seems they ain't registered." He leaned over the side of the car anxiously. Harvey recognized him as one of the men who had been drinking the previous evening at headquarters; he was sober enough now, and worried.

"Haven't they got their registration receipts? You must have a receipt if you're registered."

"Nope, they haven't."

"I was afraid of this. Y'see, Don, the Repubs. were in power in this country, and J. Frank had a lot of deputies with lists checking from house to house. That gave folks the impression they were registering people. If you were on their side, they told you to go and register; if you weren't, they left you feeling you'd been registered and that was the end of it."

"Shucks, Harvey, can't we do nothing? Look at that line." The man pointed to a line of people standing outside the entrance to the basement of the school.

" 'Fraid not. They'll have to lose their votes

and learn the hard way. That's why we went after 'em ourselves. Otherwise how you coming?"

"Otherwise just fine. We got most everyone voted, and say, Don, your kids are something! Down to Mrs. Gray's, they tended the kids, tidied up her house, did the dishes and made beds, so she and her old ma could come up and vote. And one lady on South Jackson, why, darned if those girls didn't do the wash while she was up here voting."

"Good, that's great. Where's Sandy?"

"Sandy?" He looked around. "He must be out hauling."

"O.K. Watch it, boy, these last hours are mighty darn important."

They moved away. As they did so, they heard a woman's voice calling to a boy, one foot on the pedal of his bicycle by the curb. "Take a look at my home, Earl. See if everything's all right."

They went down the street. The sun was trying hard to break through the clouds of late afternoon and not quite succeeding, though the mist had disappeared. "What time is it, Don?"

"Three minutes till four."

"Let's get back. These boys are on the job

out here." They went toward the center of town, down Indiana Avenue and up South Superior to headquarters. Cars were stopping, leaving people, moving along; others were parking, the drivers going away; kids were coming and going on bicycles. Inside the noise was as bad, the confusion as great as ever. Harvey came down the long room toward the railing, to be assaulted by half a dozen voices, and surrounded before he could remove his hat and coat. He stood listening. Then he answered, advised, suggested, arranged his forces.

"Sure, you just gotta watch that, Steve. They vote early, then they challenge lots of our voters so's we'll get discouraged and go home without voting. Watch it, that's why we put you on that precinct; it's a tough one. Cora May! Send two of your best workers to Bill Stokes in 16; he's falling behind. Bedford and South Jackson. Who called? Who? Whitey Moore? What's biting him? I thought we had the housing project all sewed up; we were counting on that."

"He thought so, too. Only the county commissioners assigned the Gardens to a polling booth way the hell and gone out on the edge of Austin Avenue, at Hose House 12."

"Austin Avenue! That's pretty nearly at one end of the Heights."

"Sure as yer a foot high! And the folks at the housing project must either walk a mile and a half through those fields, or else drive way round by the Wolf Construction plant and up Memorial Drive."

"O.K.! Dan, you and Pete get right out there and help Whitey Moore. Have Tom Shaw assign you a couple of cars, and mind you clean that up. It's a bad situation; we need the housing project the worst way; we can't win without it. There's not much time, so hustle up."

Two men went out the door. Someone spoke to Harvey.

"How 'bout 13? How you feel about 13?"

"I was a mite worried till we plugged that up."

One girl at the telephone interrupted. "Pee-dad! Harvey! Bill Hayes in 12 needs help. Says there's been a heap of discriminatory challenges coming in the last hour; he can't handle 'em all."

"12! That would be Wabash Avenue. Harry, you and I'll run out and have a look. Want to come along, Don?"

5 P.M. Dusk. On the way back to headquarters

they rode through the colored district, and slowed down by the Douglass School. There was a huge bonfire going, and a crowd stood around in the growing chilliness of evening. Hoarse gaiety and laughter could be heard as they drove past. An enormous sign was affixed to a gatepost.

BIG BARBECUE AT TRINITY CHURCH
AT 6:30.

A boy ran past, shouting in a high voice, "168 to 47 for Henderson! Henderson 168 to 47!"

"I sure hope the kid's right," remarked Don.

"Same here. No use talking, it looks like it'll be close. I felt it would be close, and it will be close. But I believe the power plant'll win out, anyway."

At a desk behind the railing in headquarters, Mary Jo sat with a large sheet before her on which to tabulate the results as soon as they arrived by phone or messenger. Soon the polls would close, the leaders in the various precincts would start coming in with their reports, usually accurate, on how things stood. The crowd waited in the smoky, crowded room, knowing by now that a handful of votes miscounted by a careless worker in a busy precinct could lose the election. It grew darker outside; then the lights came on along Superior Street, and the big EATS sign on the lunch wagon across the way illuminated the front of the building.

Suddenly there was a yell from the door.

"Here's Paul. Paul Douglas."

A Negro with a slip of paper pushed eagerly up to the railing and leaned over. "206 to 65 for Don. Yes, by 150 votes." Another yell went up. This was a good beginning.

Then a tired and dirty man in a worn leather jacket entered. His eyes were red around the edges.

"Here's 12."

"And here's 15."

Mary Jo grabbed the papers and wrote down the figures. They stood behind her watching, Harvey and Peedad and Sam Katzmann and Don and the others, saying nothing, thinking, speculating on the results to come. If we can only swing 14 . . . if Jake comes through in 5 . . . if we hold this margin in 7 . . .

The telephone rang. Carlene answered.

"Citizen's Committee for Henderson." Her face became serious, a frown came on her forehead.

"Missing! It is! Say . . . you better talk to Harvey. It's Whitey Moore."

"Hey there, Whitey. What's cookin'?"

The voice of the man was tired and husky. "Harvey, they done gone and stole the ballot box."

"Stole it! How could they with all you fellas out there, with Dan and you and Pete? How could they?"

"That's what we'd like to know. Can't locate it nowhere."

"What the hell were you boys doin'—sittin' and talkin' in the courthouse square?"

"No, sir, no, Harvey. Honest, it come up missin' when they started to count the votes . . . it was gone in no time."

"But . . . did you talk to Roscoe?"

"Yes, sir. He's been here the best part of half an hour with a detective from City Hall . . . from police headquarters."

Harvey's head hummed. The ballot box of the housing project gone. That meant they'd lose the votes from Springfield Gardens, on which they counted, which they must have. "O.K., Whitey, lemme handle this." He rang off. "Seems they've pinched the ballot box from the housing project."

Silence over the room. Someone whistled. Then a sober voice remarked, "They better find it—and quick. That's the 486 votes we need to win right now. Can't win without the housing project!"

At that second a boy edged forward. He had no cap or coat on, his sweater was frayed and worn, and his shoes were scuffed at the toes. He was breathless, excited, and red of face. The men, lost in contemplation of what it meant to have the votes of the housing project gone, paid no attention. Persistently the boy shoved through and into the circle to Don's side.

"Hey there . . . Don!"

He looked down. "Why, Roy! Hello, Roy, what's up, boy?"

"The ballot box . . . from the housing project . . . they're planning to burn it . . . and dump the stuff into the . . . Wildcat . . . below Stony Point."

Everyone turned, everyone looked. For a moment only Don took him seriously. "What makes you think so, Roy?"

"I heard 'em! I trailed 'em myself. Then I put my brother on 'em while . . . I came down here. Ya better hustle, Don, ya better move quick!"

"Your brother! You mean Jimmy? Why, he's only ten."

"Yeah . . . he's smart though. I can take you there, Don, if ya hustle."

Then Harvey stepped in. "Let me handle it, Don. You phone City Hall, have Andy ready in a police car. We'll pick him up on the way past. Come along, kid, you come along with me, and you, Sam, and you, too, George. Tom, gimme your fastest car. We'll stop and pick up Andy to make it official."

31

The room was completely jammed with the tired men from the battlefront, more tired than ever now, and snatches of hoarse voices rose in the smoky air—triumphant, downcast, excited, elated, or despondent according to the results from the various precincts. For most of them knew within a few votes how their district had gone.

"Still and all, we got eighty-five percent out . . . that's something, that is."

"Mine had eighty-nine percent."

"Mine had eighty-six."

"Hullo there, Joe, how are you?"

"Me! I'm no good, boy, I'm all in."

"I'm not much account, neither."

"Lemme tell you it'll be close; it's close all right; few hundred votes one way or the other."

". . . And so we slipped a big Republican button on the guy, and when he comes up to the table, why, we just pretended not to see him. Know what? They give him a ballot and he votes! How's 'at?"

"465 to 212. I'd call that organization, boy, wouldn't you?"

"Why, say, they was votin' dead men out in my precinct." The voice rose. "I know they was . . . I kin prove it."

There was an interruption, a break in the hubbub, as a man came through the street door. He had a newspaper in his hand, and was waving it.

"*Journal* says it's Pennington by 314."

Instantly he was surrounded. The crowd gathered around as he held the early edition at arm's length, so they could all read it. But most of them couldn't get near enough, and shouted at him to read it to them. He stood on a chair, extending the paper so everyone could see the headlines, moving it round from one side to the other.

SPRINGFIELD SAVED.
PENNINGTON BY 314.

They watched silently, the noise and conversation died away. He read:

"The city of Springfield in an election that made its citizens fighting mad, rejected municipal ownership of the local power plant, socialism and other isms in a smashing victory for law and order by electing Dale Pennington and the entire Republican ticket."

"Smashing victory . . . how's Frank Fager get that way."

"Sh . . . sh!"

The man on the chair continued. "Early returns tabulated at this office indicated a narrow majority of about 314 votes for Pennington in twenty-two election precincts of the city, with a few scattered districts, unlikely to change the final result, still to be heard from. The 'No' majority on the municipal power issue will be closer, but it is anticipated that . . ."

Someone broke away from the circle and burst into the room in the rear. It was as quiet here as it had been noisy outside. At a desk sat Mary Jo adding, checking, and re-adding the figures on a large chart. Roscoe Stallings leaned over her shoulder; Peedad sat at her side by the desk, watching with attention. Only Don, leaning back in a chair against the wall, chewing gum, and Doc Jordan, walking restlessly back and forth, were apart.

"The *Journal's* just come out with a special early edition. They give the election to the Repubs. by 314 votes!"

Doc whirled round and stood motionless. Don stopped chewing. Peedad glanced up. Mary Jo's pencil was suspended. They looked at each other. This was it.

"There go the 486 votes from the housing project. We might have squeezed through with those."

The telephone on the desk jingled. Mary Jo answered. "Citizen's for Henderson . . ."

Well, thought Don, it was close, it was mighty close; we put up a good fight, a grand good fight; by ginger, we made a fight of it. Somehow it's kinda like losing a ball game by a single basket, by three or four points. You get to thinking of all those fouls you made, and the free throws you missed and hadn't ought to of . . .

"No, we don't. No, we do not . . . nothing official . . . I say we have no official figures as yet. WSWP says the whole thing is still in doubt! Well, I'll be glad to ask him for you. Hold on a sec and I'll try to get hold of him." She placed her hand over the mouthpiece. "The *Journal* wants to know will you concede, Don?"

"Concede hell!" Peedad spoke. "Of course we won't concede! Here . . . just hold on a minute." He scribbled some words on a pad, words that rapidly became sentences. Tearing the sheet off, he handed it to her.

Again she spoke into the telephone. "Will you please take this down? Quotes. At an early hour, Don Henderson, the Democratic candidate, refused to concede Pennington's election. A spokesman for the Citizen's Committee for Henderson said. Quotes. Our standard bearer has waged a good, clean, fighting campaign. Win or lose, he has succeeded in waking this town up on some of the fundamental issues which confront America today. He also got out the largest vote the city of Springfield has ever had."

•

The police car swung down Indiana Avenue and turned into Michigan. It bumped over the tracks on the edge of the city, passed the small wooden one-story houses of Shedtown, and went out along the Frankfort road. The boy in the front seat, wedged in between Andy at the wheel and Harvey Patterson, was tense and excited. So, too, were the others, even though they could not feel the holster of Andy's pistol against their thighs.

On into the darkness. The car swept down the long, straight road, on past the farms in the misty blackness, when Roy touched Andy's arm. "It's somewhere about here, Stony Point is. We ought to be seeing my brother."

As he spoke, the car slowed down and lurched to the left. Andy slapped on the brakes and brought it to a stop. He opened the window, leaned out, and began backing up hastily.

"Like to kill the boy, like to kill the kid . . . never saw him till I was atop of him," he muttered.

Then a breathless youngster, running along with a bicycle almost as tall as he was, came up from behind. He was a tiny, forlorn figure in the gloom of the patch of trees and the wood where they had stopped.

"They're up ahead, 'bout fifty yards. To the right . . . to the right!"

Andy got the last words as the car was off and moving ahead. In second gear they went forward, cautiously searching the roadside to the right. Sure enough. There was a small clearing in the clump of trees, and a kind of pathway in through a broken-down gate. Andy swung the wheel over, and the car thumped along a muddy, overgrown path. As it swung round, the lights showed a car standing further inside the trees. A man was holding the back door open, and two men were lifting a box from inside.

Andy threw the hand brake on so hard that Roy's forehead smacked the windshield with a bang. He jumped out before the car had ceased quivering from the shock, and strode ahead, unbuckling his holster at his hip.

"You boys got anything there I'd be interested in?" he said.

32

Don came stumbling up the steps to the platform in the park, hoarse, tired, triumphant. It was a great fight, a grand good fight, and we came through.

If only I wasn't so dry and thirsty. One more speech, only one more; one more speech and it's over, and I can go home and sleep. And sleep and sleep. But I'd sure like a drink now.

"Anyone got any water . . . someone . . . a glass of water, please."

Instantly a bottle of coke and a paper cup appeared, and were shoved in his hands just as he reached the top step of the platform. Before he could drink he was pushed out front by the people surrounding him, by his friends, by the men who had done the fighting in the lines, by their officers also; by Peedad and Harvey and Tom Shaw and Whitey Moore. The whole vast throng lost in the blackness below roared out a greeting to their mayor, the new mayor. The mayor of Springfield, Indiana.

They yelled and continued to yell and yelled some more. Voices called at him, faintly familiar voices shouted his name. He stood looking into the dim light around the platform, recognizing a few faces here and there in the front row, mostly kids down front, and behind them the grown-ups; Sam Katzmann and his wife, and Roscoe and his wife, and Jackson Piper's dad and Doc Jordan and Mac and Earl and lots of others whose faces he knew but couldn't place. Now they were his people; he was responsible for them, for their health and welfare, for their children, too. For the Springfield of 1960.

Down front was his little army, Mike Cray and Roy and Perry. Carlene and Jackson and Anola and Norman Hanscomb. Chet and Dave and the Evans twins and the team, the Wildcats.

Unable to wait any more for his drink, he poured a little coke into the paper cup and started to raise it to his mouth. Then he hesitated. Taking three or four steps, he came to the front of the platform toward the mike, and held the cup in the air so everyone could see. They realized he intended to say something.

"Shhh . . . Shhh . . . Shhh . . ." The noise died away and there was silence while they waited for his first official words as mayor. The mayor of Springfield. The man they had fought and won with, when everyone laughed, when folks who knew politics said it couldn't be done, when J. Frank Shaw, the man who runs the town, said it was impossible.

He extended the cup with the coke toward them, looking them over, Americans who had fought for what they wanted—and won.

"To America . . . with love."

Turn the page to discover more exciting books in the Odyssey series.